SECRETS

OF THE

TREASURE KING

BOOKS BY TERRY AMBROSE

Seaside Cove Bed & Breakfast Mysteries
A Treasure to Die For
Clues in the Sand
The Killer Christmas Sweater Club

Mckenna Mysteries
Photo Finish
Kauai Temptations
Big Island Blues
Mystery of the Lei Palaoa
Honolulu Hottie
North Shore Nanny
A Damsel for Santa
Maui Magic
The Scent of Waikiki

License to Lie Series
License to Lie
Con Game
The Scent of Waikiki

Anthologies with Stories
Paradise, Passion, Murder: 10 Tales of Mystery from Hawai'i
Happy Homicides 3: Summertime Crimes
Happy Homicides 4: Fall into Crime
Happy Homicides 5: The Purr-fect Crime

SECRETS

OF THE

TREASURE KING

Seaside Cove
Bed & Breakfast Mystery #4

Terry Ambrose

COPYRIGHT

ABOUT THE AUTHOR

Once upon a time, in a life he'd rather forget, Terry Ambrose tracked down deadbeats for a living. He also hired big guys with tow trucks to steal cars—but only when negotiations failed. Those years of chasing deadbeats taught him many valuable life lessons such as—always keep your car in the garage.

Terry has written more than a dozen books, several of which have been award finalists. In 2014, his thriller, "Con Game," won the San Diego Book Awards for Best Action-Thriller. His series include the Trouble in Paradise McKenna Mysteries, the Seaside Cove Bed & Breakfast Mysteries, and the License to Lie thriller series.

You can learn more about Terry and his writing at terryambrose.com.

1

Alex

Hey Journal,

Guess what? Seaside Cove had a big bust last night!
Everybody in town is talking about our new deputy. Her name is
Pamela Baker and she went to high school with Marquetta. She
caught a burglar in the act and chased him down in the rain and
muck! She got totally soaked, but she got him. Marquetta says
the deputy was just doing her job, but I think it's awesome 'cause
it proves girls can do anything they want!

Today, Mrs. King, the old lady who's staying in the Jib Room,
asked me what I wanted to be when I grow up. Can you believe
it? It's like the third time a guest has asked me that! I'm only
eleven, but with everybody always asking me the same question, I
guess I'd better come up with something. I told Mrs. King I'm
going into law enforcement. She asked me why and I told her
about the murders I helped the cops solve.

If I am gonna be a cop, Deputy Baker would be an awesome
role model. Right? She's only been here a month, but she's made

a super big impact 'cause she stopped our big crime wave. Okay, it wasn't a huge wave. It was only a few home burglaries, but that's kinda big for Seaside Cove. It would be awesome to meet Deputy Baker. The cool thing about Seaside Cove is everybody knows everybody else, so that's gonna happen for sure.

OMG. I just had an idea. Maybe I could get Deputy Baker to come to our school for next month's career day? Or I could interview her for the Cove Talkers newsletter…that would be awesome! I might ask Marquetta what she thinks.

My dad's gonna be up in a couple minutes to say goodnight so I gotta go.

Bye for now,

Alex

2

Rick

THE FIRST HINTS OF SUNRISE glimmered outside the windows of Rick Atwood's office. Though it was barely dawn, he'd been at work for nearly an hour. The fifteen-year-old news article he'd been reading on his laptop had troubled him off and on during the night.

Turning his attention away from his laptop, Rick sat back in the plush leather chair that had once belonged to his grandfather. Nothing in this office—from the coffered ceiling to the mahogany desk and matching guest chairs to the bookshelves lined with first editions—had been his choice. It had all come with the B&B as part of his inheritance.

Over the past year, he'd come to appreciate the mahogany's elegance. Each day he looked forward to spending time at his desk and allowing himself to drink in the smell of the leather bindings and old paper that hung in the air like a faint perfume.

If he were being truthful, even the coffered ceiling, which felt like an ode to a man prone to extravagance, was growing on him. It was all classic Captain Jack—a man of impeccable taste and limited budget. A man who somehow played a central role in that article on the laptop.

Trading his life as a New York City reporter for that of a small-town innkeeper had brought changes Rick never anticipated—dodging marriage proposals because he'd instantly become the town's most eligible bachelor, keeping his daughter from sticking her nose into murder investigations, or falling in love with the B&B's cook. He didn't miss New York, and he'd finally accepted the Seaside Cove rumor mill for what it was, a form of reality TV in which everyone participated.

Rick planted his elbows on the desk and reread the final paragraph of the news story he'd discovered in the *San Ladron Times* archives just last week.

And so, Neal Weiss, a man of extraordinary courage and determination, sailed off in search of sunken treasure while his ten-year-old daughter waved goodbye from the edge of the docks. How tragic that a rain-soaked day was the last time a little girl would see her father. Even more tragic is the fact that Neal Weiss never found the treasure he sought. Everyone in Seaside Cove will miss Neal Weiss, whose death at sea was all for nought.

The story, written by J.K. Keneally, was remarkably bad journalism—not much more than an obituary embellished with purple prose about foul weather, men of courage, and sunken treasure. Rick's editor in New York would never have let him get off so easily. He would have been told to build a story around the photograph of two men standing in the rain looking grim and determined.

He knew from experience those were not the faces of men wishing each other well. Fifteen years after her father's death, he'd promised Marquetta he would solve the mystery of what happened between her father, Neal Weiss, and his grandfather, Captain Jack Atwood.

Rick opened the contact form for the *San Ladron Times* and filled out his request to have J.K. Keneally contact him. He closed the lid of the laptop and let out a frustrated sigh. All he could do now was wait.

It was time to start the breakfast preparations. Marquetta was most likely already working in the kitchen. He couldn't wait to see her, but wouldn't mention what he'd found until he knew more.

The quiet of the B&B hallway muffled Rick's footsteps as he made his way to the stairs and then down to the first floor. Sunday mornings were always like this. Or so it seemed. Later, when the guests awoke, the old house would spring to life. Rick wove through the living room and dining area, straightening up as he went.

Light shined through the crack between the butler door and the jamb. He stopped, closed his eyes, and listened to the sounds of Marquetta working in the kitchen. He knew her every move. When she placed her twelve-inch skillet on the stove. When she repositioned it to center it on the burner. It was those little habits he'd come to adore. The imperfections. He bit his lower lip. The fact that he knew her so well made him smile. He opened his eyes, took a deep breath, and pushed through the door.

Marquetta snuck a quick look at him, her gray eyes smiling playfully. She'd pulled her auburn hair back in a ponytail and secured it with a red scrunchy. "Well, if it isn't the town's most eligible bachelor."

Rick crossed the room, placed his hand at the small of Marquetta's back, and gently pulled her toward him. She kissed him softly, then pulled away and sighed.

"I'm not on the market. My heart has been captured by a young woman who's a remarkably good cook."

"Oh, my. Imagine all those mothers who are still holding out hope."

Rick pulled her closer and kissed her again. "That's twenty-two mothers, Ms. Weiss. Don't you forget it."

"I won't, boss." Marquetta gave him a sly smile. "Because I just heard there are still a few who are clinging to their dreams of snagging you as a son-in-law."

"Oh, God no. Please don't tell me Mrs. Ticknor is one of them."

"Absolutely. I hear she's been checking out books from the library on aphrodisiacs."

"We need to get busy," Rick said.

"She's planning on inviting you to dinner."

"You're being insubordinate, Ms. Weiss."

"You planning on firing me, boss?"

A swarm of butterflies took flight in Rick's stomach and his cheeks warmed. "Not today." Not ever, he thought. Why couldn't he go all Cary Grant on her? Be Mr. Suave? Quip something clever instead of having his mind go blank?

"Why, Mr. Atwood, I do believe you're blushing."

"It's hot in here." Rick swallowed hard and held Marquetta's gaze. Her cheeks flushed to a bright crimson. Thank goodness he wasn't the only one flummoxed by their relationship. "I'd better take care of the upstairs coffee station. It's almost six and you know how grumpy the guests get if they don't get their caffeine fix."

"Right. And Alex will be down soon."

"We don't need to give her any encouragement."

Marquetta looked at Rick with raised eyebrows. "The little matchmaker has been at it again?"

"Not in the last eight hours."

"Could be a record."

"I'm just glad my divorce has been finalized. It means Alex and I are finally ready to start a new chapter in our lives." He paused, then added, "A better chapter."

Her cheeks brightened again and she smiled. "We need to take it slow."

"I know. That doesn't mean my daughter is going to see it the same way. You know what she wants. And Ms. Weiss, I think it's you who are blushing now."

Marquetta suppressed a smile and turned back to the stove. She pretended to reposition the skillet, but it wound up in the same place where it started. She sniffled and avoided looking at him as she asked, "How's your research going?"

Rick's pulse quickened. It was the question he feared. "It's taking forever. You know how it is—tons of reading boring news stories looking for a single lead that might actually be valuable information."

There was a long pause, then Marquetta faced him. "Maybe it's a waste of time, Rick."

"This is important to you. Right?"

"The reasons behind my dad's death have haunted me my entire life." Marquetta stopped, her brow furrowing. "I've never understood why he sailed that day. It's like I can't commit to any kind of relationship until I know what really happened. Why he chose death over me and my mom."

Rick took Marquetta's hands in his and sighed. How much he wanted to tell her what he'd found, but he couldn't raise her hopes. Not yet. "We are going to bring you closure. I promise."

After an awkward few seconds in which neither seemed to want to make the next move, Marquetta said, "You'd better get started on the coffee."

Rick picked up the tray she had already prepared. In addition to the large carafes of regular coffee, decaf, and hot water—there were little packets of various sweeteners, a small carafe of cream, and another of nonfat milk. He backed out through the butler door, thankful for the assignment and the chance to delay further discussion.

3

Alex

THERE'S NO LIGHT COMING THROUGH the drapes of my window when I wake up. I say a quick, *please, don't let it be raining*, then throw back the covers and rush to look outside.

The clouds are gone! Awesome. It's the first day of spring break! And the rain stopped. That is super awesome. I guess spring break doesn't technically start until Monday. But that's cool. I'm counting today anyway.

I get dressed and slip out the door. I don't want to wake the guests, so I close my door slowly. My dad's down the hall. He's kneeling next to the coffee station. He might be tall and handsome, but he's a terrible singer. He's humming a song I don't know and it sounds awful. I don't mind, though. He's happy and that's what matters most. We keep our voices low when I pass him.

"Hey, Daddy."

He reaches out so I can give him a hug and says, "Good morning, kiddo. How'd you sleep?"

I give him a thumbs up and let him wrap his arms around me.

"Good," I say when he lets me go. I'm totally not telling him about the awesome dream I had last night. Daddy and Marquetta were already married and Marquetta was holding my new baby sister.

Daddy looks at me and says, "You look more like your mom everyday."

"I guess." I pause, then smile. "Marquetta says I got your blue eyes 'cause of their shape."

"That may be, but there's no question of where you got your red hair."

It hurts when I think of how my mom abandoned us. Then how she tried to come back into our lives. Things are getting better with her, but…

"I gotta go help Marquetta," I turn away before Daddy sees the tears I feel pressing against my eyelids. On the way downstairs, I take a few deep breaths to clear my head.

Mr. West is in the living room. His cheeks are rosy, and he's breathing kinda heavy. He has to be coming back from what he calls his morning constitutional. I don't get how his walk is related to the constitution, but maybe it's an old-person thing. That could be 'cause he's totally old enough to be my grandfather. He waves and we say hi.

"It's a beautiful morning, Alex. I hope you can tell me you have that same daily special on the menu again. It's my last day here, you know."

I totally know today's his last day. He reminded me yesterday about fifteen times. Mr. West is a retired real estate broker from LA. and says he's thinking of moving to Seaside Cove now that he's discovered us. It's funny 'cause each day he asks for the daily special. That means he wants Scotch Eggs, toast, and a side of fruit.

"Marquetta can make that for you for sure, Mr. West. We'll miss you!" I give him a big hug and his eyes get kinda watery.

"I'll miss you, too. These early morning exchanges brighten my day." He smiles at me, then looks up the stairs. "Well, better get cleaned up. I don't want to be late for my morning repast!"

On my way to the kitchen, I wonder if Mr. West is super forgetful, or if he just really likes the same thing for breakfast every day. Our daily menu changes, but Scotch Eggs haven't been the special since last month. At least Marquetta doesn't mind taking special requests. She always says that as long as we have the ingredients and the guests are okay with a little extra wait, she'll make whatever they want.

Just like I thought, Marquetta's already working. After we exchange a morning hug, I put on my apron and tell her I saw Mr. West. "He wants the same thing for breakfast again."

"No worries, Sweetie. Mr. West is a nice man. Let's make sure this last breakfast is one he really enjoys." Marquetta raises her eyebrows a couple times and smiles at me. "What about Mrs. King?"

"I think she's still asleep, but I'll totally put them at the same table for breakfast."

We exchange a high five. Mr. West and Mrs. King would make an awesome couple, so me and Marquetta have been working on getting them together.

"Today's our last day to make it happen," Marquetta says.

"I've got a plan. I'll get pictures at breakfast and email them. They'll totally have to write to each other after they leave."

"Good girl. Now, I'm going to need more onion. Can you dice?"

I give Marquetta two thumbs up. Ever since she taught me how to hold a chef's knife, she says my knife skills have been improving. I can chop almost as fast as she can, and way faster than my dad. While I grab an onion from the fridge, Marquetta pulls out a big bowl for pancake batter. Daddy's still upstairs, so it's my chance to ask about Deputy Baker.

"Marquetta? You went to school with our new deputy, right? What's she like?"

"It was high school, and I haven't heard from her since she left Seaside Cove to attend the police academy."

"Why?"

"Why what?"

"Why haven't you heard from her?"

"Let's just say we grew apart. Okay?" Marquetta's jaw gets tight, then she takes a deep breath. "Pamela was always very career-focused. She knew she wanted to be in law enforcement when she was young, so she kept up her grades and graduated near the top of her class. Hint, hint."

Even though Marquetta's not really my mom, she pays attention to my grades and what I'm doing in school, just like my dad. It's nice 'cause I know they both care. I've cut the onion in half the way Marquetta taught me and start slicing. "Has Seaside Cove High gotten any bigger since you were there?"

"No. And it won't change much by the time you get there, either."

"How come if the class size was so small you and Deputy Baker didn't stay friends after high school?"

Marquetta sets down the milk for the pancake batter and looks straight at me. It's what I call her Mom-stare. "What are you getting at, Alex?"

"I just thought you would've stayed friends. It's like a small-town thing. Right? Everybody knows everybody else."

"That's true, but when people move, things change. How

much contact do you have with your old friends in New York?"

Okay. I get that. What I don't get is why Marquetta is acting all weird. She's always good about explaining stuff, but with Deputy Baker it's like she doesn't want to talk about it. What's up with that?

"It was different when me and Daddy moved here. In New York I didn't have any close friends. But in Seaside Cove, everybody's like one big family."

"And families sometimes have problems." She adds the milk to the bowl as she's talking. "We had a little bit of a falling out, Sweetie. That's all. I'm sure it's water under the bridge. She's probably forgotten all about it."

Wow. Marquetta's being super-evasive. "Did either of you get expelled from school for what happened?"

"What? No." Marquetta looks over at my cutting board, then at me. "Have you finished with that onion yet?"

I make one final cut and move the onion from the cutting board to a prep bowl. "Yup. All done. Why did you have a falling out? Was she mean to you?" I can't imagine Marquetta being mean to anybody.

"Has anyone ever told you that you are one persistent young lady?"

"You. And Daddy. All the time."

Marquetta laughs and points to the board. "Once you get that board cleaned off, you can start the burner under the skillet."

I look up at her, smile, and raise my eyebrows. "Well?"

"Oh lord, you are impossible. Fine. There was a boy we both liked in our junior year. He was a senior and both of us wanted to go to prom with him."

"Who'd he pick?"

Marquetta closes her eyes, then leans against the counter and sighs. "He picked me because I told him she wasn't interested. I felt so guilty over stealing my best friend's date that I was miserable all night."

"Wait! What? You and Deputy Baker were BFFs? And you stole her date for the prom? I don't believe it."

"I tried to make it up to her afterwards, but she wouldn't listen. The truth is, we haven't spoken since."

I blink a couple times. Whoa. That's huge. And I don't know what to say 'cause Marquetta never does anything mean.

Marquetta waves her hand like she's dismissing the whole thing. "Like I said, she's probably forgotten all about it. I'm sure she's very competent. She certainly knows her Seaside Cove history."

Maybe my idea about talking to Deputy Baker is better than I thought. I wonder if I could get them back together? "Maybe I should write about her for the Cove Talkers Newsletter."

Behind me, I hear my dad's voice. "Who are you going to write about?"

"Deputy Baker. Since she used to live here, it would be nice to let the town know she's back."

"I'm not sure that's a good idea, Alex," Marquetta says. "We wouldn't want to make her uncomfortable."

"If you want to do a profile, maybe you should do something about a local business," Daddy says. "I'll bet there are plenty of good stories out there. Why don't you let Deputy Baker get settled back into life in Seaside Cove before you make her the center of attention?"

"But, Daddy…"

"Marquetta's right, Alex. I haven't met this new deputy yet, so I'd prefer it if I could do that before you start in on her. What about Joe Gray? He knows everything about what goes on in town. You could talk to him and see if there's a local business you could profile."

I sigh. "Okay."

A local business won't be nearly as interesting as interviewing a lady cop, but that doesn't mean I'm giving up. I'll have to think of another way. It's what our handyman Mr. Van Horn calls an angle.

I know, right? Totally persistent.

4

Rick

AT EIGHT-FIFTEEN, RICK BEGAN his morning ritual. He went from table-to-table, thanked the guests for staying at the B&B, then welcomed them to linger in the dining room for as long as they wanted. At eight-thirty, with the breakfast service ended, he bused tables and sent Alex into the kitchen to help Marquetta. When he was done, he took a last look around and went into the kitchen.

Marquetta was sitting at the kitchen island. She had a bowl of fruit and one of yogurt for herself and Rick. Alex was carrying a bowl of oatmeal to her regular spot.

"Who's left out there?" Marquetta asked.

"Just Mr. West and Mrs. King." Rick pulled out the stool next to Marquetta.

"Are they still sitting together?" Alex's face lit up in a smile.

"As a matter of fact, they are." Rick frowned and looked at Alex as he sat. "Why do you two look like a couple of Cheshire cats? Alex, what have you done?"

Alex put her oatmeal on the counter and hopped up on the

stool. "Nothing," she said casually.

"Baloney. Have you been playing matchmaker again?"

"I got their pictures and their email addresses. That's all." Alex stuck her spoon in her bowl and stirred a couple of times. She looked up and added, "I did kinda suggest they stay in touch after they leave."

"They're both widowed, and they have a number of things in common. And they get along famously," Marquetta said.

"Oh, no. Not you, too." Rick looked at Marquetta, then Alex. "Can't two people just enjoy each other's company without everyone trying to turn it into a grand romance?"

Marquetta and Alex exchanged a quick glance, then Alex gave him a thumbs-down.

"Ditto," Marquetta said. "Sorry, boss, but you're outvoted."

"This is supposed to be a bed-and-breakfast, not a…a dating facility."

Alex rolled her eyes and shook her head.

"Let me try and explain this to you," Marquetta said. "The B&B is a small place. If we have two lonely people staying here at the same time, there's a strong possibility they'll meet. And if the sparks fly, then who are we to stop them?"

"I don't remember there being any sparks right away. You two helped that along."

Alex clanked her spoon against the side of her bowl and let out an exaggerated sigh. "Daddy, chill. It's a girl thing."

Rick nearly choked on his yogurt. He swallowed, then said, "My own daughter's telling me to chill? Seriously—wait…you two have done something." He looked at both of them and wiggled his fingers. "It's not chill time, it's spill time. What else did you do?"

"It was nothing. Just a little phone call. That's all." Marquetta grinned sheepishly at Rick.

"To?" Rick demanded.

"The Crooked Mast. Last night. I told you—it was nothing." Marquetta and Alex exchanged a high five and a self-satisfied giggle.

"You totally rocked it," Alex said.

Rick massaged his forehead with his fingers. "On second thought, I don't think I want to know about this phone call. Let's change the subject. Alex, I didn't know you were interested in doing another story for the Cove Talkers Newsletter."

"I wanted to write about Deputy Baker, but you guys said I should do a business profile instead."

Rick's jaw muscles tightened ever so slightly. Since they'd moved to Seaside Cove, he'd discovered just how much Alex enjoyed solving crimes, both large and small. Her fascination scared him to death. On the other hand, he'd raised Alex to be strong. Reluctantly, he asked, "What made you want to do a story on Deputy Baker?"

"Because she chased down a burglar and showed the whole town that girls can do anything they want to."

"That's true," Rick said. "You have to remember, though. That's her job. It's what she was hired to do."

"I agree," Marquetta said.

"Business owners just do what they're supposed to do, too. How's that any different?" Alex asked.

"That's what you get to find out when you interview one of them," Rick said. "You can ask how they go out of their way to make someone's life better. I think Joe Gray would be an excellent subject."

"Marquetta, doesn't Mr. Gray do a lot of business with people from out of town 'cause they all want to find the *San*

Manuel?"

"That's true, but even the experts aren't sure where the *San Manuel* is yet, Sweetie."

"I know. That's why I'm gonna ask him how he keeps them all happy when they don't find the treasure."

"Good idea," Rick said. "All these treasure hunters come in with high expectations. Most of them get disillusioned very quickly." Good. It sounded as if they'd sparked Alex's interest. "These people come in unprepared and get the results you'd expect. There's no substitute for hard work and preparation. You know that, right?"

"For sure. I'll be prepared for when I do my interview."

"Excellent," Rick said. "Be confident, too. If Joe tells you stuff you don't understand, don't be afraid to ask questions."

Alex took her bowl to the sink, but didn't respond until she returned. "What kind of stuff?"

"Nautical stuff," Rick said.

Marquetta laughed. "Oh my God. You are so making this up as you go along!"

Rick crossed his arms over his chest and looked directly at her. "All right, Miss Smarty Pants, what would you tell her?"

"I'd say to believe in herself and do her research so she can ask intelligent questions. For instance, do you know what types of boats Mr. Gray rents out?"

Alex shook her head.

"Well, he has a variety, everything from small sailboats to large cabin cruisers. At one point he had a triple-masted tall ship replica, but he sold that about ten years ago. There was no market for something like that here after everyone started coming for treasure. Would you like me to tell you more?"

Rick cleared his throat. "Show off."

Marquetta smiled, then stood. "Don't mind your dad, Sweetie. He's just grumpy because he thought he could get away with faking it."

"I'm not grumpy," Rick declared as he stood and took his dishes to the sink. "Anyway, I always had to prepare when I was working a story in New York. A good reporter knows their subject." He returned to the island and gave Marquetta a sideways glance. "So they don't get caught by some show-off. Now, what are you up to today?"

"Me and Robbie and Sasha wanted to ride our bikes. Can I?"

"Sure. I think you deserve a little play time. Go have a good time with your friends."

"Just be back here in time for lunch," Marquetta said. "And if you want, bring Sasha and Robbie with you. I'm sure your dad won't mind hosting a little pizza party for the three of you."

"Pizza? Awesome!" Alex hugged Marquetta, then looked at Rick. "Can we? Please?"

"How could I refuse such an enthusiastic request? Of course. Now, Miss Atwood, you are hereby released from kitchen duty for the rest of this morning. Go get yourself ready to have some fun."

"Yes, sir." Alex saluted, then giggled.

When the butler door swished closed behind her, Rick moved next to Marquetta. "That was nice of you. Offering to make pizza for them."

"Who said anything about making a pizza? I'm going to order out."

Rick placed his fingertip under her chin and lifted. Their lips met and Rick's pulse quickened. "Brilliant, as usual."

Marquetta sighed. "And don't you forget it. Now, I need to get back to work. My boss let my best helper take the morning off."

"I'm just happy you diverted her away from interviewing Deputy Baker. I'd like to limit her exposure to the Seaside Cove Police Department."

"That's shouldn't be too hard; it is only two people. But, what about Adam? Are you saying you want him to stay away from the B&B?"

"Adam's a special case."

"Because he's your best friend? Or because he's now the Chief of Police?"

"Does this have to be an either-or question?"

"There you go again, making it up as you go along," Marquetta said with a smile.

"Watch yourself, Ms. Weiss. I understand your boss can get quite cranky when he's shown up."

"Then I'll try not to do that." A few seconds later, she added, "Too often."

5

Alex

MARCH 26

Hey Journal,

Not only do I get the rest of the morning off, but Sasha and Robbie are coming over for pizza. This is gonna be an awesome day. Now if I can just get Daddy and Marquetta on a dinner date, everything will be perfect! Let's face it, Journal, my biological clock is ticking and I totally want a baby sister while I'm still young enough to enjoy her.

Tell you what, I just had an idea... I'm going to tell my dad he should take Marquetta to dinner at the Crooked Mast. That way they can have a little alone time. Somebody's gotta take the initiative to move this relationship along. Right?

Bye for now,
Alex

I never had a bike when we lived in New York. And after we moved here, it took a while for my dad to agree I could have one. It's super awesome now 'cause me and Robbie and Sasha can go anywhere we want. We usually like Seaside Cove Park 'cause we can hang out on the swings and the jungle gym. But when we get there, everything's under water.

Sasha lays down her bike and walks to the edge of the playground area. "What's going on?"

Robbie puts down the kickstand and parks his bike the way you're supposed to. He's like that, always following the rules. Sometimes I wonder why I want to marry him. I mean, he's like so goody-goody, but then I look into his dreamy blue eyes and I get all mushy again.

"It's flooded," Robbie sounds super bummed out. He points at where the swing seats are floating on top of the water. "The swings look like they're coming out of a lake."

"Wow. We had the same exact thing happen at the B&B a couple days after the rain started. We had a clogged drain out by the gazebo. My dad had some guy come out to open it up. He said it was kind of expensive."

"Maybe the town doesn't have the money to fix it," Sasha says.

Robbie moves closer to the edge of the lake. "Maybe nobody's complained."

Sasha looks at me. "You totally should call the mayor."

"Yeah, Alex," Robbie says. "You should totally call her."

They're both looking at me like I'm BFFs with the mayor or something. "Just 'cause I know Mayor Carter, doesn't mean I should be the one to give her this kind of bad news. No way. I'm not gonna do it."

"But Alex, she'll listen to you," Sasha says. "She like, gave you the keys to the town."

That's a major exaggeration. But she did thank me for solving that murder. And I have to admit that of the three of us,

I'm like the one the mayor will actually listen to. It's two against one, so they eventually win and when I call, Mayor Carter is cool about the whole thing. The call only lasts for a couple minutes.

"What did she say?" Sasha asks when I disconnect.

"She said she'll get someone on it *tout de suite.*"

Robbie scrunches up his face. "What's that?"

"It's mayor talk for right away."

"How do you know?" Robbie asks.

"She told me once. Come on, let's go do something fun. I think the mayor's version of right away is a lot longer than we wanna wait."

"We should go to the marina," Robbie says.

Ever since his parents took him to the maritime museum in San Ladron, Robbie's totally gotten into boats. He knows all the different kinds and has tried to explain what makes each of them unique, but I don't have his enthusiasm. It's all like super boring.

"My mom said a huge treasure hunter boat came in. She heard the cops are not happy."

The cops? Not happy? That could mean Deputy Baker is down there now. Maybe that's how I could make my story about her. "Awesome. Let's go."

We take Main Street down to the roundabout near the marina where we can see a new boat that's docked. It's like massive. I ride straight toward it and when we're down by the water, I stop and read the name on the bow. "*The Treasure King.* It's like twice the size of everything else in the marina."

Robbie stares at the boat. "Whoa. It has to be a hundred feet long."

"Flynn O'Connor showed me pictures of one like it. She said she saw it while she was in Cartageña. They were searching for an old Spanish galleon just like the *San Manuel.*"

Robbie's eyes get all big. "Was she diving? I think diving would be awesome."

"No way. I couldn't do it," Sasha says.

I can feel my jaw drop open and it feels stupid, but I can't stop it. "What? I know you, Sash, you'd…"

"I can't swim, Alex."

"You? Can't swim? But you're down by the water all the time."

"I'm on land, Alex. I just can't like go in above my head." Sasha hunches forward and gets a worried look on her face. "I sink."

Holy moley. Sasha's never been afraid of anything. I reach out and hold her hand. Her fingers tighten around mine, and she looks at me.

I smile at her and say, "It's okay, Sash. We're not going in."

"I know," she says.

Mr. Gray is talking to a man who looks kinda like he might be the captain. But they're not just talking. The other man is all in Mr. Gray's face, and Mr. Gray looks like he's super mad. Maybe I could start my interview with Mr. Gray, and then I'd have to talk to Deputy Baker.

Robbie's still watching *The Treasure King*. It's like he's memorizing every line on the boat. "Do you think they found the treasure?"

"My mom doesn't think the treasure exists," Sasha says. "She thinks it's all a big marketing scam to bring in money for the town."

I shake my head. "No way, it's for real. Flynn told me she's still here 'cause the museum she works for wants her to find it before anyone else. And she's done all kinds of research on it, so she even knows it sank in 1568. She says it's loaded with fine china and ivory and super old artwork. It could be worth millions, depending on how much stuff they can bring up."

Sasha leans forward on her handlebars. "Well, someone's gotta find it first."

That's totally the big argument in town. The *San Manuel* is four-hundred-years-old. If it's real, how come nobody's found it? I gotta believe my friend Flynn 'cause she's a professional archaeologist and works for a museum. Flynn's cool and I like her, but she's also super smart, so she's gotta be right.

Mr. Gray is still with the other man. They sure are taking a long time. "I'm gonna go check it out. I need to ask Mr. Gray a question." I ride my bike down and stop on the other side of the big welcome sign. Mr. Gray and the other man aren't very far away and their voices are carrying, so it's easy to hear them.

"No, Captain Carroll, you cannot 'just leave her here' for a few hours. You must move to the outer dock. You're blocking three slips, none of which are designed to handle the load of a boat the size of *The Treasure King*. If you don't like it, anchor offshore and tender in."

"That's too inconvenient. We've got supplies to load and everyone will be coming and going."

"I don't care how inconvenient it is. You must move. If you don't, I'll call the police. They'll notify the Coast Guard, and you can explain why your convenience comes before safety."

Awesome! This is totally what I need. My dad always says conflict is the heart of any story. Our harbor is super small, *The Treasure King* is huge, and Mr. Gray is the closest thing we have to a harbormaster. Now, if he'll just call Deputy Baker. I stare at Mr. Gray, mentally begging him to make the call.

My shoulders slump when the captain turns and walks away. As Mr. Gray comes back in this direction, I walk my bike over and say hi.

"You kids shouldn't be hanging around here," he snaps.

That's weird. Mr. Gray has never complained about us coming here before. Especially Robbie, 'cause he's always like talking to him about the Navy and that kind of stuff. "Can I ask you a question, Mr. Gray?"

He looks back at *The Treasure King* and grumbles, "Not now, Alex. These are not the best people. That captain in particular is trouble. I need to watch and make sure they don't damage the dock when they move."

The man Mr. Gray was talking to is now standing on the dock yelling at a guy who's looking down from the top deck. The guy on top starts the engines. The rumble totally drowns out everything else.

Robbie and Sasha pull up next to me. Robbie's mouth is hanging open. He yells over the engine noise, "That's super loud."

There's a woman standing on the main deck of the boat. She says something to the man on top, then jumps to the dock. She unties the rope that secures the rear and when that's free, she runs to the front of the boat and does the same thing. When she's done, she starts walking to the outer part of the harbor and the big dock.

Mr. Gray looks pretty mad, but he doesn't go anywhere. The engine noise is so loud you can probably hear it all over Seaside Cove.

"Idiot," Mr. Gray says over the noise. "I swear, if they damage that dock…"

Robbie shifts from one foot to the other and hollers in my ear. "We should go, Alex."

His face is all scrunched up, kinda like he's worried about

something. I shake my head. "No way. We have as much right to be here as anybody else." Besides, I'm not done getting the background I need.

As the boat backs away, the noise level drops. I can actually hear Robbie when he tells me his dad doesn't want him getting in any trouble.

Sasha gives Robbie's shoulder a shake. "We're not doing anything wrong, Robbie. It'll be okay."

I look up at Mr. Gray and tell him we don't want to cause any trouble.

He takes a deep breath. "Sorry, Alex. I don't mean to take my frustrations out on you. Captain Carroll has been boasting that he has a map with an accurate location of the *San Manuel*. According to him, he visited it on a previous journey."

"Then how come they're not out bringing up the treasure?"

"Exactly. Personally, I wouldn't believe a word that man says."

"Why?"

"He says they docked for some perishable supplies, but they haven't even been at sea a week. There's no need for them to be here. Now, you kids need to move on. I don't trust him or his passengers."

"But we come down here all the time."

Mr. Gray looks at *The Treasure King*. Two men stand on the deck. Both of them look really mean, almost like they're a couple pirates. They're yelling at Captain Carroll and he's yelling back, but I don't think they can hear each other 'cause the engine noise is so loud.

When Mr. Gray turns back to me, he looks super worried. This is totally looking like an awesome news story.

6

Rick

RICK SCANNED THE GUEST LIST, then looked up at the elderly woman standing before him. "You're in luck, Mrs. King. We were expecting a new arrival today, but they called last night and canceled. That means your room is available for another night."

Mrs. King, a diminutive, white-haired widow with an impish smile, turned to the man standing next to her. "You're sure about this?"

"Dolores, I'm positive. We had such a lovely time at dinner last night and again this morning at breakfast. I think we definitely owe it to ourselves to extend our stays."

Rick suppressed a chuckle. It appeared the matchmakers had succeeded, and now he was curious about the phone call Marquetta mentioned. "So what happened at dinner?" he asked.

"It was the strangest thing," Mr. West said. "I had just ordered a glass of wine when the manager brought Dolores to my table. He said he was expecting a big rush and wondered if he could impose by having us share."

"Mr. Grayson was quite accommodating," Mrs. King said.

"He even brought me a glass of wine on the house for the inconvenience."

Rick bit his tongue to avoid bursting into laughter. Ken Grayson never gave anything away at the Crooked Mast without good reason. He suspected Marquetta had twisted his arm, or had promised to pay for the wine herself. "Ken is like that. Always thinking of his customers. So you two had a good time?"

Mrs. King's head bobbed enthusiastically, and Mr. West gave him a thumbs-up. "It was the highlight of my trip. We talked for hours. It was the strangest thing, though. The restaurant never did get very busy."

"Maybe they had a big party cancel." Rick suppressed another smile, then added, "I'm glad it worked out. Now, I believe you said you have some exploring to do. Am I correct?"

"Yes. Your daughter gave us a full itinerary at breakfast," Mrs. King said.

"That's my daughter," Rick said. "She loves having our guests feel welcome. I'll let you two get to it."

Rick suppressed another chuckle when Mr. West took Mrs. King's hand. She giggled, and they started toward the door.

"I feel like I'm eighteen again," she said.

Mr. West stopped and beamed at her. "Then that makes me the luckiest man alive."

Rick watched them leave, wondering how long the match would last. Perhaps, he thought, till death do them part. He had a sudden urge to find Marquetta. Tell her about the development with their guests. And maybe even how he wanted to move their own relationship forward. He'd spent enough time debating.

He heard the whine of the vacuum coming from the second floor. He closed the reservation book and followed the noise. At the landing, he stopped. The sound was coming from his left. He went to the corner and saw Marquetta working at the end of the hall. Her hair was pulled back and her ponytail bobbed as she pushed the vacuum forward, then pulled back.

She saw him, waved, and turned off the power as he approached. "What's up, boss?"

"I just extended the stays for Mrs. King and Mr. West."

"Yes!" Marquetta pumped her fist and followed it up with a little dance.

Rick stood back, watching her. He wanted to reach out, take her in his arms, and kiss her. That would go against their agreement to limit their public displays of affection around the guests—and especially around Alex. But if he took her out to dinner as Alex had suggested—yes, he knew what he wanted to do.

He cleared his throat. "I thought the news would make you happy. By the way, I have to go into town to set up a tour for the Carstons. They want to take the Joaquin Murrieta jeep tour."

Marquetta raised her eyebrows and locked the handle of the vacuum in the upright position. "Really? They don't want to do the *San Manuel* tour?"

"Nope. Mrs. Carston has panic attacks when she's on a large body of water. Anyway, I promised them I'd set it up for tomorrow morning so they could go into San Ladron today. I'll be back in an hour or so."

Marquetta raised her eyebrows and smiled. "Since you're going into town, could you pick up a dozen eggs and some bacon?"

Rick mentally mapped out the location of the market, the Crooked Mast, and the tour operator. Nothing in Seaside Cove was that far apart, including the jewelry story he intended to visit. He'd have to do a little backtracking so he could hit the market last, but that would only add a few minutes. "Sure. Anything else?"

Marquetta shook her head. "This will get us through the morning." She checked the hallway in both directions before kissing him on the cheek. "Have fun. And don't rush. Without any ins or outs, this will be an easy day."

"Actually, it's going to be a wonderful day." Rick walked away, humming to himself as he went down the stairs, confident that Marquetta had no idea he was about to buy an engagement ring.

The air was still crisp as Rick exited the B&B and took a right on Front Street. He followed the roundabout to the left at Main, which brought him to Seaside Cove Treasure Tours. The heart of the downtown extended up for two more blocks. Short blocks, at that. And, best of all, the jewelry store was right next door.

Seaside Cove was a hard town in which to keep a secret. And hiding the fact that he was looking at engagement rings would be even harder to conceal because the jewelry store was across the street and two doors down from Scoops & Scones— home to Alex's favorite ice cream and the town's biggest gossip, Mayor Francine Carter.

As Rick approached Seaside Cove Treasure Tours, he checked across the street. The coast was clear. Francine was not yet out sweeping the sidewalk in front of her store, which meant he could duck in to check out rings unseen if he was quick. He walked past the tour agent and went straight to the jewelers, but when he turned the doorknob, the door was locked. Only then did he read the sign hanging in the window. *Closed for the day.*

"Crap," he muttered and jiggled the doorknob. He cupped his hands to the glass and peered inside. There was nobody around.

"Double crap."

He hurried back to the tour agent before you-know-who spotted him. It only took a few minutes to make the reservation for the Carstons. When he finished, he checked for Francine again. She was sweeping her sidewalk, but had her back to him. He darted across Main St. and cut into the alley. If he had any hope of keeping the dinner with Marquetta from becoming the rumor du jour, he had to avoid Francine's prying eyes. It often felt like she had more spies than the CIA—and better security.

Rick was at the end of the alley when Police Chief Adam Cunningham called to him. He was approaching via the same route Rick had taken. Rick waited as Adam trotted toward him, his crisp police uniform giving him an official air. Adam still had the same boyish smile, but he'd updated his appearance since his promotion to Chief of Police and now wore his brown hair slicked back.

"What are you doing, Rick? Avoiding Madame Mayor?"

"You know me too well, buddy. The truth is I'm planning a nice quiet dinner with Marquetta tonight and didn't want to endure a million questions."

"Smart move." Adam pretended to check the time on his watch. He cocked his head to one side and sucked in an exaggerated breath. "This early in the day she'd have...oh, a good eight hours to spread the news."

"Especially this news." Rick looked around, saw no others in any direction, and lowered his voice. "I'm going to pop the question."

Adam's eyes widened. "Are you sure you want to do that at the Crooked Mast? The town's most eligible bachelor proposing in public?"

"I know. But I was standing there watching Marquetta

holding onto that old vacuum and doing that happy dance and…"

"Oh my God. You have it so bad. You do realize this news will go viral in Seaside Cove before you even have an answer." Adam reached out and laid a hand on Rick's shoulder. "You know how this town is, Rick. Rumors, spies, perceptions and lies."

"You're probably right. I have a bigger problem. The jewelry store is closed for the day."

"Wait a minute. You haven't talked to Markie about the ring?"

"No. Giselle made me look at fifty rings before we got married. I thought Marquetta would want to keep things simple."

"Holy smokes. You don't have the ring. You, my friend, need some tutoring in the fine art of woman wooing."

"Woman wooing? Seriously? And since when are you the expert?"

Adam did his own look around and tapped himself on the chest. "I'm the only one in this alley who's currently engaged."

"Sorry, buddy, but I went through the whole process. Rings, engagement, marriage, divorce."

"I don't think that counts. It appears the divorce turned your brain to mush. You're the one thinking of proposing before you've decided on a ring."

"Okay, Obi Wan. I bow to your superior knowledge. What's my next move?"

"As far as a ring goes, talk to Marquetta. Find out what she wants."

"But that would ruin the surprise. How about if I get an empty ring box and tell her she can fill it with whatever she wants? That's a thing now. Right?"

Adam snapped his fingers. "Tell you what. Let's create a

diversion. We can make this dinner a double-date, then if you decide to dive in later in the evening, you won't look like you're a complete doofus. You'll just look impulsive."

Rick stuffed his hands in his pockets and chuckled. "So now I'm naive when it comes to women—and I'm a doofus? Remind me again why I put up with you."

"Because I'm the Chief of Police and the mayor has forced you to be nice to me. Besides, if you go down in flames in public, you'll make me look bad. I have an image as a crack crime solver to maintain thanks to you and your daughter. I am not about to let you blow my aura."

"Please…stop. You're killing me with all this—fine, can we do dinner at six? I don't want to leave Alex alone too late."

"No worries. I have a feeling I'll be on duty later tonight. *The Treasure King* is back and that group is nothing but trouble."

A movement at the Main St. end of the alley caught Rick's attention. He looked, realized it was only a tourist, and regarded Adam. "Really? Why?"

"I'll spare you the details, but let's just say there are bound to be fireworks if my new deputy and Captain Carroll have any reason at all to get into it. And after Carroll's last trip here, I can assure you those fireworks will probably happen. If we can make it through the next twenty-four hours, my life will get a whole lot easier."

"Why? What happens then?"

"*The Treasure King* goes back to sea."

7

Alex

IT TAKES FOREVER FOR *THE Treasure King* to move to the outside dock. It's so slow. Like it's crawling. Robbie says the pilot is doing a good job, and even though Mr. Gray agrees, he watches super close until the woman on the docks gets the ropes that secure the boat tied down. When that's all over, Mr. Gray says he's going back to work.

Uh, no. That can't happen. I need more background on *The Treasure King*. I have to ask a question. Super fast. "What would have happened if they made a mistake?" I blurt.

"Duh," Robbie says. "They could have taken out the whole entire dock."

Okay, so it was a lame question. But maybe...I give Mr. Gray a big smile.

Mr. Gray stops, looks at me, and chuckles. "Robbie's right. Docking in a small harbor like this isn't easy. Not for something the size of *The Treasure King*. Our harbor is old and even a small mistake while they're moving a boat with that much mass could easily take out one of the docks."

I point to the woman who did all the work on the docks. "What's she doing?"

"Right now she's double-checking and snugging down all of the lines to make sure the boat doesn't move."

"She's one of the crew members?" Sasha asks.

"Her name's Heather Sanna," Mr. Gray says. "She's not only a crew member, but she's also the captain's girlfriend. Although, why a woman would want anything to do with those lowlifes, I don't know."

"How come nobody's helping her?" I ask.

"Because the captain feels like he's above menial labor and the first mate is busy piloting. All the work falls to her."

"That sucks." At the B&B, me and Marquetta and my dad split the work. It doesn't matter what it is—unless it's cooking for the guests. In that case, me and Daddy let Marquetta boss us around.

"She's the only girl?" Sasha asks. "How many others are there on the boat?"

"*The Treasure King* will bunk up to twelve. There's a total of nine passengers and crew on this trip. One of the passengers is running around here taking pictures like there's no tomorrow. Every one of those men only care about the treasure of the *San Manuel*, so you kids need to stay away from them."

I look out at the lady who's now helping a couple of the men off the boat. It totally looks to me like girl power rocks. I wonder if she'd talk to me.

8

Rick

RICK'S BREATH QUICKENED AS HE grasped the weathered door handle for the entrance to the Crooked Mast. The old wood, cool and smooth to the touch, felt damp. But that, he suspected, was the result of his own nervousness.

It was five-forty-five p.m. on the dot. The restaurant was probably teeming with patrons here for the early-bird specials. And most of those patrons were locals. The wisdom of Adam's cautions this morning suddenly felt very weighty. If things went wrong, this dinner could become very awkward.

Rick pulled open the door for Marquetta, waited for her to enter, then followed. Inside, he took her coat. Dressed as she was, in a short gray skirt and white, lacy blouse he'd never seen before, he felt the gravity of this dinner. In a big city, dinner out as a couple would be nothing. In Seaside Cove, it was everything. "Ready for this?" he asked.

Marquetta laughed nervously. Glanced around. "Probably not."

The aroma of grilling steaks and seafood filled the air.

Though rustic by big-city standards, the nautical theme that ran throughout the restaurant—rough-hewn shiplap walls, driftwood and brass accents, along with fishing nets dotted with shells and starfish, evoked a sense of a distant port in the South Seas. In contrast, the vintage china and silverware added a sense of elegance.

Rowdy voices and laughter broke out from deeper inside. "I always tell our guests that the Crooked Mast is both quaint and elegant. It's not feeling like much of either right now," Rick said.

Marquetta squeezed Rick's hand. "They're not even that busy. Ken must have a big party."

"I hope Adam was able to get us a table away from all the noise." Rick scanned the area as they waited for the hostess to greet them. When a girl with glossy dark hair approached with two menus cradled in her arms, he asked, "Fiona? What's going on?"

"It's the dudes from *The Treasure King*." She sighed, a look of disgust on her face, then smiled politely. "They're super rowdy. And they're not happy about being in town." She lowered her voice and let her gaze bounce between Rick and Marquetta.

A sudden tightness seized Rick's throat, then he realized Marquetta had tightened her grip.

"Are you two, like, together now?"

Rick stole a quick look at Marquetta.

"We're just casual," she said.

Rick smiled at Fiona, then added, "We're meeting Adam and Traci."

"Cool," Fiona said. "They're back here. Follow me."

When Fiona was out of hearing range, Rick whispered in Marquetta's ear, "I'll bet you five bucks she's texting all her friends about us in about two minutes."

"I'm not taking that bet. Fiona's a nice girl; her mother's the terrible gossip. I don't think we'd make the Seaside Cove High rumor mill, anyway. You're too old for that crowd."

"Ouch. Wait. I'm too old?"

"You heard me." Marquetta flashed Rick a quick smile, then stopped at a table where Joe and Angela Gray were seated.

Fiona waited at the end of the table where Adam Cunningham and Traci Peterson sat next to each other. She cradled the leather-bound menus in her arms and smiled politely. Rick signaled that it would be fine to let them seat themselves. Fiona placed the menus in front of their seats and quickly retreated to her hostess station, where he fully expected her to launch rumors about the 'new couple' in town.

Across the room, a table filled with five men he didn't recognize were talking loudly and complaining about being stuck in port. Rick tried to block out the rambunctious table as he turned his attention to the conversation going on between Joe, Angela, and Marquetta.

"They've been like that since we got here," Joe said.

"What's up?" Rick asked.

"I was asking about the rowdies over there." Marquetta cut a glance across the restaurant. "Joe says they're the ones from *The Treasure King*."

"I thought so," Rick said. "If things get out of hand, we have an in with the police chief. Meanwhile, I guess we'll have to tough it out."

"At least Captain Carroll's not here. Given how much they've had to drink, I don't know what would happen." Joe paused. "Enough about them. The kids got a bit of a show today. They were down at the docks and witnessed firsthand the long process of navigating a large boat in a small harbor."

"Alex couldn't stop talking about it," Marquetta said.

Rick patted Joe's shoulder and chuckled. "She said you faced down a real-life pirate."

"She did not!" Marquetta rolled her eyes. "All she said was there was a problem with where the captain wanted to dock, and that you straightened him out. She did not call him a pirate."

Joe picked up his wine glass and raised it. "Might as well call him what he is. The man's hoodwinked these jokers, and I think they're starting to realize it. You get that much dissatisfaction in a confined space and there's going to be trouble."

To Rick's relief, the server approached with an armload of plates. "It looks like your dinner's arriving and we're just another table down. Stop by and see us before you leave." He put his hand at Marquetta's back and eased her away.

"You ended that quick," she whispered.

"You know Joe. Once he gets going, he doesn't stop until he runs out of gas."

They exchanged hugs with Adam and Traci. Before Marquetta could reach for it, Rick pulled out her chair.

"You've got him trained well," Adam said.

"What's the buzz at the Bee's Knees?" Rick asked.

Traci wrinkled her nose and gave him a mock sneer. "Good grief. That is so old." She pointed at the bottle of Chardonnay on the table. "If Rick's telling bad jokes, we're going to need another."

"We may need it just to deal with the noise," Rick followed Adam's gaze as he cut his eyes to the table of five men.

"I haven't talked to any of them yet, but I know their names. The little guy with the Hollywood hair?"

"You mean the blond tips?"

"Yup. That's Matthew Redmond. I don't know much about

him, but the one next to him on his right is Isaac Longstreet. He's a bartender from LA and is expecting to make it big on this trip. He seems to think he'll be able to retire when this is all over."

"Did anybody tell these guys they might not even have legal claim to that treasure?" Marquetta asked.

Adam's jaw tightened, and he raised his glass. "I doubt if it was in the travel brochure. They all have unreasonable expectations—in my opinion." He drained the last of the wine in his glass and picked up the bottle. "Baker said she'd cover for me tonight."

"Good to know," Rick said.

"The guy who looks like he's carrying about a hundred extra pounds? That's…um…Silverstein. Ed. He's a computer service tech and the loudest of the bunch. The other two—the ones who are just talking to each other—I think their names are England and Shelley." Adam tilted the neck of the bottle toward Marquetta, asked if she wanted a glass, then poured and did the same for Rick.

While Adam poured, Rick said, "Let's talk about something other than treasure hunters. Bad jokes aside, how's business, Traci?"

"March is a swing month. We don't have any major holidays and the tourist season hasn't started. Things are slow, but when the tourists get here, business at the Bees Knees will be buzzing."

"I was not about to go there again," Rick shot back.

Traci waved away the comment with a quick flip of her hand and a laugh. "I figured I'd nip any urge you might have in the bud."

"I saw a couple of those new candles you got in this week," Marquetta said. "We have to get some for the B&B. Their scent is divine."

"You're placing an order with her at dinner?" Rick chuckled. "I was trying to avoid talking shop with Adam."

"Did you have something more important you'd like to talk about?" Marquetta looked directly at Rick, piercing his resistance with her innocent look.

There was no way he could propose in the midst of all this chaos. He wanted to make that moment special and not have to compete with rowdy men only a few tables away. "Nope, nope. Nothing more important. How many candles were you thinking of?"

Fortunately, the entrees for *The Treasure King* passengers arrived at the same time as the wine Rick ordered. Though the noise in the restaurant faded, there were still plenty of other diners quietly checking them out. He suspected he and Marquetta had become the center of attention the second they walked through the door. So far, he'd been correct. It was one reason they'd put off going out in public together for so long. Rick's thoughts were interrupted when Adam let out a loud groan.

"Oh, crud. Don't look now, but Captain Carroll just came in. I think everything's about to hit the fan."

9

Rick

AT THE TREASURE HUNTER'S TABLE, it was almost as though time stopped. They all turned their attention to the captain and the woman who walked behind him as they followed Fiona.

"If it isn't Captain Do Nothing." The comment came from Ed Silverstein, whose saggy jowls jiggled when he spoke.

"I can't believe that guy is one of the treasure hunters," Rick whispered. "He looks like an old sumo wrestler who hasn't seen the light of day in months. How's he going to survive any kind of dive?"

"Beats me. Maybe he just came along for the ride." Adam spoke in low tones. "Baker told me the girlfriend's name is Heather Sanna. She's the only woman on the boat."

Marquetta snickered. "Oooh…lends new meaning to the term first mate."

Rick planted his elbow on the table, propped his chin on his hand, and regarded her. "Why, Ms. Weiss, I had no idea you could be so catty."

Marquetta picked up her wine glass; a smile played across

her face. "There are many things you don't know about me, Mr. Atwood."

Tempted as he was to surprise Marquetta and kiss her in front of everyone, Rick grabbed his glass and raised it in a toast. "Let's drink to always learning new things."

"How about we change that to always avoiding trouble?" Adam said. "Looks like Carroll's had a few and he's headed straight for Joe Gray."

A heartbeat later, a booming voice silenced the hum of activity in the restaurant. "Do you know how much trouble you caused me, Gray?"

"So much for Baker covering," Adam muttered as he pushed back his chair.

"You sent that cop to hassle me because you didn't like the way I moved my boat? You pompous old goat!"

"The way you moved was fine. It was where you docked initially that was the problem. All I asked Deputy Baker to do was stop by and establish the ground rules in our marina."

Rick turned in his seat, wondering if Adam, or maybe even the two of them, might have to escort Carroll outside. This was a mismatch if Rick had ever seen one. Carroll had to be about six foot tall and easily weighed in around two hundred. He had a large gut that emphasized his physical size. A brown-eyed brunette stood behind him with her hands on her hips.

The scraping of wood-on-wood pierced the air as all five of the passengers rose at once. Two of them headed for the exit, but the remaining three threaded their way through the tables toward the captain.

"Hey, Carroll," bellowed Silverstein. "When are we getting out of here? You never told us that old crate of yours was falling apart and would need a port of call."

Carroll sneered back, then turned away and spoke over his shoulder. "Shut up, Ed. You're drunk."

Joe Gray stood, a small stick figure compared to Carroll. Traci grabbed Adam's arm and urged him to contact Deputy Baker.

"It's your night off," she said with emphasis. "Please."

Rick looked at Adam. "Your call, buddy, but Joe wouldn't stand a chance against someone who weighs so much more. And you know Joe won't back down."

"Sometimes he's too scrappy for his own good," Adam said as he stood.

The brunette stole a sideways look at the three remaining passengers, then reached out to grab Carroll's upper arm. He swiped her hand away, then turned back to Joe. Carroll clenched and unclenched his fists as he edged closer to the smaller man.

Adam cleared his throat and spoke loudly. "Captain Carroll, you need to take a step back. If you have a complaint about what happened today, you should be talking to me. Not Mr. Gray."

Carroll ignored Joe and focused on Adam. "Well, well. If it isn't the podunk police chief. What are you going to do, Mr. Police Chief? Arrest me for having a conversation?"

"I might consider arresting you for drunk and disorderly conduct," Adam said.

"Good idea, Sheriff," Ed Silverstein said loudly. "Lock him up and give us the keys to the boat."

"Shut up, Ed, or I'll throw you off and send you packing."

"I've had it," said the brunette. "Morris, if you don't let this go, I'm leaving right now."

Adam stepped forward and stood nose-to-nose with Silverstein. "It's Chief Cunningham, Mr. Silverstein. And if you don't hightail it out of here right now, I might just lock you up, too."

Silverstein and the other two men grumbled, but made their way to the exit.

"I'd have to do something disorderly for that charge to stick." Carroll seemed to ignore Joe completely and focused on Adam.

"I'm out of here." The woman with Carroll threw up her hands, turned, and marched away.

On her way to the door, she passed a petite woman in a police officer's uniform. That had to be Deputy Baker, thought Rick.

Joe steadied himself with one hand on his seat back and inserted himself into Carroll's path. "You're the one who docked without permission."

Still seated, Joe's wife implored him to step away from the argument. "Joe. Please."

But Joe shook his head and continued. "I warned you when you radioed in, but you didn't pay attention. I had Deputy Baker pay you a visit to let you know I was serious."

Carroll waved away Joe's comment. "Get over yourself, you pipsqueak."

"That's enough," Adam said and moved toward Carroll.

Joe jabbed his finger into the bigger man's chest. "You're a pompous, arrogant..."

Carroll bellowed something unintelligible and shoved Joe. Off balance, Joe staggered backwards. Rick reached out to break his fall, but was too late. Joe landed in Rick's lap. The impact drove Rick sideways into Marquetta. She screamed, the wine glasses toppled, and when Rick checked to see if she was okay, his heart sank.

Her entree, a broiled salmon with glazed carrots, now swam on her plate in a small pool of spilled Chardonnay. He started to apologize, then saw her blouse. It was soaked in wine. As was her skirt. Even the tile underneath her chair had a small pool forming from the wine dripping off the tabletop. Rick groaned and uttered a string of apologies despite Marquetta's comments that it wasn't his fault.

Rick's first impulse was to demand an apology from Carroll, but he couldn't do that with Joe Gray still stuck in his lap. He watched helplessly as Adam secured Carroll and then turned control over to Baker.

"Everybody stand down." Deputy Baker gave Adam a curt nod, which he returned, and then said, "I can escort Mr. Carroll outside if you'd like, Chief."

The big man stood more than a head taller than Baker, and Rick could picture him picking Baker up and tossing her aside like he might a can of beer. Then again, she was the one who had his arm pinned behind his back. Of course, what would happen the second she let loose her grip?

"Take Mr. Carroll in for drunk and disorderly conduct," Adam said.

"Respectfully, Chief. Mr. Gray is technically the one who provoked the attack."

Adam looked at Joe, who finally seemed to realize he'd not helped the situation. "I got too worked up. Sorry, Adam."

"About time somebody in this berg got a little sense," Carroll said, then yelped when Baker pushed his arm up almost imperceptibly.

"Do not test my patience, Captain," she snapped. "You will leave this establishment now or I will lock you up as the Chief instructed. By the time you get before a judge, you'll have lost all your passengers. Do you understand me?"

"Yes!" Carroll grimaced at another change in pressure on his arm.

Ken Grayson worked his way over to where the altercation had taken place. At six-foot-four, Ken was the taller man, but even he looked almost frail compared to Carroll's presence. "You, Captain Carroll, are not welcome in my restaurant. I called Deputy Baker because I know a troublemaker when I see one and you, sir, are nothing but trouble." Ken surveyed the scene, then faced Adam. "I don't see any severe damage. However, as the sign on the door says, we reserve the right to refuse service. I'm refusing to serve this man, Adam, and I do not want him in here again."

"Works for me," Adam said. "Baker, take the captain outside and let him go. But, Captain, if you do anything to cause more trouble in my town on this trip or any future trips, I will make sure you spend time in jail. Get him out of here."

With one swift movement, Baker forced Carroll to pivot and walk toward the front door. On her way, she paused and said, "Sorry for the interruption, folks. The show's over." Over her shoulder, she added, "Enjoy your dinner, Chief." With that, she pushed Carroll forward and out the door.

Ken Grayson brought over a handful of white bar towels. While Marquetta blotted at her blouse and skirt, Ken and the busboy mopped up spilled wine from the table and removed the ruined dinners.

"Send me the dry cleaning bill, Marquetta," Ken said as he removed her plate.

She shook her head. "It's not your fault. And I don't even know if the dry cleaner can fix this."

Traci reached across the table and laid her hand on Marquetta's arm. "Are you okay? That was a total shock."

"I just need some time to unwind," Marquetta said. "Rick? Can you take me home?"

"Sure." Rick pulled back her chair.

"Do you want company?" Traci asked. "I can stay with you for a while."

"Thanks, Traci, but I'll be okay. I think I need a little time alone."

Rick's spirits sank. How quickly his plan for the evening had fallen apart. One minute, he'd been planning a proposal, the next he had the wrong person on his lap. This was not his evening.

They exited the Crooked Mast and walked along Front Street. Pink, red, and charcoal-gray streamers rippled across the sky. Rick watched the array of colors deepen as they walked. Marquetta stayed quiet, but held his arm. When he suggested she take a look at the sunset, she craned her neck to see past him.

She smiled weakly and tightened her grip. "It's nice."

"That Captain Carroll, he's a real jerk."

"Yes."

"Adam certainly seemed pleased by the way Deputy Baker handled him, though."

"Pamela's always been efficient."

Rick looked closely at Marquetta. Her words had been so stiff. As though forced. Her grip on his arm had also tightened the second he mentioned the deputy. "So she used to live here?"

"You're as bad as Alex."

"I'm sorry."

"No. It's not your fault. I'm just upset by the whole incident." She swallowed hard. "Pamela grew up here. We went to high school together."

"Were you friends?"

"For a while."

"What happened?"

Marquetta pulled back and wrapped her arms over her chest.

"I'd rather not talk about it."

"In some ways, I wonder if Deputy Baker will be too big-city for Seaside Cove," Rick said.

They made it to Marquetta's front door, then stood awkwardly, Rick hoping to get her to open up, she, not saying a word. He took her hand. She looked up at him.

"Rick, I…"

He pressed a finger to her lips. "It's okay. We don't have to talk."

"Thank you."

She turned and unlocked her door, then Rick pulled her close. He kissed her softly, then said, "I love you."

"I love you, too." She turned away and slipped inside.

10

Alex

Hey Journal,

I'm still waiting for my dad to come home from his date with Marquetta. I've been super busy since they left. Part of the time I helped Mr. West and Mrs. King make dinner arrangements. They both said they wanted something more casual than they could get at a restaurant, so I told them about our local pizza place.

They called in an order and ate in our dining room. Guess what? They're still down there playing checkers. I suggested they go watch the sunset, but Mrs. King said she gets cold easy. She also said she's seen sunsets from all around the world, so she didn't mind missing one when she was staying in such a comfortable place.

I also got a text from Sasha. She said her mom warned her to not go near the marina again as long as Captain Carroll's boat is here. Her mom remembered him from the last time. Now Sasha's mom is gonna text my dad and Robbie's dad and tell them to keep us away. Why do parents have to be such *worrywarts? Now I'll never get to talk to the lady crew member.*

You know what? When my dad was a reporter he used to say journalists shouldn't be kept away from their sources. I agree! And if Daddy says I can't go near the marina, I'm gonna remind him of what he said. Freedom of the press! Right?

I'm gonna text Mr. Van Horn and tell him I've got a story for the Cove Talkers. I'm not gonna tell him what it's about unless he asks. He's kind of an old worrywart, too.

Alex

Rats! I sent the text and Mr. Van Horn wanted to know what my subject was. When I told him, he said he'd get back to me. While I wait for him, I decide to make myself some hot chocolate. On my way down the stairs, I hear voices and music. It's Mr. West and Mrs. King. They're still at the dining room table. They've turned up the lights and Mr. West is playing music on his phone. I wave when they look at me and Mr. King calls me over.

"Hey. How are you guys?"

"Saddened that we must leave tomorrow," Mr. West says.

"I have a ticket for a cruise that's leaving in two days. William has volunteered to drive me to San Francisco. When I board, he'll fly back to Los Angeles." She looks at Mr. West. Her eyes are kinda sad, like she'll miss their time together.

"You should totally go on the cruise, Mr. West. The two of you would have an awesome time. All that free food, the shows." I point at the board and all the checkers. "Cruise ships always have games, too."

Mrs. King looks at me and smiles. "Why, Alex. I'm surprised you know so much about cruises. Have you ever been on one?"

"Nope. But a lot of our guests talk about it. I think it would be awesome to go sometime." I look at Mr. West.

All of a sudden, he realizes Mrs. King is looking at him, too.

"Dolores? Would you want me to go?"

Mrs. King gets all flustered. Her cheeks turn pink, but she's also holding back a smile.

"She totally wants you to!"

"Alex," Mrs. King says like she's gonna scold me. "You're putting words in my mouth." A second later, she looks at Mr. King again. "It would be lovely, but I don't think you could even get a ticket at this late date."

"We have an awesome travel agent in town."

Mr. West snickers as he rests his elbow on the table and looks up at me. "Are you always this persistent, young lady?"

"Totally. My dad always says I need to follow my dreams."

"And what is your dream, Alex?" Mrs. King cocks her head to the side. She reminds me of a friendly grandmother I saw in a movie once.

It doesn't take me even a second to respond. I know my dream. I've known it for a year. "Help my dad be happy again by having him marry Marquetta."

"You are quite the little matchmaker, aren't you?" Mrs. King says.

"I think she's got an admirable dream. And if there's anything we can do to help make it happen during the remainder of our stays, just let us know. Would you agree, Dolores?"

"Absolutely."

Mr. West takes Mrs. King's hand in his. "I'll go see the travel agent in the morning. Who knows? Maybe we can make that sailing together. But only if you'd like me to try."

Mrs. King looks at me. She's got a funny little smile on her face. "I think you said it well, Alex."

"She'd totally love it!" I say, then my phone pings me. It's

Mr. Van Horn. "I gotta go. I'll take care of this stuff for you." I pick up the trash can with the dirty napkins and the empty pizza box and go into the kitchen. I put the trash can on the floor and read Mr. Van Horn's message.

—*I have a few minutes now. What is this about wanting to do a story about those treasure hunters? I don't think that's a viable option. They're a rather unsavory group.*

   —*But wouldn't it be a better story than some boring profile on Mr. Gray's business?*

   —*A lot of people in this town love Joe. Don't underestimate the value of a story about him.*

   —*A friend of mine told me Captain Carroll was here before. Was he a lot of trouble then?*

   —*If you must know, he was a great deal of trouble. The mayor threatened to banish him from the town.*

My mouth drops open. Whoa. It would be awesome to have that kind of power. It would be almost as good as waving a magic wand and making people disappear.

   —*Can she do that?*

   —*No. She was angry because two of his passengers heard one of the stories about Joaquin Murrieta's gold and decided they had better odds finding that than the San Manuel. On their last night in town, they got drunk and stole the mayor's car. They used an off-road map and drove into the mountains. It took three days to find them. The car was nearly totaled.*

   —*Did the mayor throw them in jail?*

   —*Technically, the mayor can't do that, but she had the police chief handle it for her. They disappeared before their trial. That's the kind of people Captain Carroll associates with.*

—If the mayor doesn't want him here, how come he's back?

—Because he claims to have a map showing the exact location of the San Manuel. That's the main reason you need to keep your distance. If there really is a map, these people will do anything to bring up that treasure.

If Captain Carroll has a real treasure map, then Flynn won't be the first one to find the *San Manuel*. That would be a real bummer, and it means Flynn's gonna need some help. The problem is Sasha's mom. She'll tell my dad to keep me away from the docks. Mr. Van Horn will probably tell me the same thing. What's super bad is that Flynn might not know what Captain Carroll has. And if those treasure hunters are as bad as Mr. Van Horn says, that could be trouble. I don't want Flynn to get hurt. She's my friend, and I'd feel terrible if I didn't help her.

I could do like my dad did when he worked for the newspaper in New York. I could go undercover and take on the big story. That would be awesome, but I'd need help to do it.

Sasha would help. And once she's in, Robbie will help, too. Wow. We could do surveillance. And maybe I could sneak down to the marina and ask questions. I could still talk to the lady crew member! This is gonna be off the charts awesome.

Now I have to figure out what to tell Mr. Van Horn. I text back that I'll keep working on the story about Mr. Gray. That's not a real lie 'cause he knows a lot about Captain Carroll, and I am gonna ask him questions. He might know about this map.

There are more noises out front. I look through the butler door and see it's my dad. He's talking to Mr. West and Mrs. King. There's one thing I wanna do before I go see him. I find the last conversation with Flynn O'Connor in my phone and type my message—*can you come by in the morning? Urgent. Don't tell anyone.*

11

Rick

RICK SURVEYED THE B&B grounds from his position near the kitchen sink. Long shadows cast by the early morning sun, reluctant to give up their hold, gradually gave way to the soft light of morning. He let his attention dart from the gazebo to one of the fountains and then along the winding decomposed granite paths. Even after the disaster at dinner, this morning held the promise of a beautiful day.

Standing here had become an almost daily obsession. The bank of mullioned windows gave him a view of the grounds and an opportunity to say thank you to Captain Jack. His grandfather had left him a paradise. At least, that's what it felt like.

Marquetta came and stood next to Rick. She bumped against him gently with her shoulder. "What are you doing, boss?"

"I'm letting my daughter buss the tables while I admire the view." Rick chuckled, then looked at Marquetta. "We've had enough dreary days lately with all the rain. I'm just taking in the sunshine."

"You're right. We should enjoy it while it's here."

They should, thought Rick. They should have been able to enjoy last night, too. It should have been more about being a couple out with friends, not Captain Carroll and his arrogance. Rick took Marquetta's hand, and when she looked at him, he said, "I'm sorry about last night. Things didn't go as I planned."

"We aren't always in control of what happens." Marquetta looked down at the pile of utensils waiting to be washed. Suddenly, she shook her head and forced a smile. "It wasn't your fault. Anyway, the breakfast rush is over. We should get something to eat."

"All the blame lies with Captain Carroll." Rick looked around the room. It was one of the brightest rooms in the house. White cabinets, white-and-gray marbled granite countertops. Pale green walls and overhead lighting. "How could you not love this room?" he asked aloud.

Marquetta smiled as she watched his face. "Mr. Atwood? Are you developing an attachment to my kitchen?"

"And to the person in charge of said kitchen."

He moved toward her, intent on stealing a kiss while Alex was still in the dining room, but the butler door burst open. They both straightened up and faced Alex. She had a tray filled with plates, cups, saucers, and silverware.

"The Wings are still at their table," Alex chirped, a large grin on her face.

"Wings?" Rick asked.

"It's her nickname for Mrs. West and Mr. King," Marquetta said.

Rick rolled his eyes. "Got it. Don't you ever get tired of playing matchmaker?"

"No way. It's fun." Alex set down the tray, looked up at Marquetta, and said, "Besides, we're good at it."

He was about to suggest she let nature take it's course, but stopped when the butler door swung open again.

"Knock, knock," Devon Van Horn said as he entered. He did a double take and regarded Rick. "You're here?"

"Morning, Devon. Come on in. Why wouldn't I be?" Rick asked.

Devon stammered, "No reason. I guess."

Marquetta went to the coffee maker and waved. "Coffee, Devon? I was about to start a new pot."

"I'd love some. I've got a job I'm working on today so I only have a few minutes." Devon crossed the room, pulled out one of the stools from the island, and sat, his frown obvious when he looked at Rick. "Actually, I came here because I heard about Captain Carroll."

Rick grimaced and regarded Marquetta. "It appears we've made the local news."

"How bad are the rumors, Devon?" Marquetta asked.

"Rumors? Oh, sorry. This has nothing to do with the Crooked Mast incident—although there's plenty to say about that. No, this is about Captain Carroll. He's missing." Devon cleared his throat and looked at Rick. "I assumed you'd be on the case already."

Alex drifted closer, her attention focused now on Devon. "Captain Carroll's missing? Maybe somebody killed him and dumped the body."

"That's it," Rick scoffed. "I'm officially putting you into therapy, Alex. You've got murder on the brain. Just because the man is missing doesn't mean someone killed him."

"It doesn't mean they didn't," Alex shot back. "Besides, when you came home last night you said the way he was acting at the Crooked Mast that he deserved it."

One of Marquetta's cheeks quirked up as she looked at Rick.

"That's not very nice."

Devon looked at Marquetta. "Not nice, perhaps, but Alex has a point. After the way Captain Carroll acted at the Crooked Mast, there have to be a number of people who might want him dead."

"Are you saying Mr. Gray might have killed Captain Carroll?" Alex asked.

The back of Rick's neck felt as though a spider were crawling across it. He'd been joking about Alex's curiosity and a therapist —he expected her to get over her crime obsession in time, but the question about Joe Gray concerned him. If Alex was raising that question, who else might?

"There's no evidence of foul play, is there?" Rick asked.

Devon took a sip from his cup, then shook his head. "Haven't heard of any. Other than him being missing, of course."

"It hasn't even been twenty-four hours," Rick said. "The thing is, it's pretty hard to go missing in a town this size. Especially now that Adam's got Deputy Baker. The bottom line is I'm not really needed."

"But what if you're wrong, Daddy? You should totally see if the cops need you."

"No, Alex. I'm not calling Adam. There's no reason." Suddenly, Rick wished Devon hadn't come here this morning. It wasn't that Alex liked death—at least, he hoped not. He drew more comfort from the notion that she was fascinated by solving the puzzle of who committed the crime. Or as it was in this case, if there even was a crime.

"Mr. Van Horn, have they set up a search party to find the body?"

Marquetta stood behind Alex and placed her hands on Alex's shoulders. "Sweetie, we need to leave this to the police. And, as your dad said, Captain Carroll may be alive and well."

"But Daddy always consults with the police."

"Those days may be over," Rick said. "Marquetta's right. If there's any investigating to be done, it will be a police matter. And even if Adam does ask me to help, I don't want you getting involved. Do you understand?"

"But I need to write a story for the Cove Talkers and this is huge."

"Listen to your dad, Alex," Devon said. "I was at Crusty Buns this morning when I heard the news. It got me to thinking about that story you we're asking about."

"The one on Joe Gray?" As soon as he asked the question, Rick knew from the look on Alex's face that wasn't the story she'd talked to Devon about. Once again, he suspected Alex was following her own path. "What story?"

"Well…you wanted me to do it on Mr. Gray."

"And…" insisted Rick.

"He had that big argument with Captain Carroll, and so I thought I could ask questions about *The Treasure King*."

Rick shook his head firmly. "Absolutely not. We agreed you would stick to Joe Gray. Besides, I got a text from Sasha's mother that has me concerned. I want you to stay away from *The Treasure King*."

Alex groaned and slumped back against Marquetta. "I wanted to do something people would want to read."

This was not going the way Rick would have liked. Then again, what conversation with an eleven-year-old did? He sighed and looked at Marquetta. She knelt next to Alex so they were at eye level. "Sweetie, your safety is what matters most. That's why we don't want you going near that boat. And now that Captain Carroll is missing, we don't know how long they'll be here. Obviously, they can't leave until he turns up." She looked back to Rick. "However long that takes."

"I should probably be going." Devon raised the mug and finished his coffee. "Looks like I've caused enough trouble for one day."

"Actually, it's probably good that you did." Rick looked directly at Alex and said, "I wasn't aware of what happened, but now I can take steps to ensure we aren't interfering in police business. Right, Alex?"

"Yes, Daddy."

Rick didn't miss the rolling of the eyes or the heavy sigh. Clearly, Alex wasn't happy about leaving this situation alone. Nor was he comfortable that she really would.

After Devon left, Rick, Alex, and Marquetta settled in for breakfast. Their talk felt subdued to Rick, as though they were each distracted by their own issues. He could only guess what was distracting Marquetta, but was confident Alex was thinking about Captain Carroll. Despite what he'd said earlier, he decided to call Adam. He might as well ask if he was still the department's unpaid, unofficial consultant. Maybe, with Deputy Baker on board, he'd be off the hook. If nothing else, maybe he could determine if there had even been a crime.

Midway through her bowl of cereal, Alex's phone pinged. She looked at the display, her eyes lit up, and she stood. "May I be excused for a minute?"

"Your cereal will get soggy," Rick protested.

She nudged the bowl away. "It gets that way anyway. I'll only be a minute."

"Go ahead." Rick watched as Alex hurried through the butler door. "What do you suppose she's up to?"

"I have no idea, but I think we might want to keep her busy for the next few days."

"Definitely. The last thing I need is my daughter launching another of her shadow investigations. I'd much rather have her learning math than trying to find the elusive Captain Carroll."

12

Alex

FLYNN O'CONNOR IS WAITING FOR me at the front desk. She's
wearing her deep blue camp shirt and khakis. I love that shirt on
her. The blue is a totally cool color for her. She's reading
something on her phone and doesn't see me until I'm almost next
to her.

"Hey, Flynn."

I give her a big hug. She hugs me back, then pulls away.
"What's this all about, Alex? You said we need to keep
something quiet, but you didn't say what it was."

"It's *The Treasure King*. They have a map that shows the
location of the *San Manuel*. I thought you should know."

Flynn looks down at her phone, makes a face at it, then stuffs
it in her back pocket. "I've heard the scuttlebutt, but I don't
know how much of it we should believe."

"That's why we need to find out."

"We?"

"Yeah. If there is a map, I can totally help. Somebody else
having a map would really mess up your project. Right?"

"It would force me to play defense, which I hate. But, this is something I need to deal with. If there's one thing I know about treasure hunters, it's that they're concerned about results, not methods."

"I think that's why Captain Carroll's dead."

"Excuse me? He's dead? Where did you hear this?"

"From Mr. Van Horn. He was here and told us Captain Carroll's missing. But with all that treasure at stake, he's gotta be dead."

Flynn frowns at me. "Alex, I think you're making a big leap. There's a huge difference between missing and murdered. Don't be putting the cart before the horse."

"What's that mean?"

"It's an old expression that means you can't be assuming a man has been murdered when there's no evidence."

"But there is! It totally makes sense. Captain Carroll has a map that's super valuable, and he disappeared just a couple days before he was going to bring up all the treasure. Either that, or the whole map thing is a fake-out so they can spy on you."

"Whoa, girlfriend. Slow down. Have I taught you nothing about a methodical process? When I take charge of an excavation, I can't assume anything. I have to take one step at a time—observe, evaluate, decide on a course of action. Isn't that what the police have to do, too?"

"Yes, but…"

"It's a clear-cut process, Alex. I know you've solved murders by interpreting the clues differently than the police—and even your dad. But those were different situations. These people are… dangerous. And if Captain Carroll has been murdered because of a treasure map, his body will turn up. At which point there will be an investigation. And as for spying on me, I don't think they have the patience. Promise me you'll stay away from this whole thing."

"But, Flynn, we need to find out if there really is a map!"

Flynn's face gets kinda splotchy and she starts breathing real fast. "No. You need to let the police handle this. I suppose your dad will be called in, but you cannot be asking questions of these people. Some of them are criminals."

"But…"

"No buts. We have a special relationship. I don't want anything to happen to you."

"What about the *San Manuel*? They might get to it first."

"Not if I can help it. And if they do, I have legal remedies."

"You can't watch them 24/7!"

Flynn lets out a big sigh. "You're forcing me to do something I don't want to do, Alex, and that's breaking our trust. Please, leave this alone."

She's super worried. I can see it on her face. Her voice is getting super frantic. I totally don't want her going to my dad, so I guess I have to agree—for now. "Okay. You don't need to worry about me."

"Thank goodness. I don't think I could bear it if something happened to you." Flynn lets out a breath and crushes me next to her. "By the way, why aren't you in school?"

"We're on spring break."

She steps back and looks at the door. "That's nice. Enjoy it while you're young. I have to be going."

This is getting super complex. Now I have to investigate without Flynn's help? Whatever. I'm totally gonna crack the secrets of *The Treasure King*.

13

Rick

AT NINE-THIRTY, RICK TOLD Alex it was time to go to Seaside Cove Market. On his first visit to the town's only grocery store, he'd been surprised at how much the owners squeezed into such a small space. The brand variety was limited, but he and Alex had quickly adapted, thanks to a crash course in grocery buying Marquetta had given them. Over time, they'd devised a simple division of labor for the list. Alex handled the produce; Rick took the rest.

While they waited in line behind a man Rick didn't recognize, Rick looked over the items Alex had added to the cart.

"That's a lot of apricots, kiddo."

"Marquetta said she needed two dozen."

"Okay. Ours is not to question why. I'm sure she has her reasons."

The stranger, who wore jeans and a Whaler's Cove tee-shirt, looked at Rick. "You're a local?"

"We moved here about a year ago."

"Can you tell me how to get to the lighthouse? I'm on foot,

but I heard it's a good place for a picnic."

"It's a bit of a walk, but not too bad," Rick said, then gave the man directions. The line inched forward. The stranger thanked Rick, and placed his purchase on the conveyor belt.

Alex bumped against Rick's hip, then cocked her head toward the stranger.

"What's up, kiddo?"

Alex whispered, "That man's from *The Treasure King*. He's one of the crew members."

"How do you know that?"

"Me and Robbie and Sasha were watching when they docked."

Rick grimaced. The last thing he wanted to do was start lecturing Alex in public, but he also needed to deal with this while it was a fresh subject. "You and I need to have a little talk later."

"Okay," Alex said absently.

It frustrated Rick that she was paying more attention to the conversation between the crew member and the checker than to him. He made a mental note to deal with that at the same time.

The man ahead of them in line, who had been silent until now, spoke in a loud tone. "What do you mean our account's been closed?"

"It hasn't been closed, sir. There never was one. For your purchase, we can take cash or credit card."

"Captain Carroll told me himself he opened the account. You must be wrong."

"I'm not wrong, sir. There's no account for anyone by that name or for *The Treasure King*."

"I'll have him come in later and settle up with you," the man insisted. "Just give me my items now."

"I'm sorry, but I can't do that. Would you like to speak to the manager?"

Rick had resigned himself to a long wait when one of the other checkers grabbed the front of his cart and led them to a different station. "Thank you, Maisy," Rick said.

"No worries. That's probably going to take a while." Maisy stopped, watched the crew member walk out, then scanned the next item. "Or not."

"I'm still thankful you pulled us away." Rick pointed to the end of the checkout stand. "Alex, help Maisy out and bag, would you?"

"Okay." She opened the first of their four bags and began adding the heavier items first.

As Alex bagged, Maisy said, "I heard they have a map to the *San Manuel*."

"If they had a map, why wouldn't they be out diving?" Alex countered.

"Good point. But every army must be fed."

"He wasn't buying that much stuff. If they were going out for a long time, they'd need a lot more food."

Maisy looked at Rick as she scanned the next item. "Pretty sharp little girl you have there, Rick."

"Yes, she is," Rick said as he beamed at Alex. "A little too inquisitive for her own good sometimes, but very bright."

"My teacher says being inquisitive is what makes me a good student," Alex chirped.

"Your total is $92.92, Rick."

Rick put his credit card into the terminal slot and waited for the authorization process to complete. He looked up at Maisy. "I'm going to have to have a talk with Mrs. Rawlings. She must not realize the monster she's helping to create."

"My son had Mrs. Rawlings. That was back when she first started teaching, but she never told me he was too inquisitive. He was always the opposite."

"How's he doing?" Rick asked as he signed for the purchase.

"Okay, but he's thirty and feels like he's stuck in a rut. What a shame for someone so young." Maisy handed Rick his receipt, then closed down her register. "You two have a good day."

Rick and Alex said their goodbyes to Maisy and stepped out into the sunshine. The air was still cool, which was one reason Rick liked doing the shopping early in the day. At the next corner, they stopped to wait for a car turning left in front of them.

"Daddy? Do you think Captain Carroll came here to spy on Flynn?"

"Why would you say that?"

"It just seems weird that they showed up here. Mr. Gray said they should have had enough supplies, so they have no reason to be here unless they're up to no good."

"Did he say this while you were at the docks?"

"Uh huh."

As they were making their turn onto Front St., Rick said, "So that man in the market works on *The Treasure King?*"

"When Mr. Gray made them move the boat, he's the one who ran it."

"I'm concerned about you going near that boat, Alex. After what Sasha's mom said, I don't want you going back to the docks until they leave Seaside Cove."

"But we only go there during the day. There's people around, so it's safe."

"This is one of those times when I have to pull rank on you, kiddo. I avoid it when I can, but you're more trusting than I am. Do not go near anyone from that boat."

14

Alex

Hey Journal,

I've got thirty minutes before I have to go help Marquetta. We've got a room to clean and then we'll have to prep for lunch. After me and Daddy talked on the way home from the market, I started thinking about how much I like Seaside Cove. I didn't think it was going to be any fun 'cause it's such a little town and I wasn't gonna know anybody. But before we ever moved here, Marquetta asked my dad what my favorite colors were. Teal and purple, of course! It turns out they're Marquetta's favorites, too.

But what's totally awesome is that she painted my room teal with purple trim before we moved in. She even decorated the room with white bedroom furniture and accents that match the room colors. After I told her I loved the furniture, she got all teary and told me it was hers when she was my age. She even made my favorite meal, Mac n'Cheese, for our first night here.

I was hoping my dad was going to ask her to marry him at last night's dinner, but I guess Captain Carroll totally messed that up. My dad's got good intentions, but, just between you and me, he's kinda out of practice in the whole romance department. Now I have to come up with another plan to get them together. I also wanna help Flynn find out what's going on with the treasure hunters. I know she said she doesn't want me to be involved, but that's just her being super cautious. I'm gonna text Sasha and see if we can meet this afternoon. Maybe we can do a little spying on the docks to see if we can answer the question about the treasure map!

Bye for now,
Alex

—*Hey Sasha, need to spend time watching the marina this afternoon. Wanna find out what's up with that treasure map.*

—*My mom says I'm not supposed to go near there. Did your dad talk to you?*

—*He said he didn't want me going near the treasure hunters, but didn't say I couldn't watch from Front Street. It's gonna be like a real surveillance!*

—*Awesome! I didn't think about watching from there. We're gonna need binoculars. Got any?*

—*Got one pair.*

—*Can get my dad's. He won't care. What about Robbie? Are you gonna ask him?*

—*Totally. He'll do it if I ask right.*

—*What time?*

—*Surveillance starts at 1:11!*

After I know I've got Sasha on board, I text Robbie. He's kinda reluctant at first, but he finally agrees to meet at the scheduled time. The whole thing of convincing Robbie everything was gonna be cool takes longer than I thought it would, so I have to hurry to catch up with Marquetta. She's super fast and probably has a couple of the rooms done already.

15

Rick

RICK SAT BEHIND HIS DESK contemplating the bookshelves along the walls. How many secrets had they heard over the years? Probably more than he would ever know about. He brought up the news story by J.K. Keneally. Was it possible the event that had made Neal Weiss and Captain Jack look so grim had taken place in this room? Could the bookshelves have witnessed that event? If only they could speak.

He checked his email and messages. There was nothing from the *San Ladron Times*. It was either too soon or they'd deleted his original request or…it was even possible his message had never been received. Keneally might have left years ago. Still, there was no harm in sending a second request to show his determination. He opened a new window, brought up the contact form, filled it out, and was double-checking his contact information when someone knocked on the door.

Rick quickly checked his email address in the form, took a breath, and hit the send button. "Come in."

The door opened a crack and Adam Cunningham poked his

head through the opening. "Got a minute?"

Rick gestured at one of the visitor's chairs. "Sure. Have a seat. What's up?"

"I hate being the bearer of bad news, but we found a body floating in the marina this morning. It was Captain Carroll."

"Crap," Rick muttered. "Alex was right."

"About?"

"Carroll being dead. He might have been a complete jerk, but he was too young to die."

"He didn't do it on his own. Someone helped him along."

Rick let out a deep sigh. "Murder?"

"He was shot in the chest with a speargun."

Closing the lid on the laptop, Rick regarded Adam. "After last night, I suppose I'm on the suspect list."

"No way. You're my sounding board. And maybe my consultant, if you want to be."

Rick suddenly felt two emotions ramping up inside him—relief because he wasn't a suspect, and apprehension because he would need to keep Alex away from the investigation. "What happened?"

"After that dinner altercation last night somebody found Captain Carroll, shot him in the chest, probably at very close range, then dumped the body in the water. We've got a rough window for the murder of between six and nine p.m."

"Makes sense. It couldn't have happened before six because Carroll was in the Crooked Mast making trouble. After that, he probably would have been back aboard."

"Exactly. Baker escorted him out at 6:03. Fortunately, the body landed in the water face down, The air was trapped in the lungs and it didn't sink. The killer must have decided to shove it under the docks. What they didn't count on was the tidal action.

By eight this morning the outgoing tide sucked it out and it was floating in clear view when Jennifer Martin spotted it."

"Is she the woman who runs the bait shop? I haven't met her."

"Sharp lady. Watch yourself when you talk to her. You make a mistake and she'll call you on it. She told me twice that I needed to keep up." Adam chuckled. "You'll see."

"You want me to talk to her? What about Deputy Baker?"

"You'll be working with her. The mayor has me on a special project. I'd rather work this with you, but we don't always get what we want. Do we?"

Rick gazed around the office. The B&B wasn't what he'd wanted, not at first. But circumstances had brought him and Alex here. Now, this office, the B&B, and life in Seaside Cove were exactly what he wanted. "Things work out sometimes. I'll want to take a look at the crime scene."

"Of course. This lays out the general theory." Adam pulled out a letter-sized sheet of paper. Rick recognized his friend's handiwork immediately. Detailed. Shaded properly. It looked more like an artist's pencil sketch than a crime-scene diagram.

"Looks like you've been drawing again."

"Frustrated artist," Adam joked. He held his finger over the paper. "Here's the dock, and this is where the body was found. The water there is still, except for the tides. This arrow shows where we think the body would have been concealed."

"We?"

"Joe Gray. I spoke with him before the coroner arrived. He's the one who came up with the idea of the hidden body. The entire distance isn't much, maybe ten feet or so. Joe's theory is that whoever killed the captain used the speargun to push the body under the dock."

Rick said, "Joe's lived here all his life. He knows that marina inside-out, so if he says it's possible, I believe him. If the body was in the water, how'd you narrow down a time of death?"

"Joe said the tides started coming in shortly before five p.m. and didn't start to recede until eleven. If the killer pushed the body in the water early in the evening, it would most likely have stayed put until the tide started to recede. At that point it could have drifted out from under the docks."

"But you said the window was between six and nine."

"Baker went down there at nine to make sure everything was quiet."

"Of course she did," Rick said. "Do you think the killer is someone aboard *The Treasure King*? How much time is there? Before they sail?"

"I've ordered them to stay in port until the investigation has been completed. If they try and skip out, I'll bring in the Coast Guard. You'll have as much time as you need."

Between Adam showing up at the B&B unannounced, the sketch, and Joe's theory, Rick felt compelled to help. He didn't mind the investigation, not really. What he didn't want was Alex hearing about this. But how did he keep what would be the biggest news in town away from an eleven-year-old who was plugged into the town's gossip mill? The short answer, he knew, was that he couldn't. He watched a wispy cloud drift across the clear, blue sky. Having it snow this afternoon was more achievable than keeping Alex out of this.

"I have a problem, Adam."

"The junior detective in the house?"

"There's no way I can keep her from finding out about this, so how do I keep her from getting involved?"

Adam rested his elbow on the arm of the chair and rubbed his jaw. "Based on past performance, I'd say that wouldn't be the worst thing that could happen. She has provided some valuable insights."

Rick couldn't believe what he was hearing. Nor did he really know what to say. "You can't be serious."

"I'm not saying I want to hire her as a junior consultant. All I'm saying is you know she's going to want to dive in. Why not let her do it, but with oversight? Keep her on a tight rein, don't let her get near the bad guys, that sort of thing."

One of Rick's few memories about Captain Jack was when he'd brought Rick to this office and told him the books represented the wisdom of the ages. That's the kind of wisdom he felt he needed now to deal with a precocious daughter. "I'm listening."

"Alex looks up to Marquetta. They work well together, and you know Marky's not going to let anything happen to that little girl. If you asked, I'll bet Marky would be happy to help."

With his pulse pounding in his ears, Rick considered Adam's proposal. Everything he said was true. To a degree. "I don't know, Adam. Marquetta's reaction last night in the restaurant was off. It wasn't like her at all."

"It was a brand new blouse that got ruined. Maybe that's all there was to it."

"I don't think so. She was upset about the blouse, but she wouldn't talk about anything that happened after Deputy Baker showed up."

"Baker? She was there to keep the peace. Why would Marky have a problem with her?"

"I don't know. It's just a feeling. Do you think Traci might know something—no. Forget what I said. I think all I can do is wait until Marquetta's ready to open up."

"Have it your way. As far as Baker's concerned, you won't have a problem working with her. She's got solid training, and I've explained how valuable you've been in the past."

"I hadn't even thought about how that would go. You sure she'll be okay sharing information?"

"Absolutely."

Rick's shoulders felt like they were tied in knots. He did not need to get on the bad side of the town's new deputy. "From what I saw she's pretty take-charge."

"I have already talked to her. She expressed some concern about working with a civilian, but she'll go along with the program."

"How much concern?"

"Some."

"Is that police-chief speak for you're ordering her to cooperate with me?"

"It will work, Rick. I guarantee it."

The words were there, but the hesitation in Adam's voice made Rick recall the old expression often attributed to Benjamin Franklin about there being no guarantees in life except death and taxes. He already paid taxes, and now they had a death to deal with. Maybe Franklin had missed one other guarantee—the fragile nature of the human ego.

16

Rick

AFTER ADAM LEFT, RICK WALKED the perimeter of his office while contemplating what to do next. He stopped before the west-facing windows. From here, he could see the breakwater. Waves crashed against the rocks, sending up huge plumes of surf and spray. He'd almost died out there once after turning his back on the ocean. It was a lesson learned—a frightening encounter with the force of nature. In a way, he felt the same fear at the thought of looking into the murder of Captain Carroll. Or maybe it wasn't the thought of him investigating the death as much as it was condoning some sort of part for Alex.

There was no point in putting this off. He had to deal with his daughter. Get her under control. He sent her a short text asking her to come to his office, then waited, watching the waves crash against the breakwater until there was a soft knock and the door inched open.

Rick waved Alex in and gestured for her to sit in the same seat Adam had used minutes before. The best approach was the direct one, at least, that's what he hoped. Rick rested his elbows on the desktop and prepared to share Adam's suggestion, but to also be firm in his restrictions. Before he could say a word, Alex inched forward and beamed at him.

"Are you gonna ask Marquetta to marry you? Is that why you wanna talk?"

Rick felt a pang of regret, a sharp reminder of last night's little fiasco. "No, kiddo. Things have just been a bit off since last night. You wouldn't want me to propose while Marquetta is slaving away in front of a hot stove or vacuuming, would you?"

Alex scrunched up her face. "I guess not."

"I have to wait for the right time, and so do you. This is a big deal. It's not every day that I ask a woman to be my wife."

"Maybe I should ask!" Alex's face lit up with a smile. "I could just say, Marquetta, will you be my mom? She'll totally accept."

"That's an unusual approach, but I'd rather deal with the question myself. Look, that's not why I asked you in here. For the time being, I need you to leave the proposing marriage end of things to me. Do you remember what I said earlier about me having to pull rank on you?"

"Uh oh. Am I in trouble? Did I do something wrong?"

Rick smiled. Shook his head. "Nothing like that. However, something bad has happened."

"Did something happen to one of the guests?"

"No. They're all fine. Actually, Marquetta will have to be consulted on this, too, because it involves both of you. This has to do with Captain Carroll. Adam just told me that his body was found floating in the harbor. He's dead."

"I was right?" Alex's eyes widened. "Are you gonna investigate? Is that why Chief Cunningham was here?"

"Yes, that's what he's asked me to do." Rick sighed. "He

wants me to work with Deputy Baker, but that's not what I'm concerned about. The bigger problem I see isn't my investigation, it's yours."

Alex did a double take and her eyes got even wider. "Am I on your team? That is so awesome! Wait'll I tell…"

"No, you're not on the team," Rick said firmly. "However, I know you, Alex, and as soon as you walk out that door you will be thinking about how you can find the killer faster than me and Deputy Baker."

At first, Alex's enthusiasm faded, then her smile returned. "Is that what Chief Cunningham said? That I'm a good investigator?"

"Slow down, kiddo. Given the risks you've taken in the past, I should probably lock you in your room until this is over. However, grounding you hasn't worked. Adam proposed a different solution, which I've decided to try. I'll be working with Deputy Baker. You will be working with Marquetta. Just as the deputy is my lead, Marquetta will be yours. That means she's in charge, not you. And all this assumes she's okay with the idea. If she says she doesn't want to be involved, I'll have to think of another solution. Maybe boarding school."

Rick could barely contain his laughter at Alex's reaction. She blinked several times. Her jaw dropped. Then she stammered, "Is that, like, a real thing? Not just in movies?"

"In Europe," Rick added, then chuckled. "I'm kidding about boarding school. I would never want to send you away. But I'm serious. If doing this makes Marquetta uncomfortable, I will not force her. Do you understand?"

"She'll totally do it. We're a good team."

"I know you are. But this is a murder investigation, not meal planning. What concerns me most is how you don't worry about consequences when you start asking people if they were involved. That's why I'm going to ask Marquetta if she'll work with you. As I said, if she says yes, then you have a role. Otherwise, I'll find another solution."

"But, Daddy…"

"Alex, you don't seem to understand. Now that you have a bike and can get out in the world, you're more exposed than ever. It used to be you were always here, and that made it easy to keep tabs on you. You're still a child. Quite frankly, your impulsiveness concerns me. You leap before you think. That's why you need supervision and it's my job as your parent to see that you get it in the most effective manner."

"So all that stuff about believing in myself doesn't count?"

"It counts tremendously, but part of believing in yourself is learning when to trust your instincts and when to question them. You're still too young to be able to separate those out. And honestly, it can be difficult for adults, too. So for now, I have one question for you. If I agree to let you look into Captain Carroll's death under Marquetta's supervision, are you going to be okay with that?"

"I'm totally good with it."

"Then I'll talk to Marquetta. That's the next step. I probably should have asked her first, but I wanted to get to you before you heard about this through the grapevine. In a way, I'm surprised you haven't heard about it already."

Alex's brow creased again as she thought, then asked, "How did Captain Carroll die?"

He went over the details of the killing—the speargun, the tides, and the estimated time of death. When he was done, Alex squirmed in her chair.

"So when can we ask Marquetta?"

"There's no 'we' in this part. I'll be talking to her in a few minutes. Until then, I want your promise that you won't do anything."

"But Daddy…"

"No, Alex. I was just sure you'd have already heard about the killing, and I wanted to stop you from running off on your own. So, do I have your promise you'll not do any investigating until after I talk to Marquetta?"

"When are you gonna talk to her?"

"Right after we're done."

"Okay. I can wait until then." She sighed, told Rick she would wait in her room, but barely a breath later, her smile lit up. "Do you have any suspects?"

17

Alex

MARCH 27

Hey Journal,

This is super big news! My dad's agreed to let me help the cops as long as I work with Marquetta. It's like the first time ever that I haven't gotten grounded for investigating a murder. My head is buzzing with so many ideas about how I can help.

You know what? I'm gonna start by checking out social media. Everybody posts stuff without thinking about it, so that might be the killer's downfall. The cool thing is none of the adults are very good at it, so maybe I can be the expert. Then Daddy and Chief Cunningham will see how valuable my help is.

Got things to do, Journal. Bye for now,

Alex

I open the top drawer of my desk. It's not big like my dad's, but it's perfect for me. The desk was originally Marquetta's when she was my age and I fell in love with it the first time I saw it. I pull out my folder of keepsakes. Inside are a few of my favorites—a letter from Mayor Carter thanking me for helping to solve a previous murder, a note from one of my teachers commending me on getting straight A's, and my last birthday card from Marquetta.

Inside the card is the message she wrote. It's what makes the card so special—*I hope this birthday is magical. You are so amazing and I love you more than I can say. Always believe in yourself.*

I probably read the card a couple times a week. I never got a card like that from my real mom. Maybe if I had I wouldn't cherish Marquetta's so much. The words get kinda blurry as I read them again. It hasn't even been ten minutes since I left my dad's office. The cops always say the longer it takes to solve a crime the colder the trail gets. Right? I totally want to get to work. I put the card on top of my desk and wake up my laptop.

It only takes me about five minutes to find a social media page for *The Treasure King*. At the top of the page there's a photo of the boat cruising on the water. It's an awesome photo and makes the boat look even better than it does in person. There are a couple videos so people can take a virtual tour. I start playing the first one.

The tour begins on the main deck at the front of the boat and goes all the way around. There's another video for a look inside. I click the link. The video starts. It begins inside what they call the main gathering area. There's a lot of plush red furniture. It's all super old style. By the time the video is over, I'm disappointed. Other than knowing where things are on the boat, I didn't learn much, and I kinda feel like I wasted fifteen minutes. Unless…unless I could get on *The Treasure King*.

Getting on the boat would totally go against what my dad said I could do. But what if it led me to the killer? There's no way he could ground me. If I didn't find anything, I'd be in super big trouble. So that means I'm gonna have to do this on the down low. Super quiet.

I look at Marquetta's card. Read the last three words of what she wrote again. *Believe in yourself.*

I'm in. All in. I click the link to watch the tour again. By the time the video gets to the navigation deck on top of the boat my head is ready to explode. There are so many details. So many places the treasure map could be hidden. There's no question. I have to find a way onto the boat. And that means I need to know what my dad is saying to Marquetta. Right now.

18

Rick

AFTER ALEX LEFT RICK'S OFFICE, he spent a few minutes questioning his decision. The bottom line was, as long as they could keep close tabs on Alex, everything should be fine. His shoulders slumped. Since when had it ever been easy to keep Alex under control? She had a mind of her own. He was proud of her and wanted her to grow up to be strong and independent, but above all else he had to keep her safe.

Adam's entire plan depended on Marquetta's cooperation. He might as well find out. Would she go along?

Rick found Marquetta in the laundry room loading towels into the dryer. At first, she didn't hear him. He spent those first few seconds watching her. He studied the curve of her face. Listened to her hum a song he didn't recognize. He even enjoyed watching the way she fluffed the towels in the dryer to make sure they weren't all bunched up.

"We need to talk," he said when she finished.

Marquetta jumped and put her hand over her heart. "Oh my God! You scared me to death. How long have you been there?"

"Not long." He paused and took a breath. "Captain Carroll's been murdered and Adam has asked me to consult. Adam also asked me about giving Alex a...a role to play. I hesitate to call it that because I want to keep her away from this whole thing."

Marquetta's eyes widened. "Let me get this straight. Adam wants Alex to help? And you didn't tell him no? You can't be serious."

Rick ran his fingers through his hair and massaged the back of his neck. "You know what she's like. This would be more of a diversion, I guess."

When he finished explaining Adam's suggestion and how he'd agreed, Marquetta said, "You know I'll do it, Rick. At least that way I can keep an eye on her."

"Thank you. I wish there was another way."

Marquetta pulled a top sheet from a laundry basket she'd put off to the side. "Make yourself useful. Take that end." They stood far enough apart to fold the sheet lengthwise. When they came together and Rick handed off his end, Marquetta spoke again. "I'm not saying I'm comfortable with the idea of investigating a murder, but I'm willing to go along, especially if I can keep her focused on another problem."

"I don't understand. What other problem is there? I've already talked to her and explained the ground rules. She's okay with the limitations."

"So she says. She'll find a way to run around and question people no matter what. Actually, I saw Flynn O'Connor here earlier. She and Alex were talking. What if we give Alex a different puzzle to solve? One she'll care about just as much and that will keep her away from the police investigation?"

"If you can come up with something like that, I'm all for it."

"The treasure map. Maybe we could focus on finding out if

there is such a map instead of Captain Carroll's murder. That could help Flynn, and I'm sure it would interest Alex."

"Great idea. Go for it. I'm willing to do anything that will make this easier for you and help keep Alex out of trouble. By the way, I know last night was difficult for you. I'm sorry about everything that happened in the restaurant. I can't believe what a rollercoaster this has been. First, dinner turned into a shoving match. Now, the man who caused all the problems is dead."

"It wouldn't have been so bad if Adam had just handled the situation."

"What could he have done? Everything happened so fast. One minute, Joe was upright, then he wasn't."

Marquetta pulled a pillowcase from the basket. Her jaw tightened visibly. "I shouldn't have reacted the way I did."

Rick took her by the shoulders and turned her so they were face-to-face. "I love you, Marquetta Weiss. Every little thing you do interests me. When you feel pain, I feel it, too. Please, we've come so far. Don't shut me out. What's bothering you?"

With a sigh, Marquetta turned back to face the dryer and began to fold the pillowcase. No sooner had she finished than she unfolded it and tossed it into the laundry basket. "It's stupid. Not even worth going into."

"If it upsets you, it's worth getting into. Just start talking, and let's see what comes out."

"It has to do with Pamela. I don't want to badmouth her, so all I'll say is that we were friends in high school, then something happened and we had a falling out. After she graduated, she left for college."

"What did you two argue about?" Rick asked.

Marquetta retrieved the pillowcase and again smoothed it out on the top of the dryer. Rick gently took her by the shoulders and looked into her eyes.

"Tell me."

"I don't want to go into it. I really don't. Look, we don't get along, but she's a police officer and I'm a law-abiding citizen. You're the one who will be working with her, not me. So, I'll just give her space."

"That's all you're going to say?"

"For now." Marquetta paused, then continued. "No. there is one more thing. Alex is pretty enamored of Deputy Baker. I'm afraid she's put her up on a pedestal as some sort of role model. I don't want to see Alex get hurt, so you should know this. Pamela's always been very goal focused. If there's something she wants, she goes after it."

"So the argument was about a boy," Rick said with a sly smile.

Marquetta rolled her eyes. "Peripherally. Yes. But, I'm talking about today. Watch yourself. If something happens and Pamela sees a way to make herself look good, even if it's at your expense, she'll do it. Alex won't understand that yet, which makes her especially vulnerable to disillusionment. But you... you have more to lose."

"I don't see how she's going to take away anything I have, so can you be more specific? Clue me in as to what you're talking about?"

"Just keep your eyes open. Okay? That's all I'm asking."

He took Marquetta's hand in both of his and kissed it. "I will keep my eyes open at all times. I promise, but you have nothing to worry about because I'm immune to temptation. I have everything I want here, and I'm not doing anything to jeopardize that."

"I have to admit, Mr. Atwood. You are a smooth one."

Rick put his finger under Marquetta's chin and lifted. His lips brushed hers. When she pulled away, he said, "By the way, there's something else I've been putting off telling you, but I've decided waiting is a mistake. I found a news story from the day your dad went to sea. I've reached out to the reporter who wrote it. His name is J.K. Keneally. I don't know if I'll get a response or not, but I thought it could be worth giving him a shout."

"Why?"

"If you look at the photo of your dad and Captain Jack, it looks like there was something going on between the two of them. Almost as if they'd argued. Did Captain Jack ever say anything to you about it?"

"Not to me. I was ten. And my mom never said anything. To be honest, I don't remember much from those days. Every once in a while I have flashes of a memory, but most of the time that's all buried under the pain of losing my dad. My strongest memory is standing on the end of the dock in the rain watching him sail away. He stood there, waving to me from the back of the boat until the boat disappeared." Marquetta choked back a sob and removed her hand from Rick's. She swiped at her cheeks. "That's my last memory of him."

"Was Captain Jack there?"

"A lot of people were. It's all so jumbled. And I've been through it so many times in my head that I no longer know what's real and what...I've made up. I'm sorry I can't be more help."

"Maybe we can find you the truth. If that's what you want."

Marquetta hesitated, but then said, "It is. I think."

Rick picked up the laundry basket and carried it into the kitchen. He set it on the countertop, then looked at Marquetta. "Let's see what this reporter can tell me. Assuming the paper can even put me in touch with him. I've grilled you enough for one day."

"Is that ever the truth. But, you know, deep down, I think I'm finally ready to know what really happened that day. And that includes finding out if my dad and Captain Jack had a falling out. Maybe that's one of the things that's been bothering me for all these years. I guess what I'm saying is it can't hurt to ask someone else who was there."

The butler door swooshed open and Alex burst into the room, her eyes wide and a look of panic on her face. "Help! Mr. West just fell!"

19

Rick

ALEX LED THE WAY BACK into the living room where Mr. West sat on one of the gray couches next to Mrs. King, her hand stroking his arm and shoulder sympathetically. Standing behind her was Winnie Carston, and to her left was her husband, who was bent over Mr. West. The entire little group, with the exception of the man who had caused the commotion, looked visibly shaken.

Mr. West waved as Rick, Marquetta, and Alex entered. "Ah, I see you came back with reinforcements. Stephen came to my rescue right after you darted off. Thank you for trying, but as you can see, I already have plenty of caretakers hovering about."

"What happened?" Rick asked.

"It's really rather silly," Mr. West said. "I have these floaters in my right eye. Normally, I compensate for them. But Dolores and I were walking through here when I saw one of those floaters whip by in my peripheral vision. Silly me, I thought it was a bug and tried to swat at it. I lost my balance and went down. Thank goodness we weren't at the top of the stairs."

"Do you need a doctor?" Marquetta asked.

"No. No. Nothing's broken. The only real damage is a bruised ego." He turned sideways and said, "I hate to say it, Dolores, but you're now seeing the real me. I can be a bit of an old klutz at times."

"You scared me to death," she clucked. "Are you sure you're okay? We could take you to the hospital for x-rays."

"The nearest hospital is in San Ladron," Rick said.

"We do have a small urgent care center," Marquetta added. "If you have any pain, we should have you checked out. I could call the owner. He'd be happy to help."

"Thanks to everyone's quick thinking—especially this young lady's…" Mr. West stopped and gave Alex an exaggerated wink. "I'm just fine."

Rick shot a quick look at Alex. She'd said she was going to be in her room, which was on the second floor and down the hall. There was no way she could have heard Mr. West fall…unless… He sighed. She'd probably been right outside the butler door listening to his conversation with Marquetta. Given the circumstances, Rick decided to let the subject drop, at least for the time being.

Mr. West continued, "As I said, there's no real physical damage. I might be walking extra slow for the next day or two, but that's all." He tilted his head sideways toward Stephen Carston. "Thank goodness for this strong, young man. He was able to assist me with no problem at all."

"You got part of that right, William, but I no longer qualify as young. I've passed the big five-oh myself, and I have a desk job. Thank goodness I have a gym to go to. I'm not picky, though, so I'll take any compliment I can get."

"That's my husband, modest to the end." Winnie Carston looked at Rick and smiled.

There was something very comforting about her demeanor. He saw her as a calming influence in almost any situation—except those where she disrupted the norm. He still recalled their first meeting in which she'd insisted on everyone using their first names. In addition, she would not tolerate anyone calling her Winifred, but made it clear she was Winnie. Rick had tried to explain how they liked to use the guest's last names as a sign of respect, but Winnie had pooh-poohed the notion with a backward flip of her hand.

"Rick—you don't mind if I call you Rick, do you? My father always told me, 'Winnie, it's not what people call you to your face that matters, it's what they call you behind your back.' Now, I hope you'll call me Winnie—all the time." With that, she'd laughed deep and hearty.

Alex went and hugged Mr. West. "I'm glad you're okay. I heard the fall and got worried."

"You're exceptionally lucky to have such a fine daughter," Mr. West said.

The man was right. Alex was a fine daughter. And way too inquisitive for her own good. Nevertheless, he'd drop the issue of where she was supposed to have been. Otherwise, how did he tell her she shouldn't have been present when there was an accident like this? "I consider myself a very lucky man."

When Mr. West stood, he looked stiff and shaken, but he made a valiant attempt to reassure everyone, especially Dolores, that he'd survived his fall and was ready to face the day.

"It looks like you're in good hands, William," said Stephen. "Winnie and I will take our leave."

Once Stephen and Winnie were gone, Marquetta said, "Mr. West, I'm sure you and Mrs. King have a lot you want to do today, but before you go rushing off, why don't you let us bring a soothing cup of tea up to your room? I have a lovely hibiscus blend I hold out for special people, and I'm sure Alex would be happy to bring you both everything you need. It would be a nice opportunity to enjoy the comforts of home."

He wrinkled his nose as he looked from Marquetta to Mrs. King. "I'm not a big tea drinker."

"Oh, William," Mrs. King tsk'd a couple of times. "I thought you said you wanted to try new things."

Marquetta gave Mr. West's shoulder a gentle shake. "I'll bet you didn't get to try one of our croissants at breakfast. I have some left over."

"They're awesome," Alex beamed. "They come from Crusty Buns. Mrs. King, would you like to sit with him?"

Mrs. King put a hand to her chest and smiled at Alex. "How thoughtful of you, dear." She then gazed at Mr. West. "If you'd like the company."

"I would. Most definitely. And you're right, I do want to try new things."

"We're good, then," Alex said. "Mrs. King, would you like a croissant and some tea, too?"

"Some tea, perhaps?"

"Tea for two and one croissant in the Mainsail Room," Alex said.

Marquetta cocked her head towards the stairs. "Rick, why don't you escort Mr. West to his room? It never hurts to be cautious."

"Good idea. Mr. West? How about if you let me get you upstairs?"

"I think that's an excellent idea," Mrs. King said quickly.

Rick escorted the older man to his room, got the small desk cleared so there was enough space for the tray Alex would be bringing, then brought a chair in from Mrs. King's room. By then, Alex had arrived with the tray. The entire routine was over in about fifteen minutes. As Rick and Alex left, he assured them that if there was anything either of them needed, all they had to do was ask.

In the hall, Rick said, "Kiddo, I've talked to Marquetta. Let's find her and go over a few things."

The first place they looked was the kitchen. Marquetta had set out two bread pans, the canisters of flour and sugar, eggs, and a colander filled with apricots on one end of the island. On the other, she'd placed three mugs.

"Looks like we're all set for a little conference," Rick quipped.

"What are we baking?" Alex asked.

"An apple bread, but with apricots. I've used the same recipe with peaches and it worked well, so I decided to experiment."

"We have the answer to the apricot mystery, kiddo."

"I told you, Daddy. Marquetta always knows what she's doing."

Marquetta frowned and looked between the two of them. "What in the world are you talking about?"

"When I saw all those apricots at the market, I asked Alex about them. She said you had a plan."

"I also thought we might want a little tea." Marquetta looked pointedly at Alex. "We need to set some expectations."

"Can I have hot chocolate?" Alex asked.

"Of course," Marquetta said.

"I can't stay long," Rick said. "I'm supposed to meet Deputy Baker at the police station in a few minutes. Before I go, Alex, Marquetta and I are in complete agreement about how to handle this…situation." He recapped what he and Marquetta had discussed, then looked at Marquetta. "You said you wanted to set expectations?"

"I do. And you need to leave." She gave him a peck on the cheek.

"Right." Rick went to the butler door and watched as Marquetta and Alex sat on two stools. They were almost eye-to-eye.

"My primary concern is your safety, Sweetie. I will answer any questions you have, but you have to be honest with me at all times and, if I tell you something is unsafe, you will do what I tell you or I will ground you."

Alex groaned. "Okay."

Marquetta stroked Alex's cheek, then took a breath. "I'm sure you have a million questions. Where do you want to begin?"

Rick slipped silently through the butler door. For better or for worse, it was time to meet Deputy Baker.

20

Alex

MARQUETTA'S QUESTION SURPRISES ME. WHERE did I want to begin? No clue. I wrap my fingers around my mug. It's warm from the hot chocolate and makes me feel good.

"We don't want to step on anyone's toes," Marquetta says. "And I was thinking there might be another way to approach this."

"What's that?"

"The treasure map."

That's what I was thinking! The map is what the treasure hunters want most. Well, duh, except for the treasure.

"Finding it could help Flynn do her job—and it might also help the police." Marquetta lifts one eyebrow and watches me.

"So you think maybe somebody killed Captain Carroll for the map?"

"These people came here in hopes of finding the treasure. But to get that, they need the map. Captain Carroll claimed he had one, so perhaps that's somehow tied to his murder. What about Flynn? I saw her here earlier. What did you two talk about?"

"She's super worried about the treasure hunters."

"Exactly. Maybe we should be focusing on finding out if this supposed treasure map really does exist. If we found that, or the evidence of it, we could help her and maybe even help your dad do his job."

"That's a super awesome idea. If we find the map, we'll find the murderer."

"Slow down, Sweetie. We won't be confronting any killers. That's one of my ground rules. You understand my terms, right?"

Oh, so that's what they were talking about—keeping me out of the investigation. Just when I thought this was all gonna come together, too. For now, I guess it's okay 'cause I do want to help Flynn and I'm totally sure the map and the killing are related. As long as I stick to Marquetta's rules, I can also figure out what happened with the murder kinda by accident. If we find evidence that the map exists, it might also be enough to get me on *The Treasure King*.

"It's a deal. Can I do some surveillance on *The Treasure King* from Marina Park? That's only a couple blocks away and it's not even close to the boat."

Marquetta looks at me real close. She kinda frowns, then seems to make up her mind. "We have binoculars. I don't have a lot of time to be sitting in the park, though."

"I could get Sasha and Robbie to go with me. We'll be good and keep our distance."

"You promise you won't go any closer than the park?"

"For sure."

"I'll tell you what. You can go to the park, but I'm going to be dropping by to check on you. That means if you're not there, I'll come looking for you and will consider you in violation of the ground rules. Are we clear?"

"Totally."

"I'm not sure what watching a boat from the park is going to tell you about the treasure map, but if that's what you want to do, you have my permission."

"I also wanna ask Mr. Gray questions about the map. When *The Treasure King* came in, he was talking about the last time Captain Carroll was here. He's gotta know more than that."

"We can talk to him together. It would be good to have those questions written out in advance. That way we're not trying to figure out what to ask on the fly. Why don't you start a list and email it to me? If I have suggestions, I'll send them to you. Also, why don't you see what you can find online about Captain Carroll? If he really did come across a map, there's a chance someone's written something about it."

Whoa! It's almost like Marquetta can read my mind. Sometimes, how much she understands me is kinda scary. "When I was waiting for Daddy to talk to you I did some checking on social media. I can do more later, but so far I haven't found anything about Captain Carroll having a map. Can I go watch the boat now and look into this other stuff later?"

Marquetta stands and goes to the window. She's looking outside, and I'm beginning to think this whole cooperating thing might not work out. How am I gonna follow my instincts if I have to check in with Marquetta all the time?

"We have a bit of a problem, don't we?" Marquetta says. "You can't go after dark, not without an adult…"

"I wasn't thinking about at night."

"So you were only thinking about watching *The Treasure King* during the day?"

"Just this afternoon."

"That could work," Marquetta says as she looks at me and

leans against the counter. "How long were you planning on watching?"

"I dunno. A couple hours, I guess."

"Tell you what, Alex. Go text your friends and make the arrangements to do your surveillance. Also see if Robbie and Sasha can join us for dinner. I don't know if your dad will make it home in time, but you kids might as well have a nice, hot meal. You can compare notes over dinner."

"Could we just order a pizza? That way you won't have as much work to do."

"Pizza again? Okay, but remember, I'll be checking up on you, so don't leave the park."

Me and Marquetta decide to order two pizzas, one cheese and the other pepperoni. After that, I rush upstairs and text Sasha.

—*Got the green light to watch Treasure King. Marquetta's gonna order pizza for dinner. Can you come?*

—*Awesome. Told my mom and she's cool. That was too easy. You gonna check with Robbie?*

—*For sure.*

—*Hey, did you hear about Deputy Baker? My mom says she totally lost it when she heard she was gonna be working with your dad. DB thinks that since your dad's not a cop he shouldn't be allowed to help.*

—*Where'd you hear that?*

—*Mom's got a friend who knows the mayor. Guess she got dumped on by DB after Chief Cunningham talked to her.*

—*DB better watch out. Me and my dad have solved a bunch of murders. Could be game on.*

—*Totally. We gotta show her how it's done!*

* * *

After Sasha, I text Robbie. He talks to his dad and tells me his dad is cool with him having dinner here, too. The three of us are meeting in just a few minutes at the park. It's only a couple blocks from here, so we'll have a bathroom and snacks if we need them. This is gonna be an awesome stakeout!

21

Rick

RICK STOOD ON THE CORNER opposite the Seaside Cove Police Department letting the crisp afternoon air fill his lungs. Overhead, a cloud drifted past the sun. He tilted his face toward the sky and let the warmth soak in. Once he passed under the department's green-and-white striped awning and opened the door with the town seal, there would be no turning back. Once he entered through that door, he would no longer be distanced from death.

He stepped off the curb just as a woman he didn't recognize rounded the opposite corner. Dressed in an orange ski jacket and black leggings, she resembled a walking pumpkin. He watched her pass in front of the town offices with the abandon of a tourist captivated by a quaint California setting and wondered if she was even aware of the business conducted inside the nondescript building.

By the time Rick stood in front of the glass door with the town seal, the probable tourist was long gone. Somewhat reluctantly, he entered. A woman wearing a Seaside Cove Police uniform looked up at him. Her dark hair was tied up in a tight bun, giving her a severe appearance. From her intense brown eyes to her clenched cheeks, determination shown on her face.

"You must be Mr. Atwood," she said. "The chief told me you were coming. He's on the phone right now."

Rick stepped forward, extended his hand, and smiled. "Call me Rick. You must be Deputy Baker. It's nice to meet you."

The woman looked down at Rick's hand and grimaced before she took it. Her handshake was both quick and firm. She tilted her head toward Adam's desk. "Follow me."

So much for congenial, Rick thought. This was either going to be a very tense working relationship, or all business. Either way, it was going to be very different from his dealings with Adam. Rick just hoped it would not get in the way of doing their jobs. Adam gave Rick a friendly wave as they approached and returned to his phone conversation.

The deputy pointed at one of the chairs in front of Adam's desk. "Have a seat."

"I understand finding your cat is important, Mrs. Cantwell," Adam said. "However, I'm sure Tommy Cat will be home for dinner." He paused, and a few seconds later, added, "Yes, Mrs. Cantwell, we'll certainly do a thorough check of the neighborhood. I'll let you know as soon as we find him."

Adam hung his head and sighed when he disconnected the call. "Someone needs to put a tracker on that cat."

"I don't do cat duty," Baker said. "I'm allergic."

"Don't worry," Adam said with a wave of his hand. "You don't have to kiss it, just drive through the neighborhood slowly once or twice. I'll do the same. Mrs. Cantwell watches the streets like a hawk. She doesn't miss a thing. I swear that woman has a periscope in her bathroom. Tommy Cat will come home when he gets hungry. He does this at least once a week."

"Chief, I…"

"Just drive by slowly, Baker. That's all you have to do." Adam wrote an address on a piece of paper and slid it across the desk. "I know it's not the kind of police work you want to do, but she is one of our constituents. She's also good friends with the mayor, so it would behoove you to make a show of looking for Tommy Cat."

"The political realities of small towns," Rick said with a smile.

Deputy Baker glared at Rick and huffed. "Whatever."

"The bad news is the warrant to search *The Treasure King* for the murder weapon has not come through yet. I'd like you both to go see if they'll voluntarily let you do the search."

"We'll finesse it." Baker looked at Rick and cocked her head toward the entrance. "I'll pick you up out front."

If that wasn't a hint, thought Rick—Baker wanted to talk to Adam alone. Why had she even brought him over here? From what he'd seen so far, it was either to demonstrate her authority over him or to complain about working with a civilian. No matter. Adam wouldn't budge on leaving him out of the investigation. Whether Baker liked it or not, both Adam and the mayor wanted Rick on the case, so he was here for the duration.

Rick had waited on the sidewalk for no more than a couple of minutes when a Seaside Cove police cruiser pulled to a stop in front of him. He took a deep breath before he opened the door and told himself to work on building a good relationship with his new partner. He sat and looked over at the deputy. "Do you want to do that drive-by? You'd score some serious points with Mrs. Cantwell if you found Tommy Cat so quickly."

The deputy cut her eyes in Rick's direction. "Buckle up."

They drove down Main Street to the docks in silence. So much for scoring points, thought Rick. By the time they exited the vehicle, he was ready to give up on a friendly relationship and ask Baker if there was anything about her job she liked.

He decided that kind of question would only make things worse and kept it to himself. "How do you want to play this?"

"I'd prefer to have a warrant."

"Right."

They walked to *The Treasure King* without another word. The truth was, Rick didn't mind the silence as they passed the section of the dock that had been marked off with crime scene tape. At least he had time to take everything in.

The Treasure King was, at least for the Seaside Cove harbor, a monster. It had to be at least a hundred feet long. With it's clean, white exterior, and sleek design, it looked less like a dive boat than it did a luxury cruiser. Rick counted six antennas, a radar array, and a dish antenna. If nothing else, there would be no lack of communications on this boat.

The man from the market was on the top deck. He'd exchanged his Whaler's Cove shirt for a different tee, this one a dark blue. He was cleaning the glass surrounding the open-air command center on the top deck, but watched them approach.

"That's Mancini," Baker said to Rick as she motioned for the man to come down to the dock.

Mancini raised his chin in acknowledgement and disappeared from view. About thirty seconds later, he emerged from a stairwell and met them at the gangway. He took up a classic confrontational stance—arms crossed and feet spread shoulder-width apart.

"Seaside Cove Police," Baker said. "Permission to come aboard and search?"

"For what?"

"A speargun," Baker said flatly.

"Got a warrant?"

"This is a voluntary search."

"Permission denied."

This was going nowhere, thought Rick. Adam would not be pleased if they got stonewalled simply because Baker tried to force her way onto the boat. Rick held out his hand. "Rick Atwood. I'm a consultant working with the town. Your name is?"

Mancini ignored the question and eyed Rick suspiciously. "What's this town need a consultant for?"

"It doesn't," Deputy Baker said.

"Sounds familiar." Mancini ignored the deputy and smirked at Rick. "So what do you consult on?"

"I work murder investigations. And, to be honest with you, since your captain was just shot in the chest with a speargun, I'm surprised you don't want to let us aboard—unless you know the murder weapon came from this boat and you want to impede the investigation."

The woman Rick had seen with Captain Carroll in the Crooked Mast emerged from the stairwell and stopped. She seemed to evaluate the situation before she approached. "What's going on?"

"These people want to tear apart the boat. It's not happening."

"Rick Atwood." He held out his hand, which the woman took.

"Heather Sanna. This is Gavin. He's antisocial and has no impulse control."

"Fine. You want to let them come on? Go ahead. You can clean up the mess they leave."

Mancini glared at Heather. Rick remembered her large brown eyes and dimples from the Crooked Mast. Even in the heat of the tension, she'd held onto her girl-next-door look. Rick asked, "Weren't you at the Crooked Mast with Captain Carroll?"

"We were there for dinner." She said, then directed her attention to the deputy. "I remember you. You were there to get Morris under control."

"Deputy Baker. Thank you for your cooperation that night, Ms. Sanna. May we have permission to come aboard and search?"

Heather regarded the deputy, then seemed to accept the inevitable. "I don't see why not."

"No way," Mancini said.

"Would you rather have the Coast Guard, Gavin? Those guys don't ask, they just come aboard with loaded weapons and do whatever they want. At least these two are asking."

Mancini grumbled something under his breath before he stepped aside. "Whatever. Just be careful. We finally got everything cleaned up. These passengers are a bunch of pigs. Follow me." He turned and opened a door leading to the ship's interior.

Deputy Baker ignored Rick and followed Mancini through the doorway.

As Rick passed by Heather, she muttered, "She's a piece of work."

Rick suppressed a chuckle and asked, "Were you close to Captain Carroll?"

"We'd only been together a couple months. He was a hard man to get along with. I'm not sure it would have lasted. So, I guess we weren't that close."

"Losing someone suddenly is always a shock. I'm sorry for

your loss."

Heather's cheeks tightened into a grimace. "Thank you. We'd better catch up before those two get into another snit."

"Is Gavin always like that?"

"Gavin's okay. He just doesn't like it when people infringe on his space." Heather led the way through a door and down a passageway that was lined with dark wood paneling.

"He regards *The Treasure King* as his space?" Rick asked.

"He was first mate. Now, we're unemployed, I guess." Heather craned her neck and listened. "They probably went below." She led the way down the stairwell. Over her shoulder, she said, "Actually, I don't know what we are, other than stuck with a bunch of obnoxious reprobates." She laughed. "Don't worry, they're all on shore. Most of them get cabin fever here in port."

She opened the equipment room door. "This is where we keep the dive gear."

"I'm telling you, I have no idea where it is," Mancini's voice boomed.

"What's going on?" Heather asked.

"A speargun is missing." Mancini pointed at a white, plastic rack inside a cabinet. There were two other guns in the rack, but the third slot was empty. "She says it's the murder weapon."

"I said it could be. We would need forensic testing to confirm that."

"Same difference," Mancini grumbled.

"Assuming we can even find it," Rick said.

"I'll find it if I have to tear apart every inch of this vessel," Baker said matter-of-factly.

Mancini resumed the confrontational posture he'd used earlier and stood in front of Baker. "You're not tearing anything apart without a warrant."

Heather went to the cabinet, closed the door, then opened it. She inspected the hasp and gave it a gentle tug. One end pulled loose in her hand and the entire hasp hung at a cockeyed angle from the remaining screw. "We had trouble with this cabinet before we left Santa Monica. Morris wanted to go out for a dive and couldn't find the key. He took a hammer to it. What I don't understand is why it's broken again. I fixed it myself."

Deputy Baker knelt in front of the cabinet and studied it. "There's a screw missing. When did you repair it?" she asked absently.

"Last Friday," Mancini said.

Rick peeked over Baker's shoulder. She'd pulled out her phone and was taking photos of the cabinet and the hasp. Apparently, she wasn't about to reveal her line of thinking to anyone, including him. "Between last Friday and today, have there been any reasons for someone to need access to this cabinet?" he asked.

Mancini and Heather looked at each other and shook their heads.

"I can't think of a single one," Heather said. "We didn't stop from the time we left Santa Monica until we arrived here."

Deputy Baker had begun sketching the hasp. It looked like she was also annotating her sketch with notes. Her artwork was nowhere near the caliber of Adam's, but she had to think she was onto something. At least, that's what Rick hoped. He made eye contact with Heather, then Mancini. "What about this room? Who has access and what else might they be in here for?"

"It's the dive supply room. Nobody needed access. Morris insisted on keeping the room locked. Only the crew has access."

Baker frowned and looked at the doorway, then Mancini. "I

don't recall you using a key to get in here."

"I didn't need one." He looked at Heather. "She must have left it unlocked."

"No way." Heather pushed past Rick and went to the door. She opened it and tested the lock. Her jaw tightened. She stood and let out a disgusted breath. "The lock's jimmied. Anybody on board could have gotten into this room."

22

Rick

DEPUTY BAKER LOOKED UP FROM her inspection of the lock on the equipment room door. "Do you have any idea when someone might have jimmied this?"

It seemed like a silly question to Rick. Mancini hadn't even noticed the problem, and Heather had appeared shocked by the discovery. And now they were looking at each other as though the breach in security were the other's fault.

"Like I said before, I thought somebody left it unlocked." Mancini's jaw clenched and his eyes cut to the side.

"Somebody?" Heather scoffed. "Really? Deputy, that's Gavin's euphemism for saying he thinks I screwed up." She returned the look of irritation Gavin had given her. "I didn't."

"So anyone could have entered this room unnoticed and stolen the speargun," Rick said. "Who knew what was kept in here?"

"They all did," Mancini said. "Carroll insisted on giving all the passengers a tour."

"Since you docked, has anyone from Seaside Cove been

aboard?" Deputy Baker asked.

"No," Mancini said.

Heather again rolled her eyes. "For crying out loud, can't you be civil, Gavin?" She looked at the deputy. "Only passengers and crew are allowed aboard. Morris was very particular about that."

"That seems to cut down our list of suspects," Rick said. "Nobody from town had access or would have even known about this room."

"Security through obscurity," Baker said.

"Exactly." Rick eyed Mancini, then Heather. They'd both known about the room, the weapon, and had access. "Mr. Mancini, where were you between the hours of six p.m. and nine p.m. last night?"

"I know my rights," Mancini grumbled.

"Gavin…they're just doing their jobs."

"Sure. Whatever. I had an early dinner on board, then went for a walk to the lighthouse around six. I was back here by seven and in my cabin reading."

"Is it a good book?" Rick asked. "I'm always looking for recommendations."

Mancini smirked. "Boring, actually. I'm studying maritime navigation. I want to get my pilot's license."

The answer, while not exactly specific, gave Rick what he wanted—a quick response that probably meant Mancini really had been reading. "Doesn't sound like my cup of tea," he said.

"Did you leave your cabin at any time after you got back?" Baker asked.

Gavin shot a glance at Heather, stretched his neck to one side, then the other. "No. I was alone all night."

Baker made a note on her pad, then looked at Heather. "And you, Ms. Sanna?"

"After the dinner debacle at the Crooked Mast, I went for a walk, too. I had to cool off and I'd heard it was a good walk out to the lighthouse."

"Wait," Rick said. "You both went to the lighthouse? Did you see each other?"

They replied in unison. "No."

Baker seemed unconcerned by the overlap. "What time did you get back here, Ms. Sanna?"

"I got back around seven-thirty. I watched TV in my cabin until about nine, then went to sleep."

"And did you see Captain Carroll, either alive or dead, on your way back?" Baker asked.

"No."

To Rick's surprise, Baker turned and fixed him with an intense stare. "You were involved in the confrontation at the Crooked Mast. You didn't happen to run into the captain after your little dinner, did you?"

Rick put a hand to his chest and shook his head. "I took Marquetta home. She wasn't feeling well after that whole incident."

Baker grunted. "She never did deal with confrontation very well. I'll have to talk to her, too."

"You think Marquetta killed Captain Carroll? You can't be serious."

"This is a murder investigation, Mr. Atwood."

Rick held his ground with Baker, unwilling to break eye contact first. After what felt like an eternity, Baker huffed and returned her attention to Gavin. The confrontation between them heated up with Baker demanding access to the entire boat; Gavin refusing to cooperate; and Heather mediating between the two. Standing on the sidelines, Rick was thankful that Heather seemed able to moderate Gavin's hostility. If she hadn't been around, this would probably have turned into the equivalent of a battle between two roosters in a ring.

At first, Rick tailed behind as Gavin and Heather guided Baker through the boat, but as the search wore on, he grew increasingly distanced from the questions and answers—and more concerned that they would not find the answers they needed on *The Treasure King*.

Tired of the deputy's methods, Rick texted Marquetta.

—*Was Baker always a bulldog?*

—*She was always goal oriented.*

Rick considered the message. Goal oriented. That could mean a lot of things.

—*More about results than feelings?*

—*Always.*

—*She's searching the boat for a missing speargun. Feeling like a third wheel. BTW, she says she'll want to talk to you about where you were after I dropped you off.*

After a long pause, Marquetta's response came through.

—*Got breads coming out of the oven. Have to go.*

What did that mean? Was she really in a rush? Or was that some sort of code for something else? Between his questions over Marquetta's response and the bickering over every detail of the search, Rick found himself on edge. Enough was enough, he thought once they were on the main deck.

"It looks like you have this under control, Deputy," Rick said. "I'm going to talk to some of the people around the docks."

"Sure. Good idea." The deputy immediately turned away and demanded she be shown the top deck.

As Rick left the boat, he thought about who to talk to first. He scanned the marina, spotted Joe Gray working on his houseboat, and decided to get Joe's theory about the body drifting with the tides direct from the source. The walk only took a couple of minutes, and after Rick explained why he was there, Joe went over his theory about the tides and their effect on the body's location.

"So you agree that the window of opportunity for the killer was between six and nine last night?" Rick asked.

"There's no other explanation. Before then, Carroll was harassing me at the Crooked Mast. By eleven, the tides were approaching their peak and it would have been difficult to keep the body under the pier. And at nine, Baker made a pass through here."

"You don't think it's possible that the body was just out there floating and nobody noticed it?"

"Anything's possible. But I don't think it's very likely. Even at night this place is lit up. Carroll was wearing a light jacket, so his body would have shown up even in the dark. I don't think Deputy Baker would miss something like that."

Rick thought about Joe's conclusions. It all made sense, but he'd learned long ago how pliable theories could be. Only the facts mattered—and those might not be available until after they found the killer.

"By the way, we did a search for a speargun on board *The Treasure King* and there's one missing. It looks like whoever killed Captain Carroll stole the weapon, then threw it away after they used it."

Joe harrumphed and rubbed his throat. "So you think the killer was someone from the boat?"

"That's the theory as of about fifteen minutes ago. Of course, it is subject to change. It would help if the weapon turned up. I keep expecting to see it floating around in the marina."

"Not likely. Not all of those float, although there are some that do. It would be a good reason to send down a diver. Your murder weapon might be right down there." Joe pointed at the water.

"Do you think we could get one of the local divers to do it?"

"Dennis Malone has done some work in the past for the Seaside Cove PD. It's been a few years, but he's always looking for opportunities to dive and be paid for it."

"Good to know," Rick said.

"Since you're thinking the killer might be someone from *The Treasure King*, here's something else you should know. I heard another rumor this morning about all those treasure hunters. Appears they don't get along very well. There's one of them, name's Will Shelley, he seems to be the peacemaker in the group. Sounds like the others are all fighting like cats and dogs."

"Will Shelley?" Rick said. "I think he was one of the ones at the Crooked Mast."

"I can't keep them all straight. One thing I can tell you is all these people have unreasonable expectations. They figured they were going to get rich off plundering the contents of the *San Manuel*. It's been there for 400 years just waiting for someone to find it. And it could be worth millions."

"It's hard to keep that from coloring your expectations no matter who you are. Let's hope it's Flynn who finds it first. She's probably the only one who wants to do the right thing with all that treasure."

"I agree with you about one thing. Flynn is the best one to bring it up. Let's hope you and Deputy Baker can find Carroll's killer. As disagreeable as the man was, he didn't deserve what he got."

Rick grimaced. He'd forgotten about Baker. As much as he

disliked the idea of going back to look for her, he suspected he couldn't get away with interviewing too many more people before she had a fit.

23

Alex

SASHA TAKES A BITE OUT of one of Marquetta's cookies and looks around the park. "This is so boring, Alex. Even if we see something happen, how are we gonna know if it's important?"

She's right. We've only got a couple hours left. This has been a super big disappointment. "I thought it was gonna be different, Sash."

"All we've seen so far is your dad walk over to Joe Gray's houseboat and Deputy Baker get a tour of *The Treasure King.*"

I get it. Ok? Boring. I look over to where Robbie is watching the marina with the pair of binoculars I loaned him. His bench is maybe ten feet from ours, but he's like lost in another world. He's happy 'cause he's probably checking out the fishing boat that came in right before I gave him the binoculars.

I never thought about how boring it was gonna be to just sit and do nothing. It's cool being able to spend time with my friends, but we've been here for half an hour and my butt hurts already.

Robbie holds up the binoculars and says, "Hey, Alex. The

fishing boat guys are done unloading. They're doing cleanup now. Thanks for loaning me these. This is awesome!"

Sasha rolls her eyes, then looks at me.

"You're welcome." I mumble.

"What's the matter?" Robbie asks. "Are you mad or something?"

"At myself," I confess. "This was a bad idea. I totally have to come up with another way to find that treasure map."

"Oh," Robbie says with a shrug, then looks through the binoculars and starts watching again.

"You totally need to be able to search that boat," Sasha says.

"But I don't see how that's gonna happen. There's always somebody on it. This is so not gonna work."

Me and Sasha go back to munching on cookies while Robbie watches the marina. Just as I take my last bite, Robbie calls out.

"Hey, Alex? Your dad's back. He's talking to Deputy Baker."

Sasha picks up her binoculars and looks in the same direction as Robbie. I don't need any help to see that Robbie's right. My dad is talking to Deputy Baker, and it doesn't look like they're getting along.

"What do you suppose they're saying?" I ask.

"I dunno, but Deputy Baker sure doesn't look happy about it. Maybe my mom was wrong about…" Sasha stops and scrunches up her face.

"What did she say?"

"No. It's nothing."

"C'mon, Sasha, spill."

"Okay, but you're not gonna like it. My mom says that Deputy Baker wants to take your dad away from Marquetta."

"No way! Why would she want to do that?"

"Because they were like rivals in high school."

It feels like somebody just hit me in the stomach. Marquetta told me about the prom and how she stole Deputy Baker's date, but rivals? Could that be true? "I am not gonna let that happen, Sasha. I worked super hard to get them together. They're like, practically married."

"I know," Sasha says. "Maybe my mom's wrong."

"She's totally wrong." I turn away from Sasha so she can't see the tears I feel building in my eyes. I trust Marquetta, and I believe in her, but she's always been so sensitive about her past. Maybe there was more to the story than she told me.

"Maybe she has to go read the water meters," Robbie says.

Robbie and Sasha laugh, but I'm wondering why Deputy Baker came back to Seaside Cove. It seems kinda weird now. If she wanted a big career in law enforcement why come back here? This is a small town. And now that Chief Cunningham's appointment is official, there won't be any changes for a long time. Maybe Sasha's mom is right.

"Alex? You okay?" Robbie asks.

I blink a few times, then rub my nose and sniffle. "Yeah."

These guys are my friends, but I don't want to say anything in front of Sasha 'cause she might repeat it to her mom. Her mom would tell her friends I'm worried about Marquetta and my dad, and it would get all over town.

"I guess I kinda spaced out. I was thinking about when me and my dad got here and the chief was just a deputy and had to read meters while he was helping my dad solve a murder. We weren't used to a town where the police had to do other stuff. You could be right, Robbie. Maybe she's not happy 'cause she's gonna get stuck reading water meters while my dad does the police work!"

This time we all laugh. I have to admit, it is kinda funny.

24

Rick

WHEN DEPUTY BAKER'S GAZE MET Rick's, she turned and walked in the opposite direction. Even though she was on her cell phone, Rick was positive she couldn't have missed seeing him.

Obviously, she'd been pacing back and forth for some time and was deep in a conversation. But not even acknowledging his presence? Rick's exasperation with her grew as he waited for the call to end. He couldn't understand why she'd been so rude from their first meeting. He'd done nothing, other than try to help. Then again, maybe that was the point. Maybe she couldn't get past the idea of working with a civilian.

The deputy kept the phone to her ear as she marched to the end of the dock, did an about-face, and walked toward Rick. Between her tight jaw and the severe bun she used to pull back her hair, she had the appearance of someone most annoyed with almost everything. The latest was probably having to work with him. Or maybe it was the phone call?

"If that's what you want," the deputy said abruptly. She stabbed the screen and jammed the phone into its holster. "I have to leave. Chief's orders." She looked beyond the marina back towards town. "You're in charge of the interviews," she said curtly.

"Why?" Rick asked.

"I would think you'd be happy," Deputy Baker seethed. "You get a chance to work alone."

"It's not what I wanted at all. In fact, I was looking forward to working with you. You know, team work makes the dream work."

The deputy eyed Rick suspiciously. "I thought Marquetta would have told you how awful I am."

"She said very little other than that you two had a falling out in high school. She's not the kind of person who would try to make someone out to be a demon behind their back."

Baker's cheeks tightened as she regarded Rick. "Maybe I've been a little hard on you. I didn't—still don't—like the idea of working with a civilian. But from what the chief told me, you really did help him on those previous cases." She planted both hands on her hips and huffed. "I refuse, however, to work with a child."

Rick chuckled. "Apparently you've also heard about my daughter. She holds you in quite high regard. To be honest, she's itching to meet you, and, I must confess, she has ideas on how to find the killer."

"She's a child. Just tell her to stay away from my investigation."

"You don't know Alex. She's precocious, loves puzzles, and views restrictions as a challenge to be overcome. I have told her murder is none of her business, grounded her, and even threatened to send her away. Nothing stops her."

"Well, you can tell her this. If she butts into my investigation,

I will lock her up for obstruction of justice."

And if you lay a hand on my daughter, you will pay a heavy price, thought Rick. He opened his mouth to tell her exactly that, but stopped. Instead, he said. "Let's hope she doesn't force the issue. You said you had to go?"

"Interview Jennifer Martin. She's the one who found the body. We'll compare notes later since I took her original statement."

Without another word, Deputy Baker left. Rick watched her stride across the dock, past Jennifer Martin's bait shop, and to the parking lot. She never looked back once. Whatever bee Baker had up her bonnet, it had to be a big one.

From outward appearances, Jennifer Martin's store, Ugly Worm Bait and Tackle, was an afterthought—a large shack plunked on top of the docks at the whim of the marina architect. Shortly after his arrival in Seaside Cove, Rick had commented on its dilapidated appearance to Marquetta. She'd told him the shack had been through numerous phases since Seaside Cove's early days when the town had been a small fishing village.

The first signs of a new life for the ramshackle building had begun several months ago. A steady parade of tradesmen had renovated the interior and painted the exterior an azure blue with white trim. Jennifer did most of her business with the local fishermen at the newly installed service window, which was covered by a bright blue canvas awning with white lettering.

Never having been an entrepreneur prior to inheriting the B&B, Rick had no idea whether Jennifer's business model of serving both fishermen and tourists would work. If nothing else, he hoped she succeeded because the colorful building, which was no longer an eyesore, was visible from the B&B's backyard.

He went to the side door and knocked. From inside, he heard

a high-pitched woman's voice call out. "I'm closed for the day."

"Ms. Martin? This is Rick Atwood. I have a few questions about…what happened this morning. Would you open the door please?"

An abrupt response came back immediately. "Hold your horses."

A middle-aged woman with narrow shoulders and wide hips eased open the door and studied Rick. "Sorry. I thought you were a customer. Come in." She held out her hand. "Call me Jennifer. It's not like we have to be all formal with each other."

"Works for me," Rick said as he shook Jennifer's hand. He stepped inside, nearly tripping over one box as he sidestepped another. The place was a maze of boxes, aquarium tanks, and what appeared to be a glass display case waiting to be assembled. Rick had never considered himself claustrophobic, but it felt as though the walls were closing in.

"Sorry for the mess," Jennifer said. "I thought I'd be all settled in by now, but my shipments were delayed and it's been so hectic during the day I can't seem to get all this stuff done."

"You just moved in a couple months ago. Didn't you?"

"Yes, and I had time budgeted to get everything organized. Then the mayor talked me into opening early—that's when chaos took over." She gestured wildly about the store. "So here I am, flailing away."

"You'll get there."

"Some days I wonder." She laughed again and gave Rick a friendly grin. Her straight nose was filled with freckles, and her brown eyes also seemed to smile. "You said you had some questions? I heard you've worked with the police before. Adam's got you working Captain Carroll's murder?"

"He asked me to help out. I hope you won't mind going back

over the statement you gave to Deputy Baker."

"Nope. Happy to get a break from all this." Once again, she waved a hand in a wide arc.

Rick made a mental note—*keep your distance when Jennifer Martin is talking, she's a hand waver.* "Great. I heard you gave a statement to Deputy Baker, but I'd like to start from scratch. If that's okay?"

Jennifer raised her hands to the back of her neck as though she were going to pull up her red hair, but it had been cut straight at the shoulder and there was not much for her to grab. With a sigh, she lowered her hands and fidgeted as though she didn't know what to do with them. "Just chopped it all off and haven't adjusted yet." The light and cheerful tone of her high-pitched laugh reminded Rick of tinkling bells.

"I'm sure you'll like the style once you get used to it."

"It's a lot easier to get rid of a bad hair style than it is a bad hire."

"Sorry, I don't follow," Rick said.

"Deputy Baker. She's a peach. Chief's going to have a hard time undoing that decision."

Rick wasn't sure how to respond. If he even should. He scrutinized the store's interior, unable to shake the irony. Here he was, in a bait shop, and Jennifer Martin had just cast out her line. He was not going to be snared that easily. "Adam and I always found it was helpful to have more than one person talk to a witness. That way we can compare notes and…"

She cackled. "You want to see if you can trip me up."

"It's not a test, but more of a way to see what details might come out with one interviewer and not with another."

Jennifer puckered her cheeks as she seemed to contemplate his response. "What they say about you is true. You are smooth.

And I'll bet you get a whole lot more detail than Adam's deputy. My worms are better conversationalists than that woman."

Rick made a show of looking both directions before lowering his voice. He was tempted, but not willing to slip down the slope and become mired in gossip. "Tell you what. We'll just keep that to ourselves."

"Good enough." Jennifer again reached up as though she were going to rearrange her hair and sighed. "Never realized how many times I did that in a day. All right, what do you want to know?"

"Tell me what you saw. Time, date, exact location."

"If that's what you want." She went on to provide a detailed account of her morning. At the end, she added, "The marina is always quiet when I start. The serious fishermen are already out and the casual ones are just waking up. I should have been working in here on this mess, but couldn't resist a chance to enjoy a beautiful sunrise. Got more than I bargained for. That's for sure."

"So none of your customers said anything? You were the only one to see the body?"

Jennifer snapped her fingers a couple of times, then she chuckled. "Come on, Rick. Keep up. Think this through. It's dark when the commercial guys are getting ready for the day. And the tourist guys aren't here yet. They're still eating scones or whatever you people serve for breakfast."

The tips of Rick's ears burned at her friendly chiding. Adam had warned him. He just hadn't really expected to become a target for her wit. Could she take a little chiding herself? He shot back, "Crusty Buns makes the best scones in town, so we try to avoid competing."

She smiled, then patted her hips. "You're right. As you can

see, Crusty Buns is one of my weaknesses. I have a love-hate relationship with everything Angus O'Donnell makes. I love to eat it, but hate the results. So what else do you want to know?"

"Adam showed me his sketch of the area, and I saw the yellow tape out there, but I'd like to get your thoughts about how the body got where it did. Would you show me where you were standing at the time you spotted it?"

"Sure. I love to be outside. That's part of my problem. I come in here and want to go out there. Once I'm outside, I have to guilt myself into coming back in here. At least this time I have an excuse. Let's go."

She led the way out the door, crossed around to the front of the store, and strode to a spot about twenty feet away. "Right there." She pointed at the water in front of where the crime scene tape shook in the onshore breeze.

"Adam estimated the distance from the dock to be about ten feet. Would you agree with that?" Rick asked.

"Give or take."

"And you said you started work at four?"

"Same time I start most days."

"And you didn't notice a body floating out there when you walked by?"

"To be perfectly honest, all I wanted was to get started, so my mind was in there." She gestured at the Ugly Worm. "Not out here. Even later, you know, when I first noticed the body? I just figured someone was snorkeling. Then I realized he was fully clothed. That's when it hit me—the guy was dead."

"So it's possible someone else saw the body and didn't realize what it was."

Jennifer shrugged, then let out a little huff. "Sunrise wasn't until seven, so someone walking by prior to six-thirty probably wouldn't have noticed it. You know how it is, most people just want to get where they're going. For those who aren't in a hurry, it's easy to get lost in the atmosphere. The lines sway and clink against the masts. The gulls start circling overhead, watching for a free meal. But there's a stillness, too. It softens everything. Kind of like a quiet musical interlude."

"I didn't realize you were such a poet."

"Not really. All I'm saying is if there'd had been some sort of argument, everybody would have heard it. If there wasn't one—even if the killer snuck up on Carroll and shot him in the chest without warning—there would have been noise from the speargun and a splash when the body hit the water. Nobody who works around here would have missed something like that."

"How can you be so sure? People are working. They get busy."

"I'm not saying everybody would have noticed it, but somebody would have. This little harbor and marina is a jewel, Rick. We're all in love with this place and try to watch over it. If there's trash in the water because some dipstick throws something overboard, we fish it out. We're always in touch with what's going on, except for when we're not here. Somebody would have gone looking if they'd have heard anything like an argument—or a big splash."

Rick sighed as he watched the water's surface. "You're probably right. Captain Carroll was a large man. His body landing in the water would have made a lot of noise. And it would take someone who was incredibly strong to lower him into the water quietly. So you agree completely with Joe's theory?"

"There's two things I like about it. First, the timing explains how nobody heard what happened when somebody decided to shoot Captain Dead Man with a speargun. And second, it also explains how he spent the night floating in our marina without anybody noticing."

"Thanks, Jennifer."

"Not much to go on, is it?"

Rick blew out a slow breath. Was that ever an understatement.

25

Alex

BY TWO O'CLOCK, EVEN I'M bored. Robbie's going on and on about boats and Sasha's practicing yoga and dance. I'm the only one who's still paying attention to *The Treasure King*. I have to admit, this is super boring stuff. All it looks like so far is that the two crew members are working on the boat while everybody else stays away.

"Alex? Are we gonna be here all afternoon?" Robbie asks.

"We're on a stakeout. We have to be here." I grumble.

Robbie's not exactly a daredevil. Not like me and Sasha. He's more of a homebody. Who likes boats. And wants to join the Navy. And now looks super sad 'cause I snapped at him.

"Sorry, Robbie. I didn't mean…"

"It's okay."

Sasha's not watching us 'cause she's bent over backwards and kinda reminds me of a pretzel. Her bellybutton is facing the sky. She calls it a yoga backbend.

"What do you think, Sash? We still good?"

"For sure."

Her mouth moves and the words come out, but I have to stop myself from leaning over to look at her. "Sash, do you know how unreal it is talking to somebody when their mouth is on top of their eyes?"

"Totally." Sasha giggles. "That's what you are right now."

Me and Robbie look at each other and roll our eyes. He picks up the binoculars and lays down on the grass next to me. "So weird," he mutters. "What are we looking for?"

"Suspicious activity. See the man painting the railings on the sides of the boat? It's like taking him forever 'cause he's got this little brush and a small bucket of paint. He must not be putting much paint in the bucket 'cause he keeps disappearing. When he comes back, it looks like maybe he's cleaned his brush. Mr. Van Horn does that a lot when he paints around the B&B."

"So that's suspicious?"

I sigh. "No. It's not. It's boring. He's made a couple of trips now to get more paint. Each time he disappears, he's gone for about ten minutes. Then he comes back and paints some more. See the girl? She's been doing things like taking out trash."

"Wow. I hate it when I have to do that."

"Me, too," Sasha says from a different pretzel position. "Hey Alex, can you do this? It's a bow."

She totally looks like a bow. She's holding her feet with her hands and has her belly on the ground. "I don't think so." I say and make a face at Robbie.

We both giggle and go back to watching *The Treasure King*.

"Why's she got all the gear from the lifeboat out on the deck?" I ask.

"It's something they do in port," Robbie says.

I check out what's going on through the binoculars. "It looks like she's doing a major cleaning. She took three plastic bags to the dumpster before. Then she was mopping the deck, and when she finished with that she started on the lifeboat. I didn't realize how much stuff there is to do on a boat. It's like totally mind boggling."

Robbie gets all serious for a second. "A boat is a lot of work." He raises the binoculars and looks through them. "She's got like food and lifejackets and blankets."

"I know. She unpacked all that stuff, replaced some of it, and then packed it all back up. I'd totally want her in charge of the lifeboat supplies if my boat was ever going down."

"For sure."

It's twenty after two. I wonder if Marquetta's going to be coming by to check on us. She said she would. But maybe she got busy. There's a lot of stuff to do in a B&B. Maybe working on a boat wouldn't be so different.

My back is getting super stiff from laying on the grass on my stomach, so I sit crosslegged and look at Sasha. She's doing a handstand. Seriously? On a stakeout?

Then again, maybe she's got the right idea. This is the most boring stakeout ever.

26

Rick

JENNIFER RETURNED TO THE UGLY Worm, which left Rick alone to watch the spot where the body of Captain Carroll had been discovered. Closing his eyes, he imagined himself walking by in the dark with the only illumination coming from the security lighting. Black water. Calm and quiet.

Would he have noticed the body? Hard to say. What if he and Marquetta had walked this way instead of to her bungalow?

The sun had set and there had only been a sliver of a moon, so it was conceivable they could have walked right by this spot and never even noticed anything unusual. Except that Captain Carroll was most likely still alive at that time, so there would have been nothing to notice.

With a last look around, Rick retraced his path to the marina entrance. He exchanged a wave with Joe Gray as he passed by Joe's houseboat, but stopped when Joe motioned at him.

"Hey, Rick. If you want to talk to any of the treasure hunters, I just saw Will Shelley heading into Ocean Surf. You should be able to catch him pretty easily if you go there now."

"Thanks. I'll do that. I just finished with Jennifer. She thinks your theory is right on."

"I was here early myself and I've got to tell you, the entire marina was quiet. Under those conditions, only a ninja could have killed Captain Carroll and pulled it off." Joe looked to his left. "Uh oh. There's Shelley. He's in front of the store. Better let you go before he gets away."

Rick hurried up the ramp to shore, then along Front St. to Ocean Surf. Will Shelley didn't appear to be leaving, but just inspecting some of the merchandise on racks outside the store. Ocean Surf was small, but the store always did a brisk business. On most days the owner, Dennis Malone, set up racks of merchandise he tagged as on sale. In truth, Rick had seen the same things on sale for months at a time.

Shelley took a pale blue tee shirt with the image of a surfboard emblazoned on the front from the rack, inspected the price tag, then held it out at arm's length. Though Rick didn't know the man's age, he'd place him in the sixty-plus category. His craggy face was heavily lined, but his hair was still full and looked to be a natural blond. Apparently satisfied, Shelley carried his find into the store. Rick arrived just as the dressing room door shut.

Along one wall there was a counter with surfing accessories —bags, fins, board waxes. Near that was a circular rack packed with wetsuits. Boards lined the wall behind the counter. The rest of the store was dedicated to clothing.

Rick waved to Dennis, who was rearranging clothing on one of the racks toward the back. When Rick pointed at the dressing room and got a thumbs up from Dennis, he waited near a rack filled with children's wear. He found a bright purple tee he knew Alex would love, checked the size, and then the price. As usual,

Dennis's regular price was high, but the markdown significant.

"Would look great on Alex," Dennis said as he slipped between a pair of racks to stand near Rick.

"You're right, but I didn't come in to buy." Rick pointed in the direction of the dressing room.

"No worries." Dennis lowered his voice to a whisper and chuckled. "Dude's been messing up all my inventory."

"I wanted to ask him a few questions away from the others."

Dennis gave Rick another thumbs-up, then gestured at the tee. "She'd love that one. That's the tourist price—I got more in back. I'll give you an extra ten percent off. You want me to hold it for you? Since you're here."

"Sure. Can we pick it up tomorrow when we do our shopping at the market? I'd like Alex to try it on first."

"No problem."

The door to the dressing room opened and Will Shelley came out, the tee he'd selected outside draped over one arm.

"Fit okay?" Dennis asked.

"Well enough. I'll take it." Shelley seemed unconcerned by Rick's presence and lifted his chin in acknowledgement. He had intense blue eyes, a stark contrast to his heavily lined face. "How's it going?"

"Pretty good. Looks like we both found something. Mine's for my daughter." Rick handed the shirt he'd selected to Dennis.

"It's definitely not your color," Shelley said with a smile.

"I'll ring you up. You two can talk for a sec." Dennis took the tee from Shelley along with Rick's and made his way back to the checkout counter.

Rick introduced himself, explained that he was working the investigation of Captain Carroll's death, and then waited, watching Shelley expectantly. The other man apparently got the message—it was his chance to talk.

"Terrible thing about Captain Carroll," Shelley said. "So are you a cop?"

"I consult with them. You mind if I ask where you were last night between six and nine?"

"Not a problem. I rented a car yesterday afternoon so I could go to San Ladron after dinner at the Crooked Mast. I have a niece who lives there. She just had a baby and I decided to make the most of our forced landing."

"Leaving here after dinner, that's a pretty late start," Rick said.

"Not a problem for me. I usually work late. And I could always stay in their spare room."

Rick eyed Shelly, not sure how much sleep he expected to get in a house with a newborn. "So Seaside Cove wasn't a planned stop?"

"No. It wasn't planned. But I think you know that already." Shelley flashed a quick, forced smile. "I can't really say anything else. We're all covered by an NDA on the boat."

"Excuse me?" Rick blurted.

"You know, a nondisclosure agreement. Keeps us from saying anything about what happens during the trip."

"I know what an NDA is," Rick said. "I didn't realize *The Treasure King* was on a secret mission."

Shelley cocked his head to one side and grimaced. "Seemed overkill to me, too. But, there is—was—a lot at stake. I don't know what will happen now." He edged toward the back of the store where Dennis stood next to the register. "I should probably pay for my shirt."

Rick slipped in front of Shelley to block his way. "What does your NDA cover?"

"Operations of the boat, the dive, location, anything associated with finding the treasure."

"It doesn't cover people?"

"People? Oh, you mean who might have had motive to kill Captain Carroll? No, that kind of stuff isn't covered. In fact, since the captain is now dead, I don't even know if the agreement is still valid." Shelley looked around as though he were searching for an alternate path.

"We can go this way," Rick said and inched toward the back of the store. He stopped, turned, and asked, "So…who didn't like the captain?"

Shelley smirked, the weathered lines on his face forming a disquieting landscape. "Nobody liked him. Feel free to confirm it. A few of them are in Crusty Buns. At least, they were when I left."

"I heard Captain Caroll claimed he had a map showing the exact location of the *San Manuel*. Do you think that's true?" Rick wedged himself between two racks of clothing, one containing women's tops, the other filled with shorts.

"Sorry, buddy, but that's definitely a taboo subject. Until I get some sort of clarification on the status, I can't talk about anything along those lines. But I will tell you this, you might want to look into Heather. Something's not right about her whole relationship with Carroll."

"Meaning?" Rick stopped and regarded the other man.

"She was supposed to be Carroll's girlfriend. But from what I could see, she didn't act much like one. Didn't look like she enjoyed being around him or anything. I know they had… relations at least one night. But the rest of the time? It was like she couldn't stand the man. She called him a toad once right to his face."

"What happened?" Rick asked.

"It looked like Carroll was going to throw her overboard, so I stepped in and calmed him down."

"It was that serious? Do you really think he'd have done that?"

"The man had a mean streak. He irritated everybody. I was the one who had to smooth things over with the others. Somehow, I became the de facto peacemaker. Maybe it's because I'm the only one who'd stand up to him."

Rick eyed Shelley. Though he was older, he was well-muscled and lean. "I could see where you might be intimidating."

Shelley laughed. "Only looks that way, man. I was a line cook. Never been in a fight or anything. All my working out was in butchering slabs of meat."

"So you were used to lifting a lot of dead weight?"

"Let me tell you, whenever they needed someone to pull a slab off the hook in the freezer, I was the guy." He clicked his chin upwards. "Hey, I have to get checked out."

"No problem," Rick said. "One last question. How much can you bench?"

"I don't know." Shelley scrunched up his face. "Maybe three hundred? Why?"

"Just curious. That's all."

27

Rick

RICK LEFT OCEAN SURF AND headed straight to Crusty Buns. Located only a few blocks away, he hoped he could make it to the bakery before the treasure hunters left. He speed-walked up Main Street, noticing along the way that the jewelry store on the other side of the street was open. Of course they were open now. He was busy. No matter how much he wanted to cross over, pick out a ring, and propose to Marquetta, that was going to have to wait.

Crusty Buns was on the southwest corner of Whale Avenue and Main Street. Like so many other businesses in downtown Seaside Cove, it operated out of an old house. A single story bungalow with bright green paint and rust trim, Rick felt it was a classic definition of the word gaudy. But then, that was much of Seaside Cove. Old homes. Bright colors. Friendly people. He'd learned quickly that Crusty Buns was filled with those. Thanks to Angus and Mary O'Donnell's baking prowess, it was a hopping place, favored by both locals and tourists.

The two bistro tables on the sidewalk in front of the store

were occupied, one by Stephen and Winnie Carston. Stephen waved to Rick, then motioned for him to come closer.

"Enjoying the local fare?" Rick asked as he approached.

"I am going to miss this little town," Stephen said.

"My waistline won't." Winnie laughed, but immediately took a bite of a miniature muffin Rick recognized.

"Those blueberry muffins are Marquetta's favorite," Rick said. "Mine, too, for that matter. Alex likes the chocolate chip."

"Smart girl," Stephen said. "I just polished off one of those myself. Would you like to join us?"

"Sorry, but I have business inside." Rick said a quick goodbye and went through the open front door.

Inside, the sandwich blackboard gave the daily specials along with Mary's quote of the day, which was "Enjoy the sweet things in life." Judging by the crowd at the long table for ten, which was often shared by locals wanting to exchange gossip, there were plenty of customers following the sandwich board's advice. Most of the smaller tables were filled, some with individuals, others with small groups of two to four people.

It always amazed Rick how a bakery did so much business at three in the afternoon, but Crusty Buns was that way most days. Rick scanned the crowd in search of the men from *The Treasure King*. Before he finished his search, he heard the sweet lilt of Mary O'Donnell's brogue behind him.

"Looking for someone in particular?"

He turned around to greet Mary. "I didn't realize you were behind me, but maybe you can help. I'm looking for a couple of the passengers from *The Treasure King*. Someone told me they were here."

"Aye, that they are. In the back corner." Mary stuck her hands into the pockets of her green Crusty Buns apron and pulled out a small order pad. "Can I bring you something? A blueberry muffin, perhaps?"

"You know those are my favorite, but I need to make this quick. Another time?"

"We'll look forward to seeing you. Be sure to bring Marquetta and your lovely daughter."

"I will," Rick said as he inched away. "I'd better catch these guys before they leave."

"So far they haven't been in a rush. Maybe you can hurry them along." Mary winked as she returned the order pad to the pocket of her apron. "I need to turn their table."

Rick headed toward the back corner where Mary had pointed. Ed Silverstein sat with two other men that Rick didn't recognize. Silverstein had been with four others at dinner, but these two hadn't been among them. One of the men eyed Rick as he approached the table. The man had short-cropped brown hair, blue eyes, and a trim build. He leaned sideways and made a quiet comment to the man on his right. He got a nod in return, then Silverstein looked over his shoulder at Rick, who now stood almost directly behind him.

"Excuse me, gentlemen," Rick said. "I wonder if I might be able to speak to the three of you for a few minutes."

"Who might you be?" Silverstein asked.

Rick introduced himself, told them he was investigating the death of Captain Carroll, and asked if he might take a few minutes of their time for some questions. Ed Silverstein shook Rick's hand, pointed to the man on his left, then the one on his right.

"Eli England, Christopher Jenks," said Silverstein. "They're business partners. Eli's a narrow weaver, and Christopher is the QC guy."

"You're in an interesting industry," Rick said to England. "I did a story on narrow weavers once for a newspaper in New York. Quite the history."

The man's eyebrows went up and he looked at Jenks. "Can you imagine that? Someone who's actually heard about narrow weaving. When my grandfather ran the business, it was primarily just tapes and ribbons and that sort of thing. We're now expanding into everything from braids to webbings to tie downs and tubular products. We're total high tech these days. And still nobody knows who we are."

"Watch out, Rick," said Silverstein. "If you get Eli talking about his business you'll be here all afternoon."

England sneered at Silverstein. "I'm justifiably proud of my business. Everything I've done for it." He looked sideways at Jenks. "Right, Chris?"

Jenks, who was holding up his phone to capture a photo, spoke absently. "Sure thing, Eli. Sure thing."

"Always taking pictures, this guy. The good news is his passion has helped me build the brand."

"Sounds like a good partnership," Rick said. "I'd love to hear about your company, but I need to focus on my investigation right now. I only have a little time. I need to ask all of you where you were between six and nine last night. How about if I start with you, Eli?"

"Chris and I were on a conference call with a customer in Hong Kong. It was morning there. This is a big deal. Could be a million a year in business."

Rick made a note. *England and Jenks on conference call with Hong Kong. England - blowhard. Jenks - quiet. Phone records?* He looked up at Silverstein. "And you, Mr. Silverstein?"

"I was on *The Treasure King* with Isaac and Matthew. We

were playing poker."

"Who won?" Rick asked.

"Not me," Silverstein said. "I'm diabetic and my blood sugar had dropped."

Almost involuntarily, Rick glanced down at Silverstein's plate, which contained only a few crumbs.

"I know," he said. "But it was a bran muffin. I can sneak one of those now and again. Have you talked to any of the others?"

"Will Shelley. He's the one who told me you were here."

"Got no use for that one," Silverstein said. "Makes himself out to be some big problem solver, but all he does is create trouble."

Rick caught the sudden change in Silverstein's demeanor—his sharper tone, the harder edge of his jawline. There was obviously no love lost between him and Shelley. He didn't want to stoke the fires of animosity, but discord might work to his advantage. "He sounded sincere enough to me," Rick said innocently.

Silverstein waved his hand dismissively. "That's all bogus. Right, Eli?"

"He tried to mellow things out after Heather got all in a snit. But it was a powder keg there for a few days."

"What exactly was she so worked up about?" Rick asked.

Both England and Silverstein looked at each other and laughed as though they were sharing a secret.

"Captain Carroll had himself a little extracurricular activity onshore in Long Beach. Heather found out about it and really dug into him. Things have been tense between the two of them ever since." Silverstein laughed again. "Of course, that didn't stop them from scratching the itch the first night out."

Jenks shook his head at Silverstein's comment and huffed.

"She said she filed a complaint in Long Beach. Sexual harassment. Seems pretty weird to me. Saying a guy is harassing you on one hand and then turning around and sleeping with him a few days later."

"That girl's not right, I'm telling you," Silverstein said. "She's the one who got her nose out of joint, then she asked Will to mediate. They'd gotten kind of friendly, so he agreed."

"Exactly how friendly were they?" Rick asked.

England inched forward to insert himself into the conversation. "Let's not go making more out of this than there is. Will liked to talk about his niece in San Ladron and how she'd just had her first baby. Most of us could have cared less, but Heather seemed interested, so that gave him a license to go on about it with her. I sure never saw anything more serious. Right, Chris?" He looked sideways at Jenks.

"That's right. All innocent." Jenks sneered at Silverstein. "Ed just likes to make trouble."

Silverstein cleared his throat and moved his head from side-to-side. "I ain't saying she was trying to play house with the guy, but she did encourage him. I think she was trying to put the screws to the captain."

"Are you saying you think she wanted to make him jealous?" Rick asked.

"More than that." Silverstein thumped himself on the chest with his thumb. "I say she wanted the good captain to feel the threat of physical pain."

"Did Will assault him?"

"He didn't have to. Carroll was a jerk, but he knew Will could do some serious damage if he got ticked off. After that, Carroll was in a foul mood."

Rick recalled the apparent tension between Heather Sanna

and Captain Carroll at dinner. How quickly she'd left when he got out of hand. And how quickly he'd gotten into the argument with Joe Gray. "If those two weren't getting along, why was she even at dinner with him last night?"

"You'd have to ask her that, my friend," said Silverstein. "I got no idea what her motives are."

"Ed, why don't you just give her a break?" England said. "We've all had to do things we didn't want to in our lives. Right, Chris?" He glanced at Jenks, but continued on without waiting for an answer. "Chris doesn't like to gossip. Ed's got no problem with that, though. Do you, Ed?"

"Don't go all high and mighty on me, Eli. You ain't exactly above the fray. You've talked plenty of trash about the others. Besides, what else have we got to do on that boat?"

Jenks rolled his eyes and stared off into space. Rick suspected the man had plenty to say, and jotted a note next to his name about talking to him in private. For now, though, he might as well see what he could get from Silverstein and England. "Things are pretty boring when you're at sea?"

"This ain't no cruise ship," Silverstein grumbled.

"You got that right." England raised his hand, palm facing Silverstein, and the two exchanged a high five.

"Gentlemen, I've heard Captain Carroll has a map showing the exact location of the *San Manuel*. What do you know about that?"

Silverstein harrumphed. "Carroll tried to keep us all silent with some bogus NDA, but that's just a bunch of BS. The fact is, we probably know about as much as you. He sold us all on the idea of him having this valuable map, but he never would show it to any of us. Said he would take us there, but he was not about to share the map for fear we'd make a copy and go it alone. That's what he claimed."

"Now that he's dead, we're out everything we put in," England complained. "I couldn't run my business that way."

The others grumbled their agreement.

"Most of us couldn't get away with that," Rick said.

"I'll see you guys back on the boat." Jenks stood abruptly and said a quick goodbye to Rick, then wove his way through the tables to the front door.

"Guy's not a people person," Silverstein said with a laugh.

The corners of England's mouth turned down into something resembling a scowl. "Moody cuss. I can't count the number of times I've offended his delicate senses because of something I said."

Rick turned to see if Jenks had made his exit. He was nowhere in sight. "Eli, you said he was on a conference call with you last night between six and nine?"

"That's right. The call started about eight, but we spent some time mapping out our strategy beforehand. Maybe an hour. Afterwards, he went back to his room."

"Well, that should easily put you both in the clear," Rick said. But, even as he said the words, he wondered if the alibis of both Christopher Jenks and Eli England might be just a little too convenient. He could always ask Adam to get a call log for both men. Rick felt his eyes widen with a sudden realization. He could also answer that question right now. "Eli, who's phone did you use for the phone call?"

A frown creased England's forehead. "Excuse me?"

"Did you use your phone or Christopher's?"

"Mine. Why?"

"Your phone should have a record of the call. If you can show me the call log, I can rule both of you out as suspects right now."

"No way."

"I could get a warrant," Rick lied.

"Then get it. Nobody sees what's on my phone."

Silverstein snickered. "What? You got something to hide?"

"Shut up, Ed. You got no idea what you're talking about."

"Then why don't you explain it?" Rick asked.

England glowered at Rick, then stood. "You know what? I don't have to talk to you." He looked down at Silverstein. "Neither do you, Ed. If you're smart, you'll follow me out the door before he tries to pin this thing on you."

Silverstein pushed back his chair and studied Rick. His head bobbed a few times, then his jaw quirked to one side. "The man's right. Never did trust small-town cops." He followed England toward the front door.

Left alone, Rick made a couple of quick notes. *England secretive about his alibi. Could he and Jenks have done something together and be covering for each other? Silverstein— confirm alibi with Longstreet and Redmond.*

Someone tapped Rick's shoulder. He looked up to see who was standing over him. "Hi, Mary," he said.

"Looks like you didn't make any friends."

Rick laughed. "I didn't. Thank goodness that wasn't my goal. At least I'm starting to get familiar with the players. And I can tell you, they're living down to my expectations."

"Aye." Mary squinted at the front of the store. "They are a strange bunch."

Rick's phone beeped. "That's Marquetta. I'd better take this."

Mary patted Rick's shoulder again and winked. "Good idea."

Rick answered. "Hey, what's up?"

"Alex is missing."

"From the B&B?"

"No. We agreed I'd meet her in Marina Park. I said she could go there to watch *The Treasure King.* I'm at the park and there's no sign of her."

Rick's pulse picked up. It wasn't like Alex to disappear. "Have you tried calling her?"

"Yes. She didn't answer. She went with Robbie and Sasha. They're both gone, too. I checked and they're home. I'm worried about her, Rick. What if something's happened to her?"

"We'll find her," he muttered. But how? A rushing river of blood pounded in Rick's head. Where did they even begin? Better yet, what was Alex up to now?

28

Alex

I'M HIDING BETWEEN THE BIG trash cans behind the Ugly Worm. It smells kinda bad, but other than that, this is so much better than the park! I don't need binoculars or anything. Nobody can see me 'cause I'm wedged between the cans, but I can see everything that goes on.

When I came down here, the two crew members were both on the boat. Then, the girl left and the man chased behind her. Lucky for me, they stopped to talk just a few feet away. He said they should go away together, but she didn't think it was a good idea. She wants to keep things cool? That totally sounds like a boyfriend-girlfriend thing. He even took her hand once, but she pulled away.

After the argument, she stormed off and told him he needed to get back to the boat 'cause they couldn't leave it unattended. He looked back at the boat, and then he ran after her.

It's been a few minutes since they left. This is totally the best opportunity I'm gonna get. Marquetta said I should try to find the treasure map. That would totally help Flynn. If I found it, Flynn would know it really exists. She might be able to do something to make them turn it over. Or maybe I could find evidence to prove who killed Captain Carroll? If there really is nobody else on the boat, I could totally sneak aboard and look for the map. I could do my search and be gone before anybody figures out what I did. It's a big boat, but how many places could there be to hide a treasure map?

Oh man, there are so many reasons to do this while there's nobody around. But there's one big reason I shouldn't. I promised Marquetta I wouldn't go near *The Treasure King*.

I was supposed to stay in the park with Robbie and Sasha. But they got bored and left. And then I started to think about Flynn and what she needs and how Marquetta said I should focus on the treasure map. It would also help my dad because he could use the evidence to help the cops and that would force Deputy Baker to be nice to Marquetta and… This sucks. Marquetta's already called once. I didn't answer, so she left a message. She's in the park right now. And she's worried. I know she's going to ground me. I am in so much trouble. So what's it matter? Right? If I'm going to be grounded, shouldn't I at least get something for it?

I look up and down the docks. There's still nobody paying attention. If I do this now, I can totally get away with it.

29

Rick

RICK HURRIED OUT OF CRUSTY Buns and down Main Street. Marina Park came into view as he neared the roundabout at the base of Main Street. Shortly after that, he saw Marquetta continuing her frantic, and obviously fruitless, search. All during the last block of his trip, he willed her to look his direction, but she never did. When he called to her, she rushed forward and threw her arms around his neck. He pulled her close, felt her body tremble, and then eased her away.

She swiped at her wet cheeks. "I never should have left her alone."

"You couldn't have known." He winced at how naive that sounded. They both knew. Alex was fearless—and at eleven-years-old, had terrible impulse control. There was no telling what she might do once she found a reason. "I'm going to rush home and check her room. If she's not at the B&B, I'll be back in five minutes. If she's there, I'll call you."

Marquetta studied the marina. "Do you think she could be on *The Treasure King?*"

"Let's hope not," Rick said. "Is there anybody on board?"

"The crew members left a few minutes ago. Now, it looks deserted."

Deep down, Rick worried that Marquetta was right. It would be just like Alex to get caught up in the moment and not reason through the implications of her trespassing or doing an illegal search. "Let's not jump to conclusions. I'll check at home and be right back."

Rick rushed off, sneaking a glimpse of Marquetta over his shoulder as he left. She'd moved to the edge of the park where she had a good view of the marina. He made it to the B&B in two minutes. The old house was eerily quiet. There was almost always someone else around and he couldn't recall ever being completely alone inside. He rushed upstairs, checked Alex's room, his office, the kitchen, and then stood at the kitchen island with his palms resting on the counter. He whispered, "Alex, where are you?"

He called her phone, got no answer, then called Marquetta. "She's not here. I'm on my way back."

On his way out the front door, Rick sighed. "What have you done now, Alex?"

Almost as if it were divine intervention, Rick's phone rang. He snatched it up without checking to see who was calling. "Alex?"

"Um...no. This is Jason Keneally. You sent me a message about an old story I did in Seaside Cove."

Rick paused at the edge of the porch. He closed his eyes. Of all the rotten timing.

"There's not much I can tell you," Jason said. "I didn't remember the story until I looked it up. It was one of those things where I was out there on vacation when the town started making a lot of noise about this big treasure hunt. My editor liked the idea and had me cover it."

"Jason, I appreciate you calling me back. Would it be possible for me to call you later?"

"Sorry, but I'm at the airport, and I'm going to be unavailable for some time. It could be a month before we can talk again. Look. I'll make this quick. It was a foul day. Lots of wind. Rain. I took the photo that was in the story, but neither of those men would say much."

Rick took the steps quickly and turned toward Marina Park. He kept the phone to his ear and scanned the area as he walked and asked questions. "Did it seem as though Neal and Captain Jack had had an argument?"

"Yes. But, what about, I don't know."

"Was there anyone else around who might have known what they argued about?"

"I have no idea. It's been fifteen years. I'm sorry I can't be of more help."

"Did you meet a man named Joe Gray that day?"

After a brief pause, Jason said, "Yes. If I remember correctly, he's the one who told me about the big event. I met him in some bakery. Friendly guy. He was in the original photo, but my editor had him cropped out to focus on what he thought was the bigger story. I'm sorry, but they're calling my flight. If you have more questions, you can always email me, but I may not be able to get back to you for an extended period."

Operating on autopilot, Rick thanked Jason for his time. After he'd hung up, he realized he hadn't even wished him a safe trip or asked where he was going. In the distance, he saw Marquetta hurrying toward him. They met halfway.

"What are we going to do?" Marquetta asked. "I told her to

stay here and that I would be checking up on her. I decided to put together a snack for the kids, so it took longer than I wanted to get here. When I did, it was deserted."

Rick took Marquetta's hand and led her to the spot where they could see the marina. *The Treasure King* lay below them in the marina, apparently abandoned by its crew and passengers. "I don't think there's anybody on board."

Marquetta's hand went to her chest. "Oh, no. Not you, too. Rick, you can't go on that boat without permission. That's trespassing."

"What other choice do I have?"

"Call Adam." Marquetta squeezed Rick's hand hard. "He'll find a way to get you on legally."

"There may not be time for that." Rick grimaced and shook his head. "When Baker and I asked for permission, it was Heather Sanna who let us on, not the guy. Her coworker, Gavin Mancini, was very resistant to giving us access. I don't want to have to bargain with him under any circumstances."

"Rick? Please?"

Her gray eyes were rimmed in red, her cheeks, puffy. He could see the worry, both for Alex and, if he did this, for him. And yet, Alex was his daughter. It was an excruciating choice, but he really didn't have one. No matter what it took, he would do what he needed to keep Alex safe.

"I'm sorry," he said. "I have to go."

30

Alex

I RECOGNIZE THE LIVING ROOM of *The Treasure King* from the virtual tour I took. It looks smaller than it did on the video. The two red couches form a sitting area and there are tables where people can put their drinks. It's a lot of furniture for a small space. The painting on the wall with the antique-looking gold frame is super weird. It's a dog dressed in an old soldier's uniform. The drapes over the windows on the sides are open and there's a lot of light coming in.

Standing in the middle of the room, it totally looks like this is the gathering place when they're at sea. 2It also doesn't look anything like a place where Captain Carroll would store a valuable map. Time to move on. I remember Robbie saying there are always a lot of maps on the navigation deck—and maybe in the captain's quarters. I have to find both of those before anybody comes back.

There's a ladder at the other end of the room. I crane my neck to see where it might go to, but can't tell. I'm gonna have to climb to the top. I put one foot on the first rung and test it. Grab the handrail. My heart is pounding. I listen. There's no noise. I take the next step. And the next.

My jaw drops when I get to the top deck. It's like a spaceship! And even better than the video. There's a computer screen and a panel with a lot of dials and switches. There's even a huge steering wheel. The windows are slanted back and each one has a wiper.

I have the whole entire thing to myself! This is awesome! I hurry over to the captain's chair and sit. It's big and has arms and is super comfortable. The problem is I can't reach anything without sitting on the edge. At least when I sit forward, I can get my hands on the steering wheel.

There are a couple of black boxes in front of me. They each have lots of dials. The one on the left has a handset, so it must be some kind of radio or telephone. The other one's like a radar thingy. Robbie would probably know what it is. Too bad I can't ask him.

The chair even rocks and swivels. The boat creaks, and I realize I'm running out of time. It would be super fun to pretend-pilot the boat, but I have to get back to my search. If Robbie's right, this is the best place on the boat to keep a map. You could pull it out when you needed it and put it back when you didn't. But they wouldn't just leave it out. And maybe Captain Carroll didn't want anyone to know about it, so he was hiding it more than keeping it handy. If it's not inside one of these cabinets or drawers, it's gonna be in a secret place.

There are only three drawers and a couple cabinets. Even though they're all obvious places, I check those first. I start with the top drawer. Maps!

Holy moley. Maybe this is it. But, when I look at them, they don't have anything marked. It looks like they're just what Mr.

Gray calls navigation charts. He's shown me some before. They're super detailed and complicated. But if there's nothing to mark the spot, they're not what I'm looking for. I shove the charts back in the drawer and check the one below it.

This one's got a keyring and a phone and a couple of walkie-talkies along with some other office-type stuff—pens and pencils, rulers, nothing important. Rats. The boat creaks again and I freeze. I shove the drawer closed and rush over to the stairwell to listen. Did someone come back?

I stick my head out over the opening. Listen real hard. But the boat's quiet. It must have just been another wave. I'm surprised at how much *The Treasure King* moves. I look around the area again. Everything's been put away, so the place is like super organized. Maybe the map's not up here. What about the captain's quarters? Duh. I'm gonna need keys.

I go back to the second drawer and grab the keyring that's just laying inside, then climb down the ladder. How am I going to know when I have the right room? The captain would have the biggest cabin. Right? And he'd probably have a good view. And be close to the bridge…at least, that's what Mr. Gray says.

On the second deck, I go toward the front of the boat. I pass by a bar and a small seating area for four. The cabin I'm looking for is at the end of the hall. It's even got a little sign on it like what we use at the B&B. That was super easy. Now all I have to do is figure out which key opens the door. I try the first one. It doesn't fit. Neither does the second. Or the third. Just as I'm about to put the fourth key in the slot, I hear voices.

Holy crap! It's a man and a woman. The two crew members. And they're coming back. I jam the key into the lock.

My pulse races faster. The voices get louder. The door doesn't want to open.

I can barely breathe. "Please," I whisper. "Open!"

The key turns in the lock.

But it's too late.

31

Rick

ON THE SHORT TRIP TO *The Treasure King* from Marina Park, Rick thought desperately about a solution to getting Alex back—that is, something other than illegally boarding and searching the vessel. The problem wasn't Adam; it was Deputy Baker. She'd made herself perfectly clear—she had no interest in coddling him or Alex.

At one point, he was sure he saw a figure move and called Marquetta. "Top deck. Do you see her?"

"No. I thought I did once, but it looks empty now."

"Use the binoculars."

"I am, Rick. I have been since you ran off." She paused, then added, "Sorry. I didn't mean to snap at you. But there's a much bigger problem. The crew members are returning. They're about a hundred feet ahead of you and are boarding right now. One of them is the woman from the Crooked Mast. It looks like they're arguing."

Rick stopped and peered ahead. "I see them. You're right, that's Heather. The guy is the one I was telling you about, Gavin

Mancini. He's a mean one. And it does look like they're having a bit of a tiff. They don't look happy at all. There's no way I can get on board with them standing where they are. Marquetta, text Alex and tell her to find a way off that boat. I'm going to distract these two."

"There's only one way off, and that's the ramp. Unless you want her to swim."

"Fine. Tell her to hide in one of the lifeboats on the starboard side. I'll get these two inside and then she can sneak off."

"Why don't you just tell them the truth, Rick? They won't want to hurt a child."

"Alex being aboard that boat jeopardizes everything. Not only will my role in the investigation be over, but any evidence recovered will be thrown out of court because it's contaminated. The only solution is getting her off that boat before anyone finds out she's there."

"All right. I'll tell her. Please, be careful."

"I will." But it was a lie.

Careful was a luxury he didn't have.

He waved to Mancini and Sanna as he walked, but they either didn't see him or ignored him and disappeared inside the side door. Unsure of what he was going to say or do, Rick quickened his pace. He had no authority to force his way aboard, and as long as Deputy Baker was around, trespassing would land him in jail for sure. Without question, he would go to jail to protect Alex, but once he was locked away, he'd no longer be able to protect her. That meant he would break the law only as a last resort.

Rick marched up the ramp, stopping before he set foot on *The Treasure King*. Both Mancini and Sanna were still inside. Now what? "Hello!" Rick called as loud as he could. "Hello aboard *The Treasure King!*"

A door to Rick's right opened and Mancini poked his head out. When he saw Rick, he scowled and muttered something under his breath. Striding forward, he planted his feet on the deck and his hands on his hips. "What are you doing here?" he barked.

"Hoping to talk to you. I had a few questions about some of your passengers. Can I come aboard and talk?"

Mancini eyed Rick suspiciously and held his position. "What kind of questions?"

Heather came up to them and stood next to Mancini. "The man's got a job to do, Gavin. Let's just tell him what he wants to know and get on with things. Go ahead."

"Let's start with Will Shelley." Rick watched Heather's face as he spoke. "I've gotten conflicting stories about him. His version is that he's assumed the role of mediator on the boat. Ed Silverstein says he's more of an agitator. Can you clarify what kind of role he played?"

Rick couldn't help but notice the woman's body language— she visibly tightened up by clutching her arms around her. She scowled at Rick, looking as irritated as Mancini, who took a protective step forward.

"Told you, Heather. We don't have to answer any of these questions."

She glared at Mancini, but didn't move away. This was not going the way Rick had anticipated, but he didn't have any other alternatives.

"Why wouldn't you answer?" Rick asked. "If you have nothing to hide…" He let his words trail off, but held eye contact.

"You can just take your questions and go find a rock to hide under," Mancini bellowed. "Will Shelley's a major pain and he's only caused her trouble."

"Shut up, Gavin! I'm sick of you and your macho interference." Heather's jaw tightened and her tone softened. "I'm sorry. But you need to back off. I'll deal with this." She laid a hand on Mancini's shoulder. "Why don't you get back to work?"

Mancini watched her face for several seconds before he took a deep breath and walked off in a huff. Heather kept her arms wrapped around herself as she watched Mancini leave, and when Mancini disappeared through the door, his heart sank. Now what did he do? Maybe Marquetta was right. The truth was the only way.

"Look, Ms. Sanna. You seem to be very level-headed."

"Gavin's okay. He just doesn't always understand boundaries."

"Right. Boundaries." Rick hesitated. "That's my problem. I have a daughter. She's eleven. And she doesn't always understand boundaries either."

"It's a hard age," Heather said, then forced a smile.

Why couldn't he just say it? Get it over with? "You don't understand," he stammered and took a deep breath. "The problem is…"

Mancini's voice bellowed from inside *The Treasure King*. "Hey, you! Come back here!"

"Alex!" Rick yelled, then nearly knocked Heather over as he rushed past her.

32

Alex

I PUSH THROUGH THE OPEN doorway, slam the door closed behind me, and stand with my back pressed against it. The man pounds his fist on the door. Each time, it feels like he's getting madder and madder. It won't be long before he breaks it down. My heart feels like it's gonna explode.

"Open the door you little brat! Who are you?"

My phone pings. Someone's texting me? Now? Are you kidding?

The man hits the door again. Holy crap. I never thought I'd get caught. I look at the text. It's from Marquetta.

—*people coming. Find a place to hide. Run for it when your dad distracts them.*

My dad knows I'm here? Oh, man, he's gonna ground me for a month. Unless the guy out in the hall kills me first.

There's a super loud noise. The door pushes against me, but it holds. I think the guy rammed it with his shoulder. I have to do something. The only escape routes are the bathroom and a closet. The guy hits the door with his shoulder again. It almost gave way that time. What am I gonna do?

I rush into the bathroom. There's no way out. It's the same with the closet. There's not even an air vent big enough for me to crawl through. I take another look around the room and stop when I get to the hanging picture frame on the wall. But it's not a picture in the frame. It's a map. Could that be Captain Carroll's treasure map?

The door shakes again and the man yells at me. "When I get in there, you're dead!"

It won't be long now. The door can't hold forever. I pull out my phone. Take a picture of the map. Run back to the door and press my back against it.

"When I get my hands on you, kid, you'll wish you never saw this boat!" There's another huge thud.

I do the only thing I can. Dial 9-1-1. I jump at the next huge thud. A couple more times and the door's gonna give.

When the operator answers I don't even hear what she says, I just start yelling.

"Help! I'm trapped on *The Treasure King* and there's a man who's trying to hurt me!"

Another slam against the door. It's so loud I can't hear the operator's question.

"Seaside Cove Marina! Tell Chief Cunningham Alex needs help on *The Treasure King*!"

Then, I hear another voice. It's the woman who was arguing with the guy before.

"Gavin! Stop it. What are you doing?"

"There's a kid in there. I'm trying to get her out."

"Her? It's a girl?"

"Yeah. I didn't get a close look. But she had a ponytail."

"So you thought you'd coax her out by scaring her to death?

Brilliant, Gavin. Just brilliant. You can be such an idiot. Back up.
I'll handle this."

There's a gentle knock on the door. It's followed by the
woman's voice. "You can come out now."

No way. But I can't stay in here forever. And now that I've
called 9-1-1, Chief Cunningham will be here soon. I'll be safe
once he gets here.

"Alex. Open this door."

Oh, crap. It's my dad. He's using his stern voice, the one
where he wants me to think he's not mad, but I know he's so
angry he has to hold it all in. I am so dead. There's no way to
avoid what's coming. I'm gonna be grounded until college for
this. And then there's another voice. They're all talking at once,
but the new voice isn't Chief Cunningham like I expected. It's
Deputy Baker.

She'll get me out of here! I reach for the doorknob. Wrap my
fingers around it. And then someone pounds on the door with
their fist. "This is the Seaside Cove Police! You're trespassing.
Open this door and come out with your hands up."

Forget grounded. I'm totally going to jail.

33

Rick

WHAT A MESS, THOUGHT RICK. Everyone in this little hallway was ticked off. At least Mancini was now directing his anger at Deputy Baker, not Alex. Of course, that was only irritating Baker more—a fact Rick was sure he'd hear about until Adam took over—and then things would get worse.

If only he hadn't gone home first. He'd have made it onto the boat, retrieved Alex, and escaped before anyone became the wiser. Now, there would be a heavy price to pay for Alex's impulsiveness. He sighed as he watched his daughter standing there looking frightened and holding her hands in the air.

"What's your name?" Baker demanded.

"Alex...Atwood."

Baker pulled out a pair of handcuffs.

"Really?" Rick exploded. "She's eleven. Not a hardened criminal."

"Back off, Mr. Atwood, or I'll take you in for obstruction."

Mancini snickered. His body language exuded self-satisfaction in spades. He had his arms crossed over his chest and his head bobbed up and down enthusiastically.

"You're going to cuff an eleven-year-old?" Heather blurted. "Give me a break."

"You won't need those. She understands she's in the wrong." Rick's heart broke as he looked sympathetically at his frightened little girl. "Don't you, Alex?"

She looked down at the floor and muttered, "Yes, Daddy."

"I don't care what she claims to understand, Mr. Atwood. I warned you about this before. You did not heed my warning, so I'm placing her under arrest for trespassing, breaking-and-entering, and interfering in a police investigation. Obviously, you haven't taught her a child should not be butting into official police business. When I get done with her, she'll understand it perfectly."

Rick's blood boiled at Baker's little tirade. He was not going to let the deputy treat his daughter however she wanted, not while he stood by helplessly.

"Hope you've got a smaller pair of cuffs," Mancini said with a smirk. "I'm checking the room to see if she stole anything."

"Stop right there, Mr. Mancini," Baker snapped. "You will enter that room when I can go in with you and not a moment before, or I'll arrest you for entering a crime scene." She stared directly at Alex. "Where's the key you used?"

Alex pointed to a spot just inside the door. A small keyring lay on the floor. "I dropped them when he started pounding on the door. I got scared."

Rick's heart broke at how Alex's voice shook. He'd never seen her so afraid, and right now all he saw was a scared child with two bullies towering over her.

"Young lady, I'm going to handcuff you and read you your rights. Since your father's here..." Baker's irritation was obvious as she stood over Alex. "He'll be a witness to your arrest."

"Deputy, there's no need to arrest her," Rick said. "I'll take her home and keep her out of your way."

"Back off, Baker."

Everyone turned to see who was behind the authoritative voice. Baker's jaw clenched and her breathing quickened. Her voice was tight when she said, "Chief."

Rick stood to one side as Adam strode forward. He gave Rick a cursory nod, then pushed past the two crew members. Not quite sure what Adam intended to do, Rick decided to wait. He knew Adam to be fair, and to have a soft spot for Alex. He could only hope for the best.

"Everybody stand down," Adam said firmly. "Mr. Mancini, since you've alleged this young lady may have stolen something, we're going to need you to be with us when we search the room."

"You can't do that!" Mancini snapped.

"I'm the chief of police. I'll do whatever is necessary to ensure everyone gets a fair shake." Adam paused, looked directly at Mancini, then Deputy Baker. "Everyone. Baker, you will conduct the search with either Mr. Mancini or Ms. Sanna present. There will only be one person allowed at a time and the one who is not in the room is to remain here, in this hallway, until the search has been completed. Am I clear?"

Baker squared her shoulders and pointed at Alex. "What about her?"

"I will escort her home. Rick, you will continue working with Baker. You will be with the person who is not in the room."

"Got it."

"Chief, I object. This working with civilians is ridiculous. You can see that it leads to chaos and mistakes. This isn't a parking ticket, it's a murder investigation."

"Objection noted, Baker. Do your job."

"I'm trying to, but if I have to babysit…"

"Baker, enough. You can talk to me later. Right now we have to deal with the situation we have in front of us. Like it or not."

Baker huffed, but focused her attention on Mancini. "Come with me." She turned and entered the captain's quarters with Mancini on her heels.

Rick placed his hand on Alex's shoulder. "You and I are going to have a talk when I get home." He looked at Adam, and said, "Thank you. I'm glad you showed up when you did."

"You have no idea how lucky you are." Adam looked down at Alex. "Or you. Come with me, munchkin. You're going to be under house arrest for a while."

As Adam guided Alex toward the door, she asked, "Does this mean I'm gonna have a criminal record?"

"That depends," Adam said.

"On what?"

"On whether I have to use handcuffs on you or not. Now march before I change my mind."

Rick breathed a sigh of relief as Alex left with Adam behind her. He trusted Adam and was positive he wouldn't let anything happen to Alex. Rick stood next to Heather watching the search inside the cabin.

Mancini was busy rummaging around while Deputy Baker watched. From the scowl on her face, the deputy looked as though she'd about had enough. Heather was leaning against the wall, her arms folded in front of her, and rolling her eyes.

"You think this is a waste?" Rick asked.

"I know it is. Your daughter couldn't have stolen anything. She was wearing a tee shirt and leggings. Gavin's being a jerk.

Maybe I should say, he's just being himself. Do you mind if I go get a few things done? I've got work to do."

"Sorry, but you'll have to wait until your coworker is satisfied my daughter didn't steal the silverware or something."

Heather rolled her eyes again. "Whatever. Hurry it up, Gavin."

Rick kept an eye on Mancini as he flung open the closet door. He grunted, then began pushing hangers aside.

"Mr. Mancini, I'm tired of this," the deputy huffed. "What exactly are you looking for?"

There was a long pause, during which Mancini avoided looking at Deputy Baker and the tension built. Finally, he said, "I'm satisfied. Lock it up."

The deputy followed Mancini into the hallway and looked at Heather. "What about you, Ms. Sanna? Do you feel a need to inspect the room?"

"I'm good." She regarded Mancini, then indicated Rick with a upward tilt of her chin. "I already told him, Gavin's just being a jerk."

Without a word, the deputy locked the door and dropped the entire key ring into a plastic baggie. "This room is still a crime scene. We may need to do an additional search."

"I told you there's nothing missing," Mancini said. "You can't make it a crime scene just because you want to."

"You're the one who made it one when you claimed that little girl might have stolen something. I don't want there to be any question." Deputy Baker slipped the plastic baggie and key into a pouch on her utility belt and looked at the two crew members. "I especially don't want some unauthorized person entering the room, taking something, and then blaming it on a child. The room remains a crime scene until the chief or I declare it otherwise."

Rick couldn't figure out Deputy Baker. On the one hand, she'd appeared ready to lock Alex up, but now she was protecting her?

"I take it you're done for now?" Heather asked.

Deputy Baker scratched out a note in her notepad. "For the time being."

34

Alex

Hey Journal,

I got busted on *The Treasure King*! I am so bummed out. After Chief Cunningham got me off the boat, he took me up to the park where Marquetta was waiting for us. At first she hugged me and held me real tight, then she started to chew me out. Chief Cunningham didn't say a lot, but he did tell us I could be tried in juvenile court.

This totally sucks, Journal. There was nobody around when I snuck on the boat, I totally should have been able to get on and off without being seen. And then those stupid crew members came back. The man is like totally insane. At least he was slow! Ha ha. If he'd have been faster I wouldn't have made it into the captain's quarters and found the map. The map! I've gotta look at that after I finish. I tried to tell Marquetta about it, but she was super upset and said she didn't want to hear any more talk about Captain Carroll or the boat or even Deputy Baker.

This sucks. I was just trying to help. You'd think Deputy

176

*Baker would get that, but she's treating me like I'm the criminal.
I don't wanna be a criminal, Journal. The cops get mean and it's
super stressful 'cause you don't know if you're going to jail or
how long you'll be there.*

*What nobody gets is I wasn't trying to steal anything! I just
wanted to find the evidence. Now I'm like grounded and stuck in
my room until my dad gets home. Then he'll give me the speech
about being impulsive and irrational. I've totally heard it before.
The thing is, I gotta do things my way. Right? That's what he and
Marquetta are always telling me. I guess that only applies when
they approve of what I'm gonna do.*

*Marquetta didn't take away my phone or my computer. Not
yet, anyways. First, I'm gonna look at the photo of the map from
Captain Carroll's wall. If I need someone on the outside to help,
I might be able to get Sasha. We're gonna have to be super
careful to keep everything on the down low. I don't want her to
get busted, too.*

Bye for now,
Alex

I open the picture I took in the captain's quarters on my phone.
It's definitely a map. And it shows Seaside Cove. But that's only
a small part of it. There's a bunch of marks going down the coast.
When I zoom in, I can see that each one of those little marks
looks like a wrecked ship. Some of them have names, but a lot of
them don't. There must be at least a hundred little marks on the
map. Maybe more.

This is gonna take some time 'cause of how many wrecks
there are. Maybe it would be better if I transfered the photo to
my laptop? It's worth a try. I drop it on the computer's desktop
and open the file. The map's a lot easier to read now.

Some of the locations are marked with more than one shipwreck. This is totally awesome. But where's the *San Manuel*? It's supposed to be off the coast of Seaside Cove. I start north of San Francisco and read the names. There's *Celia, Northland, Catania,* and so many more it's making my eyes cross. When I get down to Southern California, I see a little island off of Long Beach has a bunch of wrecks. There are even a few Spanish ships listed—*Santa Marta, San Pedro, San Sebastian.*

My eyes are super tired, and I've gotten through most of the list. But there was no mention of the *San Manuel*. Does that mean it doesn't exist? Maybe Captain Carroll was running a scam and that's what got him killed!

35

Rick

WITH ALEX UNDER CHIEF CUNNINGHAM'S control, Mancini still grumbling about not having access to the captain's quarters, and Deputy Baker obviously unhappy over the entire incident, Rick and the deputy disembarked *The Treasure King*. They met on the dock, not far from the boat. The tightness in Baker's cheeks telegraphed her frustration, and Rick did not have high expectations for how this conversation might go.

The planks creaked beneath Rick's feet, its old wood, worn and weathered, still sturdy. Joe Gray had once told him the dock's flexibility, the give and take Rick heard and felt now, were the reason it was still standing. As he waited for the barrage he expected from Baker, Rick wondered how long he'd be able to stay calm.

"Your child is a menace to this investigation."

"Deputy Baker, I'm sorry about Alex. We'd given her specific instructions to stay clear of *The Treasure King*. I'll deal with her appropriately."

Baker's cheeks, which were now tinged with pink, puckered.

"Your daughter, Mr. Atwood, not only put herself in danger, but also this investigation. I cannot work with someone I can't trust. And obviously, no matter how good you might be at this sort of thing, you are still an amateur and your daughter is not controllable. I'll be talking to the chief about having you removed from the case. I see no point in continuing this discussion."

"It's not that easy," Rick said. "Alex made a mistake, sure. But, her mistake does not mean you should be working this investigation alone. There are still witnesses to interview. For instance, have you talked to Will Shelley? He portrays himself as a mediator, but the others see him differently. They say he caused more problems than he fixed. And his alibi is that he was in San Ladron visiting his niece on the night of the murder. We should be verifying that."

"And what would Mr. Shelley's motive have been, Mr. Atwood? He was angry over too many sea days? Or he didn't like the food? This is why working with a civilian is a very bad idea. You people have no idea of proper investigative procedures. You think you can just run around, accuse people of a crime, and they'll confess."

"You people? Wow. You are jaded, aren't you?"

"I'm a cop, Mr. Atwood. I have to do things by the book. And right now, that book involves getting you off this case. So, if you'll excuse me. I'm going back to the station to talk to the chief. We're going to get this straightened out once and for all."

Letting Baker stride away without fighting for a better resolution felt much to Rick like a defeat. Logically, he knew she was right. But, deep down inside, the way she operated didn't mesh with life in Seaside Cove. At least, not the Seaside Cove he and Alex had moved to. He turned to take a final look at *The*

Treasure King before heading back to the B&B, but stopped when he saw Joe Gray approaching.

"Can be a bit of a tiger, can't she?" Joe asked.

Rick snickered. "You might say that. I guess I'd better get used to life as a plain old civilian. What will be harder is convincing Alex she needs to do the same."

"Don't be too hard on her. She's just being herself."

"That's what worries me." Rick felt the tension building within. He hunched his shoulders, then let them drop. He did not need parenting advice from all of his friends, but that was most likely what would soon happen. "Unfortunately, this isn't playing with dolls or being in a grunge band—do those even still exist?"

Joe peered at Rick. Shook his head. "No idea. You'll figure it out. You're a good dad, and Marquetta is good for her, too."

The mention of Marquetta reminded Rick of his conversation with Jason. "I have a question for you. It's about the day the town had the big sendoff for Neal Weiss."

Joe rubbed the back of his neck with one hand, his jaw tight as he gazed off into the distance. "You really should leave that alone. Let the ghosts of the past have their peace, Rick."

"I can't. And Marquetta's okay with this. We've talked. There was a reporter there. His name is Jason Keneally. I've talked to him on the phone, and he said you were the one who told him about Neal leaving. There's a photo of Neal and Captain Jack in his article. They both look pretty grim. There's someone else in the photo, but that person's been cropped out. According to Keneally, that person is you."

"It was."

"Did Neal and Captain Jack have an argument?"

"It's not my story to tell. I'm sorry."

"Both men are dead, Joe. What difference does it make?"

"They did have a discussion. A pretty heated one, but I didn't hear it. There was something going on between those two, but I don't know what it was. That's why it's not my story to tell. I don't know what really happened. All I know is that Neal was desperate. That's why he made the trip. He was too good of a sailor to go out with the seas so unpredictable."

"When we first got to Seaside Cove, you told me Neal was confident he could find the treasure despite the conditions."

"I did...that was...at first. He'd changed his mind, but he knew he had to go out anyway."

Rick's breathing quickened. Joe's evasiveness was beginning to irritate him. The man was always willing to gossip—he was often at the center of so many rumors. "Who are you protecting?"

Joe let out a heavy sigh. "You. Marquetta. These secrets you're trying to dredge up—there's a reason they were kept secret."

"Isn't it time we all stopped hiding from the past? Marquetta's not hiding from it anymore. And yet, when someone like Pamela Baker comes back, it seems like the past is right there in our faces."

"I told you the truth. I don't know the details. What I can tell you is that Captain Jack was one of Neal's backers. There were three of them. The other two were old Navy buddies of your grandfather's. They financed much of Neal's treasure hunting."

"What?" Rick stared at Joe, his brow furrowing with confusion. "I don't understand. Captain Jack didn't have that much money."

"Back in those days, he did. He was a wealthy man by most standards. And, honestly, for a while, he made good money betting on Neal."

"You told me before that Neal's luck changed. You didn't tell me Captain Jack was helping to finance his expeditions. Is that why Neal went out? Because my grandfather pressured him?"

"I don't know. When I got there, the discussion was over. What I do know is Captain Jack was beside himself about something. Whether he was part of the reason Neal wouldn't postpone or not...I don't know."

Rick massaged his forehead with his fingertips and struggled to take in the story. "So my grandfather caused Neal's death?"

"I told you, Rick, I don't know. Captain Jack was a hard man. He could be very demanding. And Neal had been on a long losing streak. The two were a bad combination. Whatever happened between those men that day was a secret Captain Jack kept until just before he died."

"Are you saying he told somebody what happened? If it wasn't you, then who was it?"

Joe rolled his neck in small circles. "He didn't tell anybody anything. What he did do was write two letters. One to Marquetta, the other to her mother."

"That makes no sense at all. Marquetta says she knows nothing about what happened. If she'd have gotten such a letter..."

Joe held up his hands. "The letters were never delivered. Captain Jack couldn't bring himself to do it, so he told me where they were and gave me instructions on when to deliver them."

Unable to take anymore, Rick growled, "Joe, it's been fifteen years. When were you supposed to deliver these letters?"

"When Marquetta was ready."

"Ready for what?"

"To deal with the truth about her father's death."

Rick's breath caught. Now he got it. It was a simple

instruction. But, even a year ago, Marquetta hadn't dealt with her feelings. She'd been afraid of the past—of the truth.

"And you're not sure she's ready," Rick said.

"I'll answer that after you answer one question for me. And I want you to be truthful. Are you sure she's ready to deal with whatever your grandfather put in that letter? We could be talking about a dying man's confessions. So, dig deep, Rick. Are you one-hundred percent positive she's ready? Or would you rather I just carry this secret with me to my grave?"

36

Alex

AFTER I FINISH TELLING MY journal about Captain Carroll and his possible scam, I climb onto the bed to think. My eyelids are super heavy, so I decide to close them for just a minute. When I wake up, it's been like thirty minutes! Holy cow. I only take naps when I'm sick, but the break also gave me a new idea. I sit at my computer and send a message to Flynn O'Connor. If anybody's gonna know about this kind of map, it's her.

It only takes a couple minutes to get her reply.

—*Maybe the map is commercially available. Can you send me a copy?*

—*For sure.*

I attach the photo and send it. While I'm waiting, I start to wonder about what Flynn meant. Commercially available? My eyes get wide. So you could buy it online? Who sells maps? I put that in the search field. I get like millions of responses. Everything on the first page is for travel maps. Nothing for treasure.

So I search for that. Okay, I'm down to three-hundred

thousand. That's when Flynn's response comes through.

—*Definitely a commercial product. I'm looking at a website for a company on the east coast that sells cheap imitations. Might have something. See attached.*

When I click on the attachment, a web page opens up. The map I'm looking at is super similar to the one Captain Carroll had. I go back to the photo I took in the cabin and zoom down to the lower right corner. There's some faint print. I didn't notice it before. But now that I'm looking right at it, I can make out the company name. It's the same company! And there's a map number. I copy the number and put it into the search field on the company's website.

My jaw drops when the page comes up. It's totally the same map. I immediately type a new message to Flynn.

—*I found the exact, same map. Here's the link. You can buy it for $29.99.*

37

Rick

A COLD GUST OF WIND bit into Rick's skin. He rubbed his arms with his hands, wishing he'd brought a jacket. He'd walked, almost in a daze, taken a left past Ugly Worm Bait & Tackle, and meandered to the northern tip of the docks. He let his attention follow the sheer line of the coast. To his right, the B&B looked down over the marina, and to the left was the Seaside Cove lighthouse. If he looked west, the blue waters of the cove led out to open ocean, and to a string of shipwrecks that lined the California coast.

More than four centuries had passed since the *San Manuel* had sunk, and during that time plenty of other ships had joined her. The ocean's treachery, especially along the coast, was well known to sailors. But what about the treachery of men? Was that why Neal Weiss had died? Because Captain Jack had abandoned him and forced him to take an impossible risk?

Rick stuffed his hands in his pockets and turned away from *The Treasure King* and the ocean to focus on the question that had brought him to the end of the dock. Why had he not been able to answer Joe's question? Perhaps it was for the same reason he'd postponed the proposal—his own uncertainty about his and Marquetta's futures.

Before Pamela Baker had shown up, he thought he'd been certain. But now, he wondered if he'd just been fooling himself. Maybe the problem wasn't Pamela Baker or this murder or Captain Jack's dying confession, but something much deeper. Was he ready to accept Marquetta no matter what might be in her past? He shivered against another gust. He'd barely known his grandfather, and had no idea if he was the kind of man who would bare his soul before he died. Did that reticence run in the family? Maybe so, which was one reason Rick didn't know if he could honestly confront his own fears.

Taking a deep breath, Rick retraced his path to the marina entrance. On his way, he took a final look at *The Treasure King*. More an older sleek yacht than a dive boat, it seemed an unlikely choice of craft for a treasure hunter. But, at more than a hundred feet in length, he supposed it could travel wherever its owner wanted.

He stopped at the foot of Main Street and looked up the block. Standing there, feeling the ocean breeze at his back and watching the sleepy little town's main drag, he realized Seaside Cove was where he wanted to be. And Marquetta was the woman he wanted to be with. No ifs, no ands, no buts. He needed to deal with whatever cards Captain Jack had dealt him.

It only took a few minutes to walk to the B&B. When he entered through the front door, Rick closed his eyes and listened. Faint voices came from the dining area—the Carstons, if he was correct. It was nearly five, and he supposed Marquetta might be in the kitchen. Alex was probably in her room, most likely grounded. Did he deal with her first? Or talk things out with

Marquetta?

Marquetta. He wanted to find out what she'd said to Alex. As he passed through the dining room, he waved to the Carstons, who were sitting at one of the tables, an array of Chinese takeout boxes before them. The aroma filled the air, and Rick decided that if Marquetta hadn't started dinner yet, they might do the same.

When he entered through the butler door, he found her sitting alone at the kitchen island, a glass of wine in front of her.

"Hey," Rick said.

"Hey, yourself." She gave him a weak smile, then took a sip. "I feel terrible about what happened this afternoon."

He sat on the stool next to her and stroked her cheek. "It's not your fault. Alex can be…"

Marquetta raised her eyebrows, smiled. "Impulsive? Frustrating? Too inquisitive for her own good?"

"D. All of the above. She's a definite challenge. Tell me something. Did Adam show up because you called him?"

"I was afraid of how Pamela might treat Alex."

"All I can say is thank you. Both of us were on a fast track to jail. Adam shut down Deputy Baker's efforts to ruin my life and Alex's, and that wouldn't have happened without your quick thinking. So, thank you again." He paused and studied her face. Right time or not, he had to tell her what he'd learned. "There's something else I wanted to talk to you about. It has to do with the day your father set out on his last voyage."

"Talk about bad timing." Marquetta's eyebrows knitted together as she twirled her wineglass absently. Finally, she asked, "You've heard something from that reporter?"

"Yes and no. He remembered the photo, but he didn't know much about what he captured with his camera." Rick paused. He scrutinized the curve of Marquetta's cheeks, the underlying tension in her forehead. Was he making things worse by telling her what he knew? Did he even know anything worth telling? "We've talked about not keeping secrets."

"We shouldn't. It's not healthy. You know how I feel about honesty, Rick."

"So you'd tell me if you didn't want me looking into your dad's death?" He paused, again hoping for some direction.

After a long silence during which Marquetta watched him closely, she huffed. "What do you want me to say? That I'm okay with you digging into my past? If you want complete honesty, I don't know how I feel. It's confusing. For fifteen years I've buried those feelings. I can't just suddenly forget all those years of pain and hurt."

Rick took Marquetta's hands in his. "I'm not expecting you to forget everything you went through. I can't forget my marriage to Giselle or the years of anguish she caused Alex and me. I'm glad she's out of our lives, but the memories are still there. I just need to know if you want the answers—no matter what they might be."

"That sounds ominous. What do you know? Is it bad?"

He spoke slowly, choosing his words carefully. "I'm not sure. Apparently, Captain Jack wrote two letters—one to you, the other to your mother. I don't know the content of those letters other than they're the last thing Captain Jack wrote. The question I need you to answer is whether or not you want me to find them."

"How did you hear about these letters?"

"Joe Gray. My grandfather asked him to deliver them when Joe felt you were ready to deal with whatever's in them."

Marquetta's brow creased again and she reached up to retie

her ponytail. It was another of those moves he'd come to know so well. The angst on her face was driving him crazy. How had he not seen how difficult this was for her?

"I'll drop it," Rick said. "I can't bear to see you in such turmoil."

A tear formed in the corner of Marquetta's eye. She sniffled as she gazed out the windows over the kitchen sink. "You should deal with Alex. I have to think about this."

Deflated, Rick stood. He leaned forward and kissed Marquetta on the forehead. "How about cheap Chinese for dinner?"

"Good idea. I'll call it in."

Taking a deep breath, Rick looked at the ceiling as though he could see Alex's room from where he stood. "I'll go talk to her and bring her down when we're done."

"Okay."

Rick took a last look at Marquetta as he exited the butler door. She swiped at her cheek, gave him a weak smile, then turned away. He hurried up to Alex's room and knocked. Alex was sitting at her computer, but she closed the lid and stuck out her lip in a pout when she saw him.

"You're here to ground me. Right?"

"I'm here to talk. I also want to know what you're working on."

"I was messaging Flynn," Alex said defensively. "I wanted her to know what I discovered."

"Which was?"

"Captain Carroll had a map on his wall that shows like tons of shipwrecks off the coast. There's a huge group of them right out there." She pointed toward the ocean and pulled up a photo showing a map of the California coast on which there were a large number of x-marks and the names of ships. As she spoke, her tone softened and grew more enthusiastic.

As usual, his daughter's jump to a conclusion was supported by a couple of facts and a great deal of supposition. "And what's the significance of this map? Why's it matter to Flynn?"

"Because it totally could have been used to sucker the passengers on *The Treasure King*."

"Did this map show the location of the *San Manuel*?"

"No. But Flynn says that's what makes it work as a scam. He could like show people all these other shipwrecks and tell them the *San Manuel* has to be kept super secret."

Rick cleared his throat. Balancing his role as a parent with that of a consultant to the police was the most difficult part of his arrangement. "So you're thinking one or more of the passengers found out about this scam and killed Captain Carroll. It's an interesting theory, but the problem with it is you found the map by using an illegal search. Do you understand what that means?"

Alex's shoulders, along with her enthusiasm, fell. "This is the part where you get mad at me for breaking the rules. Isn't it?"

"I suppose so," Rick said. "But before I do, let me see that photo once again."

38

Alex

I CAN'T HARDLY BELIEVE IT. Daddy wants to see the map again? That's awesome! I hold out the phone so he can see the screen.

"Where did you say this map was?"

"On the wall in Captain Carroll's room."

"And you said Flynn agrees this could be the secret map Captain Carroll claimed to have?"

"Totally."

"Let me think about this. Alex, in philosophy, there's a saying about the ends justifying the means. Are you familiar with that saying?"

"I'm eleven, Daddy. We don't study philosophy in school. It's boring."

"A lot of adults would agree with you. The thing is, with the law, the ends never justify the means. You must follow proper procedures. And because you trespassed to get this photo, you've jeopardized the ability to use the photo or any information that might be derived from it."

The longer my dad talks, the worse I feel. I've watched

enough cop shows to know he's right. I totally might have made it impossible for the cops to put someone away for killing Captain Carroll. I'm totally bummed. I can feel the tears building. The room gets kinda blurry and my dad hugs me. I lean into him. I can feel my shoulders shaking because his hands are strong and warm and he's holding me like he did when my mom never came home.

I wrap my arms around him and hang on. I let all the fears I felt when I was trapped in the captain's quarters come rushing out. When I stop crying, he gently pushes me away and wipes my cheek with his fingers. "I think you've had enough high tension for one day, kiddo. Let's go have dinner with Marquetta. She's waiting downstairs."

"Okay. But there's something else you should know. Sasha told me her mom heard Deputy Baker wants to take you away from Marquetta."

"What?" Daddy laughs like he does when he's nervous. "What are you talking about?"

"Deputy Baker. I heard she's still mad at Marquetta 'cause of what happened in high school."

"It's a rumor, Alex. Don't believe everything you hear. And even if that's what Deputy Baker wants to do, it's not your problem. That's between me, Marquetta, and Deputy Baker. You're only eleven, so I don't expect you to fully understand adult relationships, but you have to trust me."

"But Daddy…"

"No, Alex. It's ridiculous. Deputy Baker exhibits a complete lack of interest in me. She's uncooperative and resents everything I do. Now, let's go have dinner. We're going with Chinese takeout tonight. Forget about Deputy Baker and what she may or may not be trying to do."

Wow. That's harsh. He's like totally mad now. I'm super confused 'cause that's how all the TV love stories start. Two people meet and hate each other and by the end of the movie they're getting married. "Can I make a note in my journal first? I kinda need to clear my head."

"Clear your head?" My dad looks at me for a second, then nods. "Sure. Just don't take too long or there might not be anything left when you get downstairs."

March 27

Hey Journal,

I only have a minute. I told Daddy about Deputy Baker wanting to take him away from Marquetta, but he didn't believe me. He's super confident everything's gonna be okay, just like I was when I went on the boat. I'm not supposed to be investigating the murder, but I'm gonna have to stay on the case so my dad doesn't work with her anymore. I guess I'm already grounded. What more can they do to me?

Alex

PS Maybe I should tell Marquetta what I heard and see if she'll help me. What do you think?

39

Rick

THE OVERHEAD LIGHTS IN THE kitchen were on when Rick pushed through the butler door. He stopped and looked around. Marquetta was gone. He called her name. No answer. He checked the laundry room. The pantry. His breath caught and he feared that she'd left.

"Marquetta?" he called, louder than before.

He turned to leave the room, but then noticed a cool breeze. One of the French doors drifted open a few inches. As another gust blew threw, the door opened further. Rick went to the door and stuck his head outside. Marquetta stood alone gazing out toward the bay and the ocean beyond. She rubbed her bare arms absently and didn't seem to notice the crunching of his footsteps on the concrete as he approached.

"Hey," he said.

She started, then turned to face him. "I didn't hear you."

"You were a thousand miles away. Penny for your thoughts?"

"You've been summoned to see Francine in the morning."

"What's the mayor want?"

"She wouldn't say. You're supposed to be at her house at seven-thirty. Sharp."

"Obviously, Mayor Carter doesn't realize I have a business to run."

"Alex and I will handle the morning rush. The hard part will be over by then. It's just keeping up with the orders for the late risers."

The breeze kicked up for a few seconds, then died. Marquetta shivered, and Rick stepped closer. He wrapped his arms around her and pulled her body next to his. "You're cold. Why don't we get you inside?"

Marquetta faced Rick and folded her arms in front of her so they were nestled in the warmth between them. "Did you talk to Alex?"

"Yes, but I don't think it did much good. She's now convinced Deputy Baker is the devil."

"You're exaggerating. As usual."

Rick kissed the top of Marquetta's head. "Okay. Maybe not the devil, but certainly up to no good."

Marquetta sighed, then pulled away slightly. "What's Evil Pamela up to now?"

"I'm surprised you haven't heard this. The rumor came from Sasha's mother. Apparently, Evil Pamela wants to ruin our lives. She wants me taken off this case and then she's going to turn me into her love slave."

"You've got to be kidding me." Marquetta stared at Rick, her jaw slack.

"That's another exaggeration, but she supposedly wants to break us up."

"She still hates me," Marquetta sighed. "When I heard she was returning, I hoped she'd decided she'd carried the grudge long enough."

"Not according to Alex. You said before that this was all over a boy? Who was he?"

"It was all a terrible mistake. I was too young to realize what I was even doing."

"Is this a secret I shouldn't know?"

Marquetta turned away and Rick waited, his hands resting on her shoulders while he took in the silhouette of the lighthouse on the bluff. He felt her shiver, but made no more mention of going inside.

"There are no secrets in this town, Rick. This is one nobody has talked about since... The boy's name was Eddie Thomas. He was dating Pamela. Then, a few days before the prom he called and told me she'd broken up with him. He asked me to the prom, and I said yes without thinking."

"So let me guess. Eddie was two-timing his girlfriend and you were the other woman."

"Worse. I saw Pamela and told her about my date. When she told me they hadn't broken up, We got into a huge fight. I should've canceled on Eddie, but I didn't."

"Let me guess. You went to the prom with Eddie and Pamela got mad."

"Pamela never got over it. I went out with Eddie once or twice after that. I suppose part of it was to spite her. It got to the point where we were always avoiding each other. My mom finally talked some sense into me and I broke up with Eddie. I told him he was immature and self-centered. He got drunk, stole his parent's car, and drove to San Ladron. But he never made it. He went off the road and died before they could get him out of the car."

"So that's why Pamela hates you so much? Because her high-school boyfriend died in a car crash?"

"It wouldn't have happened if he hadn't gotten drunk. And that was because of me."

Rick turned Marquetta around by the shoulders and looked into her eyes. Lights from the B&B illuminated her face. The colors of sunset still clung to the coast in the distance. "You don't deserve to carry that burden. A young man's stupidity is not your responsibility. If Pamela Baker can't see that, then she needs to go. I'll be happy to tell that to the mayor in the morning."

"Don't. Please, don't go to war with Pamela over me. I couldn't bear it. No matter what happened." She sniffled and pulled away. "I shouldn't have told you."

"No. I appreciate the fact that you did. Besides, I'd have heard sooner or later. Maybe even tomorrow morning. I won't bring your past up when I talk to Francine, but I will tell her I don't think Pamela's a good fit for this town. I didn't before, and I don't now. Everybody here looks out for their neighbors. Pamela's got big aspirations and only cares about herself, and after what she pulled today, I don't want her near Alex. Period."

"Daddy? Marquetta? Are you fighting?" Alex's brow was creased with worry. She approached cautiously, taking slow steps and letting her gaze bounce back and forth between them.

"No, kiddo. We were just talking about a meeting I'll be having with the mayor in the morning. It's nothing to worry about."

"Then why were you talking about Deputy Baker? Is she gonna be part of the meeting?"

Marquetta darted a glance at Rick. Though she hadn't said a word, he got the message. Trying to hide the truth from Alex was not going to work. He should have known better than to even try.

"Do you remember what I told you about Deputy Baker

when she first showed up and you were so enthusiastic about her?" Marquetta asked.

"For sure. You said she was super goal oriented."

"That's correct. Unfortunately, I left a few things out when we were talking." Marquetta shivered again. "Let's go inside, Sweetie. Our dinner should be here any minute. I'll tell you the rest of the story."

Rick stayed silent during dinner and let Marquetta tell Alex about her past with Pamela Baker. As difficult as the deputy had been, he found it hard to believe she had returned to Seaside Cove solely to wreak havoc on Marquetta's life. Who did that? Wouldn't she have just moved on after all these years? Quite honestly, he wasn't sure.

By nine, they were all yawning. Rick told Alex she needed to get to bed. Alex went upstairs, put on her PJs, and came back down to say goodnight. When she was gone, Rick felt the tension building within. There was so much going on. So many things to talk about. Perhaps the best place to start was with something easy.

"She adores you, you know," Rick said.

"And I love her with all my heart."

It was the perfect moment, Rick thought. They were alone. He could ask her right here and now. But she hadn't told him what to do about her father. It was the elephant in the room. The question that might hang up everything. "I don't know if we finished talking about your dad. You said you had to think about whether I should continue digging into the past."

Marquetta pulled on a strand of hair and her brow creased. "I don't know. I've spent so much of my life wondering what happened. And now, to find out there's some sort of letter that explains everything? It's overwhelming. When I try to think about it, my brain freezes up. And then there's this whole thing with Pamela coming back to town. It has me questioning everything I've done in my life."

"What? How can you say that? You love what you do."

"What if it's not enough?"

"I don't understand. Enough for who?"

She released the strand of hair and clutched her arms to her chest. "I need to think about what I want, that's all."

"Sure. I get it." He paused and looked at her. "Will you be here in the morning?"

"Of course. I wouldn't leave you in the lurch like that. You've got a meeting with her highness."

He reached out, took her hand, and pulled her closer. When he kissed her goodnight, she melted into him. Suddenly, Rick realized his were the priorities that had been all mixed up. Tomorrow morning, he would get into the jeweler's store no matter what. He'd waited too long to ask the most important question of their lives.

40

Alex

MARCH 28

Hey Journal,

    I can't sleep. It's super late and I'm writing this with a flashlight just in case Daddy is still up and walks by my room. I'm totally bummed about Marquetta 'cause she's so upset. Deputy Baker's a big part of the problem, but she's not all of it. Marquetta's also worried about Daddy. She thinks he might not love her enough. When I told her he wants to propose, but just hasn't found the right time, she said procrastination is usually a sign somebody doesn't want to do something.

    Could that be true, Journal? Is my dad not asking Marquetta to marry him 'cause he's having second thoughts? No way. And now that Marquetta's all upset about Deputy Baker, even if he asks, she might not say yes. This really sucks.

    Me and Marquetta agreed that no matter what Daddy does, we're still gonna be friends. I made her pinky swear that nothing would ever come between us. I'm going back to bed now, Journal. And I'm gonna dream about the day Marquetta becomes

my mom.
     Alex

41

Rick

A SMALL SIGN, NO MORE than six inches by twelve, hung from the wrought iron fence surrounding Mayor Francine Carter's home. The lettering, an ornate gray-blue over a pale yellow background, read *Cote d'Azur*. The sign was the perfect complement to its counterpart, a three-story, yellow Victorian with white-and-gray trim. Much like its owner, *Cote d'Azur* imposed itself over it's surroundings like a brass band. And, at three stories tall, it stood head and shoulders above the surrounding houses.

At seven-thirty in the morning, Rick felt the century-old home, along with its owner, could be a bit much to take. Nevertheless, with a small flick of the wrist, he flipped the latch on the gate. It opened smoothly and noiselessly. The concrete steps deadened his footsteps as he climbed to the second-floor landing. Unlike the last time he'd been here, when he'd been worried about what Francine would say to him, this time, he had his own agenda. He was tired of working with Pamela Baker. She'd been difficult all along, but her treatment of Alex had been the final straw. The bottom line was, Baker had to go.

At the front door, the polished brass door knocker gleamed just as it had on his last trip. Rick wondered if the mayor polished it herself. When the door opened and Francine stood before him, her hair perfectly coiffed and she looking ready for the day, Rick's resolve stayed strong.

"Thank you for being prompt." Francine opened the door and gestured for him to follow with a wiggle of her fingers. "This won't take long. Come along." She strode out the foyer and into the parlor.

"Why the early morning meeting, Madame Mayor?" Rick asked as he tailed along.

Francine threw her left hand in the air and continued walking. "You'll see."

Rick looked up at the ornate ceiling and shook his head. Francine and her theatrics. In the parlor, she did an immediate about-face. She planted both hands on her hips and cocked her head to one side.

"Now, what is this I hear about you and our new deputy?"

"What exactly have you heard?"

"Don't play coy with me, Rick. I've heard about her heavy-handed tactics."

"Are you referring to the incident on *The Treasure King*?"

"Why no. I was referring to the Crooked Mast. But if something happened on that treasure hunter's boat, I want to know about it."

"I don't think I should be the one to tell that story."

"Why not?"

"Because I was part of the problem…well, not problem, more like the cause of her…" He stopped, took a breath, and said simply, "I'd prefer not to sound like I'm complaining."

"Nonsense." Francine fingered the back of her hair and cast

her standard mayoral smile—closed lips, chubby cheeks curled upwards—in Rick's direction. "You'll simply be passing along valuable intelligence to the chief executive officer of Seaside Cove."

Rick studied the room. From crystal chandeliers to pink-and-black paisley carpet, it was all staged with a very Victorian feel. A portrait of Francine's grandmother, wrapped in an ornate, gold frame scowled down at Rick. A stern looking woman, Rick wondered if that's where Francine's tenacity came from.

"Okay. I'll tell you what happened. Before that, though, I have something else to say. I may not like Deputy Baker's methods, but she is the officer on the case. Can you respect that?"

Francine made a fuss. Fiddled with her hair a few more times. But in the end she agreed to Rick's terms. He went through the entire incident on *The Treasure King*, which led to more questions from Francine, and eventually, details of every Pamela Baker interaction since he'd met her.

"It sounds like what you're saying is that she's bad for the town and we should get rid of her," Francine said when he was done.

Dumbstruck at how quickly the most extreme action had become the solution, Rick found himself mentally scrambling to decide what it was he really wanted. He'd come here intending to get rid of Pamela Baker, but now that ruining her career was within reach, he was having second thoughts. Could he live with himself if he caused her to be banished from Seaside Cove? "That's pretty harsh, don't you think?"

Francine turned her attention to the photo on the wall. "Grandmother Maebelle once told me to never question your decisions if they feel right. Yours isn't the only problem we've had with Deputy Baker. Chief Cunningham has called her recalcitrant and overly ambitious. Others have also spoken up. Though they have asked for their complaints to be kept confidential."

Life would probably be much easier with Pamela Baker gone, but Rick wasn't sure it would be better. What would happen to the investigation? "I'm sure she has a large number of backers in town. You wouldn't want to isolate all those voters by firing her, would you?"

"Quite honestly, Deputy Baker has very few supporters. Most find her far more officious than friendly. And you know how residents in a small town like to be friendly."

Rick tried, unsuccessfully, to suppress a smile.

"You find that amusing? You and your daughter were welcomed with open arms in Seaside Cove. Of all people, I would expect you to understand how important it is to not step on toes."

Holding up both hands, Rick took a small step back. "I remember how well we were accepted. I also remember how much gossip there was about me. There was even a marriage competition for a while."

Francine cleared her throat and rubbed the back of her neck. "Yes. Well, it would appear the competition has ended, hasn't it? How are you and Marquetta doing?"

Immediately, Rick recognized Francine sniffing about for gossip material. She was, after all, one of the biggest peddlers of idle rumors in town. She didn't need him to give her grist for the mill. "We're doing well," he said. "I have a few things to get done this morning, so I don't have much time. I would like to resolve this question, however. Are you really going to fire Pamela Baker?"

"That decision should be made by Chief Cunningham. I'll encourage him to weigh all of the factors and we will arrive at a mutually agreeable decision."

More code, thought Rick. Francine decides and Adam agrees. He needed to talk to his friend. To warn him of what was coming. "I can live with that. You don't mind if I talk to Adam and let him know we talked, do you? I wouldn't want him to feel blindsided."

Francine made a face and huffed. "I suppose he should have all the facts," she said hesitantly.

"Then we're in agreement." Rick held out his hand. "Thank you, Madame Mayor."

"Of course." Francine flashed him another closed-lip smile, then purposefully held up her wrist. "Oh my, the time. I really must call this little meeting to an end." Without waiting for a response, she led the way to the front door.

On his way down the steps, Rick listened for the click of the front door latch. He hadn't heard it by the time he got to the bottom, so he turned and waved to Francine, who was watching him with the door ajar. She finger waved back and immediately shut the door.

Rick walked along Whale Street. Overhead, the leaves of the rosewood trees rustled in the gentle breeze. White wispy clouds dotted the bright blue sky above. This was as good as mornings on the coast got—a perfect opportunity for a walk. Rick checked the time. It wasn't even eight, so the jeweler's wouldn't open for another hour. The dining room at the B&B would only be serving for another half hour and Marquetta probably had everything under control. She'd certainly keep Alex busy until he got back. He had plenty of time to go to the police station and talk to Adam. If he wanted to be really bad, he could sneak into Crusty

Buns for a cinnamon roll and some coffee before he went to look at engagement rings.

He swallowed hard at the thought—it was a big step. And he couldn't take it alone. Marquetta would most likely say yes when he asked the question, but what if she didn't? His heart thudded in his chest and his breath caught. Was that what had been holding him back? Fear of what would happen if she said no?

Rick stopped and looked at his surroundings. He'd been walking without thought or concern for where he was. But somehow, he'd ended up in front of the police station. Maybe that was his way of avoiding the unthinkable—life without the woman he loved.

He sucked in a breath and ducked through the front door.

42

Rick

THE GLASS DOOR SLIPPED CLOSED behind Rick. Even though Deputy Baker wasn't present, the police station interior felt cold and sterile. Given his reason for coming to the station, it almost felt like the universe had decided he needed a break—a bit of good luck for a change.

"Hey, buddy, what's up with you?" Adam Cunningham strode toward Rick, his hand outstretched.

"Just have a lot on my mind." A moment later, Rick said, "No. That's a dodge. I have to face my fears, Adam. All this time I've been deluding myself. The reason I've been putting off my proposal is because I'm petrified Marquetta will turn me down. I think I'm afraid of rejection."

"You, my friend, are delusional. You're running from ghosts. Besides, what's the worst that can happen? You pop the question and she walks away? Or she laughs at you? Or she leaves Seaside Cove forever, finds some rich guy to marry, settles down with a passel of kids while you turn into a lonely, depressed, curmudgeon who…"

Rick threw up his hands and barked, "Enough! I get it. I'm being stupid. In a way, I'm doing the same thing Alex does. She blows things way out of proportion."

"I think that's called human nature—or maybe you passed along a defective gene." Adam looked as though he was trying to hold back his laughter, then turned serious. "Now, I assume your real reason for coming here is to tell me you had a discussion with Madame Mayor this morning."

Rick gawped at Adam. "You know about that?"

Adam shook his head and grinned. "Not really. I did suspect it was going to happen. The mayor loves her early morning meetings, and she has a way of inserting herself at the least appropriate time. She's got good intentions, but she lets the office go to her head. She thinks if something happened to her the town would fall apart."

"Let's not go there," Rick said. "Have you got a few minutes? I'll fill you in."

"Have a seat." Adam gestured at one of the visitor's chairs in front of his desk. "And, just in case you're wondering, Baker won't be interrupting us. She's conducting a search of the harbor."

Rick regarded Adam with a narrowed gaze. "What's she looking for?"

"The missing speargun. We believe the murder weapon was discarded under the dock. She asked me about local scuba divers, so I told her to visit Dennis Malone. He and a couple of the other locals agreed to search in and around the marina. If we find it, it could be a game-changer." Adam planted his elbows on the desk and looked at Rick. "So what happened in your conversation with Madame Mayor?"

Rick told Adam everything—from the rumors flying about

town to the mayor's reaction to *The Treasure King* incident. When he was done, he sat back and watched his friend's face. "She said she'd leave the decision up to you, but I'm concerned she might try and force you to fire Deputy Baker."

"There's a problem, Rick. Baker's a good cop. She knows her stuff. The real issue is her attitude—she knows she's good and enjoys exerting her authority. In a lot of ways, she reminds me of my predecessor. Chief Jackson was a staunch Good Old Boy. Baker's the wrong gender, of course, but there are times I think she would like to work the same way."

"It's probably not that easy to find a qualified officer who wants to have a career in a small town police department where there's only one opportunity for advancement."

Adam contemplated the wall decorated with framed photos of the town council and the mayor. He let out a long sigh before he said, "Not everybody wants to be police chief. I didn't. It was never on my radar. But when Chief Jackson retired and the senior deputy got sick, I was thrown in feet first."

Adam stopped and gazed around the room. With the exception of the photos of the town's officials, the beige walls were empty, and Rick wondered why Adam hadn't done anything about it after he'd become chief. "Love what you've done with the place," he quipped.

The comment drew a smile from Adam. "Traci said she's going to sneak in sometime when I'm gone and redecorate. The town doesn't have a remodeling budget, at least, not one I've heard of. But I haven't pushed because I haven't adjusted to the idea that I'm running this department. Maybe that's the fear of mine I need to confront. Anyway, what do you want me to do about Baker?"

"Whether she's a good cop or not, I question whether she's a good fit for this town."

"Agreed."

"And I just don't like what she did to Alex."

"I get it. That was harsh. But, it wasn't entirely uncalled for. The thing is, the munchkin was trespassing."

"She's eleven, Adam. Baker's treatment was completely over the top. I will not allow anyone to treat my daughter that way."

"Not even if she's broken the law?" Adam's green eyes flashed; he didn't appear ready to back down. "Right now I need a good cop, not an empty position. Which, by the way, I still have. The bottom line is, no matter how I feel about her demeanor, Baker's doing the job. Did she go too far with Alex? Yes. And right now I think you're going too far with my deputy. Now if you can't get along with her, or if you don't want to be involved in the investigation, just let me know."

"Are you saying you don't want me on this case?"

"I'm saying Baker is my deputy, and you're my friend. She's the cop. You're a civilian. I will not have her run out of town on a rail because of one incident."

Rick's breath caught. A civilian? Adam had never called him that before. "It's not just one incident, Adam. There's a pattern here, and apparently you're not seeing it."

Adam took a long breath. "Last chance, Rick. Do you want to be on this case, or not?"

"Since I'm only a civilian, I guess I don't have a place in it."

"Rick, don't take what I said out of context."

"No. That's fine. I will not stand by and let Pamela Baker run roughshod over everyone in her path. It sounds like we're on opposite sides of this argument."

"Let's just call it a difference of opinion."

"No. Let's call it what it is, Adam. It's a conflict of interests.

Yours is protecting your new turf. Mine is protecting my family. The two, apparently, no longer align."

"Try to look at this from my perspective, Rick. What would you do if you were in my shoes?"

The urge to shoot back a quick retort about making a more thoughtful decision was strong, but Rick held back, and instead thought about the problem. Finally, he said, "I don't know what I'd do. What I do know is this. I don't want to lose you as a friend, Adam. So maybe my role as a consultant for the police just needs to end here and now. I've got a business to run, and maybe if I'm not chasing down killers Alex will lose interest. At least I'll be home to supervise her."

Adam watched Rick with one eyebrow raised. He rubbed his neck, then blew out a slow breath. A ping from his phone caused him to check the display, then let out a heavy sigh. "Maybe you're right."

Rick stood, held out his hand, and said, "Good luck with Deputy Baker, Adam. And the case. We should get together again. Socially."

"Yeah. Good idea." Adam grimaced and tilted his head in the direction of the phone. "By the way, that was Baker. They didn't find the speargun in the marina."

Ten minutes ago, Rick felt like he would have sat back down and brainstormed with Adam. But their positions were clear, and he didn't think the police needed any more of his interference. "I'm sorry to hear that. It could have made things easier for you."

The main phone rang, Adam sighed, and picked it up. "Seaside Cove Police Department."

Rick waved and backed away. As he was opening the front door, he heard Adam assuring Mrs. Cantwell that Tommy Cat would find his way home soon.

43

Alex

DADDY CAME HOME A LITTLE while ago. He was super bummed out 'cause him and Chief Cunningham got into a fight over me and Deputy Baker. None of this would've happened if I hadn't gone on that stupid boat. Now, everything's messed up. My dad's not gonna work for the police anymore. I'm grounded. And Marquetta and my dad are kinda avoiding each other.

I've got my window open and I'm looking at the lighthouse out on the bluffs. The waves are super intense today and they're sending up huge clouds of spray. The salt in the air is so strong I can smell it. Someone knocks on my door. It sounds like Marquetta. Hers is softer than Daddy's knock.

"Come in."

Marquetta sticks her head into my room and slips inside. "Do you have a minute?"

That's funny. I'm grounded. What am I gonna do? "Sure."

I plop down with my legs crossed on the bed. Marquetta sits across from me. Her hair's tied back in a ponytail with a red scrunchy. I've got mine done the same way, but my scrunchy is purple. Her eyes are kinda red, but I don't think she's been crying. If I made Marquetta cry, that would make things even worse.

She reaches out and takes my hand. "Sweetie. You need to understand this thing with your dad and Adam isn't your fault."

I pull my hand away and wrap my arms around myself. "How can you say that? I'm totally to blame. Deputy Baker got mad because I trespassed, and then Daddy defended me, and…"

"Stop." Marquetta takes one of my hands, then the other. "Someday you'll figure this out, but you need to understand right now that just because you did something wrong doesn't mean everything that came afterwards is your fault. You take things in and assume responsibility for all of it. You do not control how Deputy Baker acts. You didn't force her to treat you the way she did. Your dad disagreeing with Adam. That wasn't under your control, either."

"But…"

"Hush." She brushes my hair back with her fingertips. "You went through a lot before you came to Seaside Cove. The way your mother behaved, ignoring you and your dad for the sake of her career, that wasn't right. It wasn't fair to either of you, but especially you because it caused you to feel like what you did drove her away."

My bottom lip is trembling and there's a lot of pressure behind my eyes. I can hardly breathe. "No matter how hard I tried…" A tear trickles down my cheek. Marquetta pulls me into her arms.

"I know, Sweetie. I know." She holds onto me while I cry.

I put my arms around her. She eases me down so I can lay with my head on her lap while she keeps holding me. I can smell her hand lotion. It's kinda citrusy. It makes me wonder what it would have been like growing up with a mom who held me like this when I skinned my knee or failed a test or just did something stupid.

"Marquetta?" I croak, then push myself up to face her.

She's got tears in her eyes and her cheeks are all stained with mascara. When she smiles at me, she sniffles a couple times. But through it all, she holds my hand.

"What, Sweetie?"

"How do I fix the mess I made?"

"That's a very good question. I'm sure if we put our heads together, we can come up with a solution."

44

Rick

THE INSCRIPTION ENGRAVED ON THE side of the pencil read *Seaside Cove Bed & Breakfast*. It was just one of the many little extravagances Captain Jack had spent money on. Rick didn't know how many of those pencils his grandfather had purchased, or even when he'd bought them. All he knew was that the B&B still had a lifetime supply of unsharpened pencils in the bottom right drawer of the desk.

How things had changed, he thought. Captain Jack hadn't kept good financial records. It was one of the first things Rick had changed, and through careful management of expenses, they'd turned the corner to profitability. The debt Captain Jack had incurred for his massive remodel and his many little extravagances, while still hanging over their heads, no longer crushed them. In fact, that reversal of fortune was how he could now afford a ring.

He pulled a three-inch strand of bright red yarn from his top left drawer. Felt it's softness. Twirled it around his finger. Marquetta had tied it around his finger on his second day after he'd forgotten to fill the upstairs coffee carafe. A warm glow spread through his chest. He hadn't realized it at the time, but that was the moment he fell in love with her.

With the yarn wrapped around his finger, he looked at the map of Seaside Cove on the wall. Quietly, he spoke to the empty room. "What secrets lie behind that map, Captain Jack?"

He put the yarn back in the drawer, stood, and crossed the room to stand in front of the map. He'd always thought of it as another of Captain Jack's whims. It was a cartographic work of art. Framed elegantly in mahogany and covered by glass, the map itself had been drawn by hand. It was scaled perfectly. The calligraphy flowed effortlessly from one letter to the next. He'd barely paid it any attention—until now.

On his way home from the police station, Rick had gone by the jewelry store, found it closed, and continued on to Gray's Sailing Charters. He walked in the door and, before Joe could even greet him, said, "I want to propose to Marquetta, but we can't move forward until we both know what happened between my grandfather and her father. You were there that day. Please, tell me what happened."

"I wondered how long it would take," Joe said. He smiled, hugged Rick, and whispered in his ear. "The answers you're searching for are in the letters behind the map of Seaside Cove in Captain Jack's office."

How had he just taken this for granted for so long? What other secrets were there in this room? Or the entire house? He reached for the frame to remove it from the wall and stopped, Joe Gray's words echoing in his mind. No matter how certain he was, only one person should read those letters—Marquetta.

Rick returned to his desk and took a deep breath. Focus. He had to focus on something other than those letters. Deal with the problems at hand. What to do about Alex's meddling? Find a ring. Propose.

Solve a murder.

"I'm no better than Alex," he said to the empty silence. Letting out a long breath, he picked up his phone and dialed Flynn O'Connor. He waited, expecting voicemail. Instead, she answered almost immediately.

"Hey, Flynn," Rick said. "Sorry to bother you, but I have a few questions about the *San Manuel*."

"No bother at all, but this is kind of funny. I guess you're not aware I'm coming over to have an early lunch with Alex and Marquetta."

"Uh…no. I wasn't." Great. Alex was grounded—how did lunch with a friend fit into that sort of punishment? "When did you set this up?"

"I just got off the phone with them."

"Them? They conference called you?"

"Sure did. I'm surprised they didn't tell you. It's okay, isn't it? Alex isn't grounded or anything like that, is she?"

Rick rolled his eyes. "Alex is almost always grounded. At least, that's the way it seems. But since Marquetta was in on this, I know it's not just my daughter scheming. By the way, what are we having?"

Flynn's laugh sounded a bit self-conscious, but she was upbeat. "My favorite lunch in the world—grilled cheese and tomato soup. So…can your questions wait a bit? I have a feeling I'll be answering some of the same ones at lunch."

"They can wait. See you later."

With the call disconnected, Rick closed the accounting program for the B&B and shut the lid on his laptop. He checked to make sure the red yarn was in his top left drawer and closed it.

Returning to the map on the wall, he studied it, then touched the protective glass cover. For all he knew, there was nothing behind the map. Captain Jack might have had second thoughts about those letters. It would have been just like his grandfather to change his mind and not tell the man responsible for carrying out his orders.

There was only one way to find out, and he would not do that alone. He turned away and left his office in search of Marquetta. As he crossed by the upstairs coffee station, he stopped and checked the supplies. It was still fully stocked.

Down the hall, Winnie Carston exited her room. Her eyebrows went up and a smile crossed her face when she saw him. "This has been such a delightful stay, Rick. Between the delicious breakfasts and the scrumptious cookies in the afternoon, I've probably put on five pounds."

"I doubt that, Winnie. You look as trim as the day you arrived."

"Believe me when I say, my clothing is telling me otherwise. However, Stephen and I will most definitely be returning." Suddenly, her brows knitted themselves together. "This murder business. How terrible is that? It's not a common thing here, is it?"

"Don't worry. Seaside Cove is a very safe place. Are you meeting Stephen now?"

"Yes. He wants to visit Crusty Buns again. We're meeting William and Dolores there for a midmorning snack. When we get home, Stephen and I are both going on a diet." She laughed, then hurried down the stairs.

Rick looked down the hall toward Alex's room. It was decision time. Deal with her first? Or find Marquetta? He headed downstairs to the kitchen. If he talked to Marquetta first—and all went well—they could present a united front with Alex. On his way through the dining room he noticed a pair of empty coffee cups and crumpled cloth napkins on one of the window tables. He tidied up the table and carried the dirty dishes into the kitchen. He backed through the butler door, but when he turned around to take the dishes to the sink, noticed the overhead lights were off. The counters had been cleaned and were ready for the next meal prep. The stools at the island had been pushed in.

His shoulders slumped as he realized how empty this room felt without Marquetta in it. He placed the dirty dishes in the sink, then went to the French doors that led to the patio. They were closed and locked. Next, he checked the laundry room. It was also empty.

Rick walked slowly back into the cooking area. He took a final look around. Apparently, he'd be dealing with Alex on his own.

45

Rick

NO SOONER WAS RICK THROUGH the butler door on his way to Alex's room than he heard Marquetta's voice coming from the front of the house. It sounded like she was talking to Alex. Rick stopped, put his weight against the buffet table, and waited.

Alex came into the dining room first, followed by Marquetta. Rick's breath caught at the sight of them together. So different, yet so similar. He felt the pressure of tears building at the significance—Marquetta was helping Alex become a young woman, and that meant his little girl was growing up.

"Daddy?" Alex asked. "Are you crying?"

Rick sniffled, then brushed his cheeks with his fingertips. "I was actually looking for the two of you. Looks like I found you."

"Nuh-uh. We found you," Alex countered. "We were just gonna start on lunch. Flynn is coming, too."

"I know." Rick tugged on Alex's ponytail. "I called her and she told me we were having grilled cheese sandwiches and tomato soup." He glanced at the clock on the wall. "It's not even eleven-thirty. How much work can it be to throw together a grilled cheese sandwich?"

Marquetta let out an exaggerated gasp. "Obviously, boss, you have been taking my grilled cheese sandwiches for granted. And we're not just pulling some old can of soup off the shelf. We have work to do."

The two of them exchanged a high-five, after which Alex looked up at Rick. "This is gonna be a gourmet lunch!"

"Far be it from me to stand in the way of the work that needs to be done. I do need to talk to Marquetta for a minute, though."

"Okay," Alex said.

"Alone," Rick added.

Alex scrunched up her face, then looked at Marquetta. "You want me to get started?"

"Go ahead, Sweetie. You remember what we talked about?"

"For sure." Alex slipped past Rick into the kitchen.

Suddenly, Rick's pulse pounded so hard in his ears he couldn't even think.

"What's up, boss?"

"Can we sit for a minute?"

Marquetta reached for one of the chairs. Without thinking, Rick moved behind her and pulled it out.

"What's going on with you, Rick?"

He pulled out the chair next to hers and sat. "I...um...do have something to talk to you about." Rick leaned forward and rested his elbows on his knees. "I did some more research about your father's last day here in Seaside Cove. That photo of your father and Captain Jack? There was a third man there when it was taken. It was Joe Gray. I wanted to see if that changed your thoughts on the letters Captain Jack wrote."

Marquetta pulled back and sat up straight. Rick waited while she seemed to process what he'd said.

"I knew Joe and Captain Jack were tight. I guess I didn't realize how close they were. You said before that one of those letters was addressed to me and the other to my mother. Do you have any idea what's in them?"

"Nobody knows for sure. Joe says they're behind the map in my office. I don't even know if they're really there. I was going to check for them, but if anyone is going to decide what to do, it should be you. Assuming you want to, of course. I think you should decide about the one to your mother, too. If reading it would distress her too much, we can always destroy them."

"I'd have to talk to her." Marquetta seemed to scan the room. She looked up at the chandelier overhead. Smiled. Took a breath. "Captain Jack chose that chandelier because he thought it would impress Francesca."

Rick gazed up at the fixture. Francesca Devereaux. The last great love of Captain Jack's life. "I still can't believe he remodeled this entire B&B just to impress her."

"It's real, Rick. He did so many things to impress her while she was here. And he never understood until the day she left that she wasn't really interested. My mom couldn't take it anymore."

"I don't understand. Couldn't take what?"

"The chandelier was the tipping point for Mom. She said she couldn't stand around and watch a man ruin his life over a woman." She smiled weakly. "I guess that's because she watched my dad do the same thing over sunken treasure. After all these years, maybe that letter will provide answers to the questions she's been living with. I'm not sure yet, but I'm thinking about reading them."

"Whether you even want to see them is completely up to you. But you're okay with it? Reading them?"

"Maybe."

"Do you want me there when you do this?"

"You're rushing me."

"Sorry, what I was getting at is those letters are to you and your mother. Anytime you want to use my office, with me around or not, feel free to do it."

Marquetta's jaw tightened. She murmured, "I need to get into the kitchen to help Alex. It's awfully quiet out there."

"Okay, but before you do that, I have one other question." Rick sucked in a quick breath, then slipped off the chair and onto one knee. He took Marquetta's hand. "I was going to ask this when Alex was around, but I've decided I can't wait a second longer. Marquetta Weiss, I am completely in love with you. I want you to be my wife, my lover, and my partner in life for everything. I also want you to be the mother of my children. And yes, that means I want more. So, would you, will you, marry me?"

Marquetta's hand flew to her chest and, after what felt like the longest moment in Rick's life, she blinked back her brimming tears. She stammered, "I...I..."

A small voice startled them both. "Say yes."

Rick turned on his knee. Alex stood with her back to the butler door biting her lip in anticipation. The look on her face melted his heart and any thoughts of making a comment about eavesdropping. And after all her matchmaking efforts, she deserved to be here for this. Marquetta turned her attention from Alex to Rick.

"Are you sure? I mean, we only met last year. There are so many things about me you don't know. I can be moody and unpredictable and..." Her voice trailed off and she darted another glance at Alex.

"You're right, there are plenty of things we don't know about each other," Rick said. "There's one thing I do know for sure. And it's the most important one of all. I am hopelessly, helplessly, in love with you. It's like I've fallen into a giant cavern. I can't touch the sides. I can't see what I'm falling toward or where I've been. All I know is not only is there no way for me to stop my descent, but I don't even want it to stop. I just want to freefall forever."

Marquetta extended her arm. Alex slipped next to her, never taking her eyes off Marquetta's face.

"What about you, Sweetie? Are you sure you want to be stuck with me as your stepmother."

Alex shook her head. "No. I don't want you to be just a stepmother. I want you to be my mom." She wrapped her arms around Marquetta's neck and hugged her.

When the two pulled apart, Marquetta's weepy gaze settled on Rick. "Yes, I will marry you. On one condition."

"What's that?" Rick's heart pounded in his chest.

"I want to adopt Alex. She and I are…"

"Yes!" Alex blurted.

"I guess there's your answer. I…we…want you in our lives forever." Suddenly, he realized he still hadn't made it into the jewelry store. "There is one problem. I don't have a ring yet. I'll go there as soon as we're done."

"Do I get a say in what ring you choose?" Marquetta raised her eyebrows as she regarded Rick.

Alex poked Rick in the arm. "Daddy! Marquetta's already got a ring."

Confused, Rick shook his head and frowned. "I don't understand. You already bought an engagement ring?"

Marquetta slipped her arm around Alex's shoulders and pulled her close. "If it's okay with you, I'd love to use my family's heirloom engagement ring. It was passed along from my grandmother to my mother, and she's been holding it for me."

"Um...sure. I never thought about...I mean, I thought you'd want something new...yes, of course. If that's the ring you want, it's the one you should have. Where is it?"

"With my mother, silly." Marquetta leaned over and kissed him.

As their kiss lingered, Rick sensed Alex at his side and put his arm around her. When he and Marquetta parted, she sat back, a sly smile on her lips.

"What?" Rick asked.

"Someone will have to ask Mom for the ring," Marquetta said.

Suddenly, Rick felt like he was about to go on his first date ever. He'd never met Marquetta's mother, and now he had to ask her for the engagement ring? "You drive a hard bargain, Ms. Weiss. But I think I have a secret weapon to help me convince your mother I'm worthy of her daughter's hand." He looked sideways at Alex.

"Awesome," she whispered. "I get to meet my new grandma!"

46

Alex

THERE'S A KNOCK ON THE wall of the dining room. Flynn
O'Connor is standing in the doorway, looking like she's not sure
whether she should come in.

"Flynn!" I rush over to greet her.

"Am I interrupting? We can do this another time," she says.

I'm so happy my heart is ready to explode. "We're getting
married!"

Flynn seems super surprised, but looks at Daddy and
Marquetta. They both smile and the next thing I know we're all
exchanging hugs. After that, Marquetta drapes her hands over my
shoulders and stands behind me.

"Sweetie, we need to get started on those sandwiches and
soup. Unfortunately, we're behind schedule now." Marquetta
looks at Daddy. "Someone threw my timetable off kilter."

We go into the kitchen to start on lunch, and even Flynn
volunteers to help. Daddy starts setting the table outside; Flynn
gets put in charge of slicing cheese; I'm working on putting
together the tomatoes; and Marquetta is pulling out the rest of the

ingredients. It takes us about thirty minutes, but when we sit down outside and dig into the gooey cheese sandwich and that creamy soup, we're all in food heaven, and I'm finally gonna get to ask Flynn about the treasure hunters.

I pull out the photo of the map and show it to her. "You said this is a fake?"

Flynn shakes her head. "Not exactly a fake. It's more like a decoration. It doesn't really show coordinates to a specific site. Even these other ships that have sunk, they're not marked exactly. It's not to scale and it's more artwork than it is a real treasure map. You found it on the wall of Captain Carroll's stateroom?"

"Yup. I walked in and was looking around. It was so obvious I almost missed it."

"Could there have been another map somewhere in that room?"

I think back and try to picture what I saw, but I can't be sure. "Maybe. I dunno. I tried looking where they steer the boat and I didn't find anything that looked like it was a treasure map."

"Hmmm…doesn't surprise me." Flynn takes a couple sips of her soup and rolls her eyes. "This is so good." Then, she looks at me. "So much is done digitally these days. It would have been easy for Captain Carroll to have a GPS that could guide him to exactly the location of a sunken ship. With all the communications advances, he could have even done that with his phone."

Daddy laughs. "Back in the old days, when I was reporting in New York, we didn't have a GPS. Everything was done with paper maps or you stopped and asked for directions, which wasn't always the safest thing to do."

Flynn shakes her head and waves a hand. "Rick, you had it

easy. Some of the places I've gone on digs? The only way to find it was with a local guide. And sometimes, they were armed for protection."

"You win." My dad throws up his hands in surrender. "I never needed an armed guard. But, I'm curious. Has the digital revolution changed the way you do other things in the field?"

"Of course. It's easier to document and communicate. We can store so much more data now than we could even a few years ago. A lot of the ocean dives aren't even done by people these days. Submersibles with cameras are commonplace. Did you see anything like that on board?"

I can feel my eyes get real big. Does she mean what I think she does? "Like a little submarine?"

"Kind of. Call it part submarine and part robot."

"That's awesome. I wish I could've seen the whole boat 'cause there was a lot of cool looking stuff. But I dunno. I didn't get to see everything."

"Cameras," Daddy mutters. "Oh my God. I just realized how we can find the killer."

We all look at him and he's got his sandwich halfway to his mouth. There's gooey cheese kind of oozing out the edges of the browned bread. These came out totally awesome. Daddy puts down his sandwich and looks at me. "Alex, what areas of the boat were you in when you were on *The Treasure King*? Did you see any kind of security camera system?"

I close my eyes and picture where I was. "I think so...yeah. I was on the top part of the boat. That's where I found some charts and other stuff. It's where they steer the boat. There was a TV monitor up there. It was kinda small for a TV, but there's not a lot of room. It totally could've been for security cameras."

"Makes sense," says Flynn. "The captain would probably

want to be able to monitor the public areas on a boat that size. Alex, was there a TV monitor in the captain's quarters?"

I have to close my eyes again and picture the room. "I think so…yeah. The same kind that was up on top."

Daddy picks up his sandwich again. He's nodding now and looks happy. "I'll pass that along to Adam. I expect he already knows about the cameras. Deputy Baker probably spotted them. By the way, she had some of the local divers search the marina and they didn't find the speargun. If that speargun came from *The Treasure King*, there should be a video recording of who took it. If Adam can get a search warrant for the surveillance equipment, it's possible he might actually have video of the thief in action."

We finish up our sandwiches and soup, then go back into the kitchen. Me and Marquetta volunteer to do the cleanup, but Flynn says she wants to help again. We form a production line with Daddy washing, Marquetta and Flynn drying, and me putting everything back. Flynn tells us about the next dive she's planning for the *San Manuel*, and then she stops in the middle of drying a plate.

My dad's washing up Marquetta's twelve-inch skillet, but stops when he sees Flynn is staring out the window. "Are you okay, Flynn?"

"I was just thinking. Do you believe the motive for Captain Carroll's murder was to find the exact location of the *San Manuel*?"

"It was either that or someone found out he didn't really know where it is and killed him in a fit of anger."

"That doesn't make a lot of sense," Marquetta says. "If it was a crime of passion, why were they carrying a speargun? Wouldn't that make it premeditated?"

My dad nods. "You're right. The problem with this being something that happened in the moment is, why were they carrying that kind of weapon?"

"They could've been going scuba diving," I say. "Maybe they were going out to spear fish for dinner."

"It was probably dark, kiddo." My dad spreads his hands to his sides, then brings them together. "Visibility in the water would have been like this. Near zero. And what kind of fish are they going to find in the marina?"

"They totally could've been on their way back."

"You have to admit it's possible, Rick," Marquetta says.

Yay! Marquetta's on my side.

"You're right. It is possible." Daddy looks at Flynn. "Have you done any diving in the marina?"

She shakes her head. "I never had a reason to. Unless I'm testing equipment, I prefer a more scenic environment."

"Anyone who was spearfishing would probably need a boat," Marquetta says.

"There was a lifeboat on *The Treasure King*. I saw it. It was covered up."

"Pretty standard," Flynn says.

Daddy finishes up with Marquetta's skillet and hands it to her to dry. She tilts it on its side to let it drain, then looks real close at it and hands it back. "You missed a spot, mister. Don't be expecting me to put my tools away dirty."

"Sorry." He takes the skillet and sticks it back into the soapy water. As he's washing, he says, "If someone did go out to fish, they'd have probably rented a boat earlier in the day. We can easily check. There are only a couple of places with rentals. But, my money's still on there being video footage showing who took that speargun."

We all agree he's right. And this time, when Daddy gives the skillet to Marquetta, she gives him a thumbs up. Now all we have to do is get Chief Cunningham to get the warrant. Let's hope that's as easy as the cleanup.

47

Rick

After finishing the lunch clean up, Rick went to his office to call Adam. The greeting he got was professional, but not necessarily warm. "I'm sorry about what happened earlier," Rick said." You have every right to run your department the way you best see fit."

"No worries, buddy. And you were just taking care of your family. I get it. In all honesty, I have to say you're right about Baker. I guess I was reacting to someone being critical of my first hire. I'm not sure how I'll handle her, but I'll figure something out. By the way, Madame Mayor has left me two voicemail messages. What's up?"

"I proposed, and she accepted."

"Congratulations. That's fantastic. You found a ring then?"

"She wants to use the family heirloom. Do you think that's… appropriate? Maybe she's just saying that so I won't have to spend money…"

"Oh, that ring. I'd forgotten all about it. I was in fourth grade when Markie read a story about it in school. I've seen it a few times, but I never connected the dots."

"What's the story?"

"First off, that ring is gorgeous. The main stone is larger than the one Madame Mayor wears. But that's not the reason Markie will want to wear it. Her grandmother gave it to Markie's mother. Now, with you in the picture, I guess it's time for it to be passed on. Consider it an honor that she wants to wear it in public."

"Okay. Thanks for the background. I feel better knowing it's not just a pity decision."

"This ain't no pity party, buddy. You'll understand when you see that ring."

Rick crossed his fingers and regarded the map of Seaside Cove hanging on the wall. If Joe Gray was correct, what was behind that map had the potential to undo all of the progress he and Marquetta had made. Or, it could help them lay to rest the ghosts of the past. That, however, wasn't something he felt he could share. Not yet, anyway.

"There's something else," Rick said. "We had Flynn over for lunch—actually, Alex and Marquetta set it up. I think I was lucky to be invited. Anyway, Flynn was telling us about all the uses of technology on treasure boats, and Alex mentioned that she saw surveillance cameras around the boat."

There was a long pause, then Adam said, "She actually saw cameras?"

The surprise in Adam's voice caught Rick off guard. "Deputy Baker didn't tell you about the security system?"

"No, she didn't. She said she saw a couple of monitors. One on the top deck, the other in the captain's quarters."

"Flynn says the cameras could have been installed by Captain Carroll because he wanted to keep tabs on his passengers."

After a few moments of silence, Adam said, "If these

cameras and this security footage exist, it could show the killer with the murder weapon. That's the reasoning?"

"Exactly. We thought maybe you'd want to get a warrant for the surveillance footage and the GPS."

"Why the GPS? The boat was docked at the time of the murder."

"It goes to motive. Alex came up with another theory. What if Carroll was just scamming his passengers? Maybe he didn't really know the location of the *San Manuel*. We don't know what Carroll was charging for this little treasure hunt, but it was probably substantial. If someone found out they'd been scammed —maybe they killed him for revenge."

"Hang on a second."

While Rick waited, he pulled out the strand of red yarn Marquetta had given him. The clicking of a computer keyboard on Adam's end of the call was followed by a loud sigh. "I don't think that would work, Rick. According to the passengers we've talked to, *The Treasure King* left out of Long Beach three days before they got here. When the captain called in to dock, he told Joe they had an engine problem. That's supposedly why they made an unscheduled stop in Seaside Cove."

"What if Carroll just said that to delay things?"

"If someone figured out Carroll really didn't have an exact location, they'd have to have been clairvoyant."

"Or known about his previous trip and that it was a failure."

"So you think our suspect list is down to Sanna and Mancini?" Adam said.

"Not necessarily. Loose lips sink ships. Maybe this is a case where someone's loose tongue got their captain killed."

"Which means we have a new line of questioning. I'll have Baker go back and talk to the passengers. Maybe something will break. What does concern me is having her do this on her own."

"What are you saying, Adam?" Rick held his breath, not sure how he felt about a possible reversal of his removal from the case. He'd reconciled himself to no longer working with Adam—mostly for Alex's benefit—yet deep down he found himself itching to dig back in.

Adam hesitated, then said, "This is just between you and me, but Baker's strong suit seems to be enforcing the law."

"You're thinking she doesn't have the patience to be a good investigator?"

"I've said more than I should, but I need someone to talk to —someone who's judgement I trust."

"You know I'm always here for you, Adam."

"Unfortunately, you've got a conflict of interest in this particular situation."

"This is about Alex going on the boat?"

"In part, but it's also about the way Baker handles people."

Resisting the urge to say, "I told you so," Rick simply said, "Oh?"

There was a huff, and then Adam said, "I'm going to have to go. Madame Mayor is about to walk through my front door." Barely a second later, Adam's voice turned professional again. "I'll get back to you as soon as we find something out. Thanks for calling."

Rick reclined in his chair and mentally reran the conversation with Adam about *The Treasure King*. It was the second time he'd heard someone mention Long Beach. If the boat had been anchored there for any period of time, records would exist. And what better place to look for a record than in a place people used frequently, but never thought about what they wrote? Social media.

Rick sat at his desk, opened his laptop, and brought up the browser. He chuckled as the first profile filled his screen. "You've probably already thought of this, Alex. But I'll bet you didn't know your old man had skills, too."

48

Alex

MARCH 28

Hey Journal,

Me and Marquetta talked about Daddy not working for the police anymore. She says it's not my fault. She also says if Chief Cunningham and my dad can talk as friends, they'll heal their professional relationship.

Marquetta's super smart about people and stuff, so I'm hoping she's right. We did figure out a way to kinda get Daddy and Chief Cunningham on friendly terms again. We're gonna use girl power to get a redo of the dinner at the Crooked Mast. Me and Marquetta are going into the Bee's Knees this afternoon to ask Traci if they can all try the dinner again. Marquetta thinks if they can go back to where this whole problem with Deputy Baker started, they should have a fun time and get to talk.

Marquetta just texted me. She told Daddy that the candles she ordered from The Bee's Knees are in. Gotta run!

Alex

* * *

The colors in the candle I'm holding are blue and tan. The tan's on the bottom and it blends into the blue on top. It's like looking through the glass in a huge aquarium. When I hold it up to my nose, close my eyes, and sniff, it reminds me of the way the ocean smells. It's salty and fresh.

"Isn't that beautiful?" Marquetta asks.

"It's awesome! It totally smells like the beach."

Traci smiles and does a little fist pump. "That's what I was going for. I'm thinking of starting a new line of candles—reminders of the world we live in. My next project is a rain forest, but I haven't quite got the scent figured out yet."

I hand the ocean candle to Marquetta and she smells it. "That's perfect, Traci. I'll take one of these, too."

While Traci is ringing up the sale, I wander around the shop some more. I'm standing at the front window looking at the display when four men walk by. I recognize a couple of them from *The Treasure King*. They're headed up the street, like they're going somewhere together. I jump when Marquetta puts a hand on my shoulder.

"What's up, Sweetie?"

I'd sure like to know where those guys went. "Can we go up the street?"

"Okay, what for?"

Uh-oh. What for? Um…I take a wild guess as to where the men might be going. "Maybe we could get a snack at Crusty Buns?"

"You and your sweet tooth. Okay. Let's go."

One of the things I love about Seaside Cove's downtown is how all the businesses are in old houses. They've all got little porches out front and the merchants do different things. The Bee's Knees has like a little bistro setting that looks like it's in a garden. It's super romantic and gets a lot of attention from tourists. Standing on the porch, I can see all the way up and down the street. The men are gone. I hope I'm right about them going to Crusty Buns.

I grab Marquetta's hand and pull her down the steps. When we get to Crusty Buns, the men are in line waiting to order. We get behind them. The one in front of us has lots of tattoos. One of the other men calls him Isaac. He doesn't even notice me standing so close that I can hear what they're saying. Right now, it's boing. They're just talking about the menu.

Marquetta cocks her head to one side and looks at me. "What's up with you?"

"Guess I'm just hungry." I smile.

"Really." Marquetta lets out a little huff, then looks up at the menu board. The men finish with their order, then we place ours. When we're done, Marquetta looks at the front of the store. "Do you want to sit outside? It's a beautiful day."

The men sit on one end of the table for ten. There's a two-top right next to it.

"Nah, let's stay inside." I go over and pull back the heavy chair on one side of the small table. The tabletop is white and Mrs. O'Donnell keeps it super clean so it always looks nice.

While we're waiting for our order to be delivered, Marquetta starts asking me if I like the Bee's Knees. I tell her it's an awesome shop and we talk about all the different candles. I'm only kinda paying attention 'cause I'm still trying to listen to the men at the big table.

Mrs. O'Donnell delivers our order—a couple of miniature chocolate chip muffins, a hot chocolate for me, and tea for Marquetta. Before she goes, she leans down and whispers.

"These men from *The Treasure King*. They're nothing but

trouble."

"Why's that?" I whisper back.

Marquetta raises her eyebrows and looks at me real close.

"They call themselves treasure hunters, but all they do is sit around complaining about how much they feel taken advantage of."

I edge closer to Mrs. O'Donnell. "What do they say?"

"Mostly that they don't think Captain Carroll ever knew the location of the *San Manuel*." Mrs. O'Donnell stands up suddenly and looks around. "Angus looks like he needs help at the counter. I'd better get back to work before he fires me." She laughs, then walks away.

"I'm going to ask you again, Alex. What's up?" Marquetta frowns at me, then adds, "And don't tell me nothing. I know you're up to something, and I want to know what it is."

I slant my eyes over at the table with the treasure hunters, and Marquetta nods like she understands. She whispers, "That's why you picked this table. Isn't it?"

"Yes." I am so busted. I didn't think Marquetta would catch on so quick. "Are you gonna make me go home now?"

Marquetta turns her head just a little, listens to the men talk, then winks at me. "Not yet." She slants her eyes toward the table with the men and sips her tea.

Mrs. O'Donnell was right. These guys complain a lot. So far, it's all about Captain Carroll and how he lied to them about the *San Manuel*. It's like they don't think anybody else is here—the one called Will is talking real loud to the one with all the tattoos.

"I'm telling you," Will says. "They're looking at all of us."

"Calm down, Will. You weren't even in town."

"I didn't see anybody, so I can't prove that," Will says. "You guys were smart, claiming to all be together. Whose idea was it to coordinate?"

"Doesn't matter whose idea it was," the tattoo guys says.

Marquetta looks at me. Her eyes get wide.

"Does that mean they're lying about where they were?" I whisper.

Marquetta shushes me with a finger on her lips.

Awesome. She's totally gone into spy mode.

49

Rick

RICK SPENT ABOUT THIRTY MINUTES researching social media accounts for the passengers and crew from *The Treasure King*. When he was done, he'd even found an account for Captain Carroll, which was not much more than an advertisement for his treasure hunting charter service.

Of all the accounts Rick found, only three were social-media regulars. Matthew Redmond posted a few times prior to the departure from Long Beach. He complained about his last job as a prison guard. Now, unemployed, he was broke. Even before the trip began, he'd come to believe Captain Carroll had swindled him out of his retirement savings. Almost every sentence included something about himself expressed as an absolute. The one that caught Rick's attention was, *I never should have booked this ridiculous treasure hunting cruise. That jerk captain says he'll never give me my money back, so I have to go.*

The latest postings from Heather Sanna gave a different impression of Captain Carroll. Hers were a series of photos chronicling her day in Seaside Cove. She'd taken a selfie of her and the captain at Ocean Surf trying on new tee shirts, another of her and 'Morry' having an ice cream at Scoops & Scones, and a third of her alone standing in front of the lighthouse.

The picture was of Heather with the ocean in the background. The tone, however, was reminiscent of Redmond's. *Grumpy didn't want to walk all the way out here to see this awesome view. Shore leave almost over, but maybe things will be different at dinner tonight. Love the solitude out here.*

The lighthouse post came half an hour after they'd been at Scoops & Scones, which meant it was a safe bet that 'Morry' and 'Grumpy' both referred to the captain—and that the relationship might have been a rollercoaster.

Eli England was also a prolific poster, but his tended more towards self-aggrandizement. Like Redmond, England's posts were all about him, but the tone was the complete opposite. According to social media, England's accomplishments in building his business were legion. He had put up a photo of *The Treasure King*, but even that had been what Rick now thought of as All About Eli. *This boat is a treasure-hunting debacle. I can't believe the mismanagement. Tried to tell the captain how to fix things, but he's too set in his ways.*

Rick stood and raised his arms above his head. He stretched to the point that his body quivered, then relaxed. Looking down at the laptop, he shook his head. This was getting him nowhere. What they needed was some sort of chronicle of what had happened on Captain Carroll's last day, not complaints about his management style or *The Treasure King's* time at sea. He looked at England's post again. All About Eli. It was the same pattern he'd seen when they'd met in Crusty Buns.

The one who was missing from this list of social posters was Christopher Jenks. England had said his business partner was taking photos all the time. Was that what they needed? The photos taken by Jenks? Rick did another search, this time looking for variations of Jenks's name. He still came up empty.

A knock on the office door jarred Rick's concentration. "Come in," he called, then swiveled his chair to face the visitor.

Adam Cunningham opened the door and peeked into the room. He was decked out in full uniform and had his hat tucked under his arm. "You got a minute, buddy?"

"Of course." Rick gestured at one of the visitor chairs. "Sorry, I know I shouldn't interfere, but I can't get my mind off this case. I guess I know where Alex gets her single-mindedness from."

"No worries. In fact, that's exactly why I'm here. We didn't get to finish our conversation earlier. After I spoke to the mayor, I had a visit from Baker. She basically told me I either needed to back her up by throwing the book at a minor who'd committed a felony or she was leaving."

Rick's breath caught. "What did you tell her?" he croaked.

"Don't worry. I'm not about to send Nancy Drew to juvie because she got carried away."

Rick let the herringbone pattern on the rich hardwood floor serve as a way to focus his thoughts. He'd worried Alex would someday go too far. And yet, he hadn't found a way to reel her in. He looked up at Adam. "She was trespassing. A jury would find her guilty of breaking-and-entering."

"Whose side are you on?" Adam tugged on his right ear. His green eyes locked onto Rick's. "Do you want me to send her to jail? Sure would make Baker happy."

"No! That's not what I meant. I just can't believe you stood up for her after our disagreement."

"She made a mistake, Rick. She's still a child—something I

think you sometimes forget. She needs to learn some impulse control, and, to be honest, I think what she did has a lot to do with the way she was raised."

Rick bristled at the implication. "So my parenting is to blame for her curiosity?"

"That came out wrong. What I meant was, she had an absentee mother and a father who worked his tail off as an investigative journalist. You taught her what it means to be tenacious and to never give up on a story. The impulse control, however, is just her being a kid."

Rick swallowed hard and stared at the floor again. His brow creased as the memories of what they'd been through came rushing back. "You're right, Adam. I do forget at times. Alex had to grow up way too fast. I worry about her so much and when she does something like sneaking aboard that boat after I told her to stay away—it just rips me apart." Rick stopped, closed his eyes, and took a steadying breath. "If you can figure out how to instill some impulse control in her—I'm all ears."

"This is the single guy talking, buddy. Maybe it's only a phase. You know, like dolls or…that kind of stuff."

"I don't think waiting for her to lose interest in crime is going to be very effective, but I don't have a better solution so I'll cross my fingers and hope for the best. In the meantime, I'm sorry to hear about Baker. I was hoping for your sake that she'd work out. Are you pulling her from the investigation?"

"Pretty much have to. She wouldn't be around for a trial, so I'm taking over. You said something about not having been able to let go. Did you find anything?"

"Not something, but maybe someone." Rick described the process he'd gone through, how he'd checked the social media profiles of the passengers and crew, discovered only Matthew

Redmond, Heather Sanna, and Eli England posted with any regularity, then brought up Christopher Jenks. "If he really is taking photos all the time, that record could be as good as—maybe even better than—security footage."

"You're right. He could go places where people wouldn't expect a camera, but what's that going to prove?"

"I don't know. Maybe he caught a couple of them conspiring to revolt. I think it's worth a try."

Adam steepled his fingers, letting his eyes dart around the room as he seemed to consider their options. Just when Rick thought his friend might disagree with him, Adam tilted his head toward the door.

"Let's go talk to him," Adam said. "We might get lucky and the man with the camera saw something that will help us."

50

Alex

ALL THE TREASURE HUNTERS ARE talking now, except for the one closest to me. His name is Matthew, and he's totally different. All the others talk and complain, but he's super quiet. The tattoo guy has a habit of cracking his neck a lot. He's kinda scary 'cause he reminds me of a bad guy in those old movies my dad likes. He talks in a loud voice, like he's used to telling people what to do.

"What about it, Matthew? You getting cold feet?" the tattoo guy asks.

The guy named Ed puts his elbows on the table and totally gets into Matthew's space. He sounds super ticked off. "No way. You can't back out now. We already gave our statements to that deputy."

I guess that's more than Matthew can take 'cause he explodes. "Shut up, Ed. The only reason I went along is because you shot off your big mouth to cover yourself."

"We all agreed to say we were together."

"Yeah, well, maybe I changed my mind."

"I'm not about to go back and tell her I made a mistake,

Matthew. You're in this whether you want to be or not."

I look at Marquetta. She cocks her head toward the table. I get it. We're gonna keep listening.

"I don't need trouble with some small-town chief of police. For that matter, neither do you," Matthew says.

"Look at you, going all moody on us again," Ed says. "You better get your stuff together. If the cops find out you suffer from depression and that the good captain suckered you out of your last dime, you might find yourself on the other side of those prison bars."

"Screw you, Ed." The man grumbles something to himself, then stands up. "I'm tired of taking your crap. You're always acting like you're so high and mighty. I've had enough. At least with the cops I know where I stand. I'm out of here."

He walks by and doesn't even look at us, but it's like there's a cold chill that follows him around. That dude is super angry— and scary.

"What do we do about him?" Ed asks the tattooed man.

"He'll sink himself. I've seen it a thousand times. Guys would come in, try to drown their sorrows in a bottle, but all the time they're just digging themselves in deeper. Matthew's in a down spiral and probably won't get past it until he crashes and burns. I've seen some of them make it out. Others, not so much."

"It'd be a shame if he offed himself over this," Ed says.

I look at Marquetta, but instead of saying anything, she motions for me to keep listening.

The tattooed guy takes a sip from his cup, then leans forward and lowers his voice. "Forget about him for now. Did you get it?"

"I got it," Ed says. "Took me a little while to crack the password, but I got in. Lemme tell you, it's a lot of data. It's going to take time to process. There was a lot more in the GPS than I thought. By the time I'm done, we'll have the coordinates."

Coordinates? Did I hear that right? I totally want to ask what they need coordinates for. Could it be the *San Manuel*?

The tattooed man asks, "You're sure it will lead us to it?"

"There's no guarantees. If that treasure is for real, and if Carroll found it on a previous trip like he said, it will be on this list. We have to figure out a way to get a boat outfitted for a dive without having to share this. If we have to give away a few percent here and more over there, next thing you know we're down to almost nothing for ourselves. Let's get going. We're running out of time."

Both men stand. The tattooed man, the one named Isaac, walks right by me, but the other one, Ed, stops and stares at me.

"Hey, Isaac! This is the kid the cops busted on *The Treasure King*. What are you doing here, kid? Are you following us?"

My jaw drops. I push my chair back from the man towering over me. Then I feel Marquetta's hand on my arm. "Stay where you are, Sweetie." She stands and faces the man. She's shorter than he is and he totally weighs more than Marquetta, but she doesn't look concerned. "Here's the thing about small towns, Mr. Silverstein. Everybody knows everybody. The police chief and I grew up together. And if there's one thing I can tell you about Adam Cunningham, he hates child abusers. Come to think of it, they take a dim view of them in prison, too. I suggest you join your friend and leave. Right now."

The man named Isaac comes back, grabs his friend's shirtsleeve and pulls. "Come on, Ed. There's no need to stir up the locals. Sorry for the misunderstanding, Miss."

"Fine." Ed follows his friend toward the door. I can hear him complaining about small towns as they leave.

Marquetta falls back into her chair and takes a deep breath. "Oh my God, that was awful!"

"No! It was awesome! You totally shut him down."

Mrs. O'Donnell comes to stand next to Marquetta and refills her cup. "This young lass is correct, my dear. You were incredible." She winks and smiles at Marquetta. "You make a fine mother."

With that, she turns away, leaving me and Marquetta looking at each other. My eyes get all watery and I sniffle.

"What's wrong, Sweetie?"

"Nothing. It's all perfect." I get up, walk around to her side of the table, and wrap my arms around her. Between another couple of sniffles, I manage to say, "I just realized how great of a mom you already are."

51

Rick

RICK SAT IN FRONT OF Adam Cunningham's desk staring at the
stark walls of the police station while Adam talked to the District
Attorney's office in San Ladron about a warrant for the
surveillance equipment on *The Treasure King*. So far, it didn't
sound like the conversation was going well. In fact, it all
reminded Rick of the argument about the chicken and the egg.

"Yes, ma'am," Adam said quietly. "No, ma'am. But if we can
get a look at the surveillance footage we might be able to
determine who actually stole the speargun."

Adam winced as he listened. He shook his head, sighed, then
said goodbye.

"The bottom line is no warrant. She says once we have the
murder weapon and can prove it came from the boat, we can get
the warrant. Otherwise, we're on…as she put it…a fishing
expedition."

"Ouch. If we can't get a warrant, we definitely need to find
Christopher Jenks. His photos could be critical."

"Don't get your hopes too high. We don't have any idea

what's in those photos."

Rick chuckled. "Marquetta and I are always telling Alex to believe in herself. I think it's about time I trusted my own instincts. Something tells me those photos will help us break this open. So, how do we go about finding this guy?"

"Shouldn't be too hard. Baker got his number during her interview with him. Let's find out where he is." Adam turned his attention to his computer screen and began typing. A few seconds later, he clicked the mouse, then pulled out his cell phone. He dialed, introduced himself when Jenks answered, and explained the reason for the call. When he finished, Adam said, "We're meeting him at the lighthouse. It appears Mr. Jenks is taking photos as we speak. Let's go."

It took only a few minutes to make the drive in Adam's police cruiser. They parked in the scenic overlook lot, which contained two parked vehicles. Rick pointed at the nearest one. "I recognize that car. It belongs to a couple staying with us. They're from Oregon. Nice people."

As Rick and Adam got out of the cruiser, a family of four appeared on the trail. They had two small towheaded boys who bounded forward only to be recalled by the mother. It was almost like a repeating game of tag with the boys jumping forward, then returning.

"Those two have lots of energy," Adam whispered.

"I assume you're talking about the kids," Rick chuckled.

"Oh, yeah. Mom and Dad look happy, but bedraggled."

"I have an idea." Rick walked quickly toward the parents and waved. "Mr. and Mrs. Hope—I see you're checking out our local sights."

"Rick, I almost didn't recognize you outside of the B&B. What are you doing out here?" Mr. Hope asked.

"We're looking for someone. A man near the lighthouse taking photos."

"He about scared me to death," Mrs. Hope said.

"Oh, Rachel, don't be so dramatic. The guy was hanging out over the edge trying to get a good shot of the lighthouse. That's all." Her husband cocked his head back along the path. "He's around the first bend where the path goes near the cliff."

Rick and Adam exchanged a quick look, said thank you, then hurried toward the lighthouse. The bend in the trail was less than a hundred feet from the parking lot, and there, on the opposite side of the safety fence, was Christopher Jenks. He was lying down with his chest on the ground, his shoulder over the edge of the cliff, and his cell phone held out in front of him.

"Mr. Jenks," Adam called. "Can you come back on this side of the fence, please? That cliff you're on can be dangerous."

Jenks sighed and made a face, but stood, came back to the fence, and climbed over. "I was only trying to get a better shot."

"I understand," Adam said. "But the town put this fence up because there were a couple of accidents out here."

"Do you take all of your photos with your phone?" Rick asked.

"The best camera you own is the one you have with you." Jenks smiled. "I heard that once and thought, the guy's right. I could be a photographer, too. I love nature, but capturing people when they're not expecting it is kind of a thing with me."

"Do you take photos everyday?" Rick asked.

"Try to. I've got this app. It encourages me to shoot, and then it takes a photo from each day and creates a video composed of one-second clips. At the end of the month, it's a cool way to remember what happened."

Adam stepped back and cocked his head toward Jenks a

couple of times. Rick got the message. It was his cue to keep asking questions. "Have you been shooting on *The Treasure King*, too?"

"It was a little weird at first, but they all got used to it. It's funny how people don't notice someone with a camera these days." Jenks grinned. "I got some good ones."

"I see. We're investigating the death of Captain Carroll, and we're trying to reconstruct what happened since *The Treasure King* departed Long Beach." Rick shot a quick glance at Adam, hoping he wasn't about to overstep. "We also have questions about the alibis you and Mr. England gave."

Jenks swallowed hard and his tone turned serious. "So this is an official visit? Didn't think you two came out here for the ambience." He forced a laugh, looked around, and his gaze settled on the path to the lighthouse. "Plenty happened," he said absently.

Interesting how he skipped over the comment about alibis, thought Rick. They'd definitely have to press that subject later.

Stepping forward, Adam said, "Mr. Jenks, I'm Chief Cunningham. Let's talk about those photos. Would you mind sharing the ones you've taken from the past few days? They might help us to get a handle on…the dynamics involved."

Jenks laughed. "You mean who hated who, don't you, Chief?"

"Hate is a strong word, but we are talking about murder. Would you mind?"

"We could really use your help," Rick added.

Jenks looked down at his phone. After a short hesitation, he said, "I don't mind helping out, but I need a charge. My phone's down to just a few percent on power. Unless one of you can get me plugged in, you won't get much."

"Adam, the B&B's not far. I could walk with Mr. Jenks, and you could meet us there. We can get him plugged in while we have some tea."

"Got any joe?" Jenks asked. "I need a good caffeine fix."

"No problem. My…" Rick hesitated, suddenly realizing he was no longer sure what to call Marquetta. "My cook makes some of the best coffee in Seaside Cove."

"Really." Jenks regarded Rick with one raised eyebrow.

"It's true," Adam said. "Take it from someone who drinks a lot of coffee."

Rick and Christopher Jenks walked to the B&B via the lighthouse path. The trail, paved with decomposed granite in the section they currently walked, ducked inland through the trees. Deep shadows cast by tall firs and pines shielded the path from sunlight.

"Gets chilly in here," Rick said as he stuffed his hands in his pockets.

"You live in a pretty great place," Jenks said.

They stepped into the clearing. Before them, the lighthouse stood looking far out to sea.

"Wait." Jenks stopped, pulled out his phone, and stepped back into the trees. He snapped a quick photo, gave Rick a half-hearted apology, and then asked Rick to lead the way.

"We just follow the trail. Come on."

The meandering path edged closer to the cliffs before it tucked inland. Eventually, the decomposed granite trail terminated near the back yard of the B&B. As they approached the house, Rick saw Adam at the French doors leading to the kitchen.

"We can go in the back way."

Jenks stopped. "Wait. I need a picture. Make that a dozen."

"Thanks," Rick said. It seemed like a nice compliment—unless it was a way to stall.

52

Alex

ME AND MARQUETTA ARE WALKING by Marina Park when Marquetta stops. She crosses the grass like she's been hypnotized or something. I ask her if she's okay, but she doesn't seem to hear me. The only thing she seems to want to do is look at something down on the docks.

I reach out and touch her fingers. She looks down at me, takes my hand, and smiles.

"I think I'm ready," she says.

"For what?"

"To read Captain Jack's letters."

"What letters?"

Marquetta's chin puckers and she looks like she's trying to figure something out. "Before he died, your great-grandfather wrote letters to me and my mom that tell us why my dad didn't wait for better conditions to sail. They've been kept secret for all these years."

My heart is pounding 'cause I want to be there when she reads them, but I'm afraid she'll want to be alone. I'm not sure if

I should even ask. I'd totally want Marquetta there if someone wrote a letter like that to me.

All of a sudden, she's kneeling next to me and her eyes are all watery. "I thought I'd want to do that alone, but I want you there with me."

"For real?"

She nods.

I throw my arms around her neck. "I totally want to be there!"

She gives me another hug, then stands and takes my hand again. "Come on. Let's break into your dad's office."

The B&B is quiet when we walk in the front door. We don't hear any voices. There's nobody sitting in the living room. My dad's not around, so maybe he's up in his office. I run upstairs and knock, but there's no answer. When I get back downstairs, Marquetta is standing behind the front desk looking super tense.

"He's not there," I say.

"Let's do this before I lose my nerve."

Marquetta opens the top drawer of the desk where my dad keeps a key to his office for emergencies. We've never had an actual emergency, but I suppose this kind of is. She clutches the key in her hand, and we go up the stairs. My dad's office is right next to my room.

Marquetta knocks on the door and gives me a weak smile. "Just in case."

I give her two thumbs up and look at the doorknob. She puts the key in the lock, turns it, and pushes. I've been in my dad's office lots of times, but he's always been there. Without him in the room, it feels different. All the wood on the walls reminds me of an old museum.

"Have you ever been in this room by yourself?" I ask.

"Of course. When I was your age, sometimes Captain Jack would let me come in here after school. He and my mom were doing the same sorts of things that we do now. I remember one time, it was a hot day in September. My mom had a doctor's appointment that afternoon, so Captain Jack left me here while he worked around the B&B. There was almost no breeze, so the room got very stuffy. My eyelids were so heavy that I curled up on the sofa and took a nap. When I woke up, he was sitting at his desk pretending to read a book."

"Pretending? What was he really doing?"

Marquetta lets out a little laugh. "He was taking a nap. His chin was on his chest and he was snoring."

We both laugh, then Marquetta crosses the room to the framed Seaside Cove map hanging on the wall. "Joe Gray said this is where Captain Jack hid the letters." She fingers the gold necklace me and Daddy gave her as she stares at the map. Takes a breath. Then she lifts it off the wall and turns it over.

It looks like any other framed picture except that it's got two sand-colored envelopes taped to the back. I recognize the paper. It's called linen, and it's the same kind of paper the B&B still uses, but this looks a lot older. The envelope on top has Marquetta's name written in a cursive style. The handwriting flows from one letter to the next. The letters are all perfectly formed. It's a lot like Marquetta's writing, but it can't be hers. She didn't know about the letters.

"That's Captain Jack's writing," she says. "He had perfect penmanship."

My heart is racing as we look at the envelopes. "Do you think the other one's to your mom like Mr. Gray said?"

Marquetta takes a deep breath. She swallows. "Let's find out."

Slowly, she pulls the tape from the cardboard backing on the map. She winces when some of the top cardboard layer pulls off with the tape. "Darn it. I was hoping that wouldn't happen."

"It's only the back. Right? It's okay."

"That's true, but it still feels like I'm defacing a part of history."

"But they're your letters."

Marquetta pulls off the last of the tape and rolls it in a ball. She tosses the wad into the trash can and lays the two letters on the desk. Just like Mr. Gray said, the second letter is addressed to Madeline Weiss.

"Is that your mom?"

"Yes, Sweetie. Her name is Madeline. And she's going to love you as much as I do."

"She's got a pretty name." Wow. I'm going to have a Grandma Madeline. "Are you gonna open both letters?"

Marquetta doesn't answer me. Her eyes are super teary, but she blinks them back and reaches for the envelope with her name on it.

53

Rick

CHRISTOPHER JENKS NOT ONLY WANTED photos of the B&B, but the fountains and gardens. Though Rick was proud of the immaculate grounds, he found the man's procrastination irritating. He wanted to indulge Jenks to avoid losing his cooperation, but he also wanted to move Jenks along. Every now and again, he spotted Adam at the French doors, who waved his hand in small circles, a subtle hint for Rick to speed things up.

"Mr. Jenks, I'm so happy you find our grounds so interesting, but Chief Cunningham has been waiting for us and we shouldn't be wasting his time. You're welcome to come back out here after he has a chance to review the photos. Maybe after you've charged your phone."

"Okay, let me get this last shot." Jenks squatted near the fountain on the south side of the house everyone referred to as the Three Maidens Fountain. He appeared to be in no hurry, but then grumbled and held his phone in the shade so he could see the screen. "Rats. My battery just died."

Irritated that the man's delays had brought them to this point,

Rick said curtly, "Come on, Mr. Jenks. Let's see what we can do about a power source." He turned and led the way to the French doors where Adam stood shaking his head.

As Rick passed Adam, he spoke low enough so only his friend could hear. "Thank goodness. He ran out of juice." In a louder voice, Rick announced that he was going to get the coffee. He darted through the butler door to the dining room coffee station. Balancing three cups on a tray, he returned to the kitchen. Jenks and Adam were sitting at the island talking. Rick set down the tray and went to the drawer where they kept a phone charging cord. After plugging in the phone, the display eventually lit up.

"So what kind of photos do you want to see?" Jenks asked as he punched in his security code. "I'm guessing you don't care about the ones I shoot for work."

"No," Adam said. "We want to see people."

Rick signaled his agreement and added, "Let's qualify that. Candid people photos."

"That's the only kind I shoot," Jenks said smugly. "Waste of time and effort when everyone's standing there with a pasted-on smile." Jenks tapped a few times on his screen, then tried to pass the phone to Adam. "Cord's not long enough."

The two men switched places, and Rick stood directly behind Adam, who was already flipping through images. When he got to the third photo of Gavin Mancini and Heather Sanna together, he stopped and examined it closely. He turned the screen so Jenks could see it.

"Oh, yeah. Those two. Never could quite figure out what was going on. Heather was supposedly with the captain, but she sure did spend a lot of time around Gavin. I never caught them doing anything, but the way he sometimes looked at her? It struck me as odd."

In the next photo, Will Shelley was sitting in the captain's chair on the bridge. He was hunched over a screen and keyboard.

"That was taken the day we arrived in Seaside Cove. Captain Carroll and Heather had gone into town and Gavin was busy working on the engine. That was the reason we came here. An engine anomaly. Sounded like BS to all of us. The boat was running just fine, but Carroll insisted Gavin work on it while he was off galavanting around with Heather."

Rick pointed at the photo. "What's Mr. Shelley doing?"

"He was trying to hack the GPS. Guy was obsessed with knowing where *The Treasure King* had been before it picked us up in Long Beach. He never did realize I was there."

Rick and Adam exchanged a frown. Rick said, "When I talked to him, he never mentioned that interest."

"He wouldn't," Jenks said. "Will holds his cards very close. He's in everybody's business, but nobody knows his."

Interesting, thought Rick. Depending on who you talked to, Will Shelley had either been a mediator or a meddler. "How would you describe his interactions with the others?"

"You mean was he a buttinsky?" Jenks laughed. "Yeah. He's one of those people who likes to stir the pot. Just when things were settling down, Will's there to rile everyone up."

Adam regarded Jenks for several seconds. "Why were you following him?"

"What?"

"It's a simple question. Why were you following Will Shelley?"

Jenks turned away and made an odd noise, then cleared his throat. "Okay, Ed kind of thought if Will was going to find something, we should all share in it."

"Ed Silverstein?" Adam asked.

"He kind of...clashed a few times with Will."

"So you were following Will because Ed thought he was up to something? And that something was hacking the GPS?" Rick let his question hang in the air.

"Look, I thought you guys just wanted to see some of my photos. I don't really like the idea of..." Jenks stopped and gritted his teeth.

Rick was about to offer 'squealing' as the word Jenks had left off, but the man continued before he could say it.

"You know what? None of us will ever see anything now. Will was always sticking his nose in other people's business and that grated on Ed's nerves. Ed wanted to get rid of Will, and the only way he could see to do that was to have Captain Carroll throw him off the boat. Ed tricked Will into trying to hack the system, then asked me to shadow him. I was supposed to get the evidence to prove he was trying to get into the boat's systems. Ed was going to talk to Carroll that night. He figured with my photo of Will on the bridge, it was a sure thing."

Rick recalled the moment Captain Carroll had shown up at the Crooked Mast. It was as though he'd been drinking heavily. Had Ed talked with him and that's why he started drinking? Or did they meet up later and things went badly? "Did Ed talk with the captain?"

"I don't know. Really. I don't. He hasn't said anything."

"Did Shelley ever get into the GPS?" Adam asked.

"I doubt it. It's not like he was an expert or anything."

Adam jotted a quick note, then looked at Jenks. "Did Mr. Silverstein know where the dive equipment was located?"

"We all did. It was supposed to be a locked room, but the lock was broken."

"So anyone could have entered the room?" Adam asked.

"That's right. You could check easy enough. Just look at the security video."

Adam grimaced, and Rick felt his frustration. They were having zero luck with the District Attorney. If only they could get a warrant, they could probably solve this case.

"Adam? Did Deputy Baker dust for fingerprints?"

"She was able to get permission from the crew members to dust the cabinet. She found at least seven sets of prints, maybe eight. One was a partial. In addition to the two crew members and Captain Carroll, there were prints for four other individuals." Adam cut his eyes in the direction of Jenks.

Rick understood immediately. Adam didn't want to reveal who those prints belonged to. If he even knew.

"I'm sure you found mine on there," Jenks said. "There also would have been prints for Will and Ed and maybe Matthew. We were all in there at one point or another. There were life jackets in that room as well. And on the first day out, the captain had us all do a drill with the dive equipment. You'd find prints for almost anyone on board if you looked hard enough."

Adam returned to flicking through photos on the screen, but from the look on his face, Rick suspected they'd just hit on a big part of the problem with the DA. Too many suspects and too few ways to prove anything with what they might find.

"I'd like copies of some of those photos. Is that okay, Mr. Jenks?"

"Sure. Why not?"

Adam pulled out his phone, and they started transferring the photos Adam wanted. While the photos transferred, Adam looked at Rick. "We can try talking to Will Shelley again. I think maybe there's a flaw in his alibi." He looked at Jenks and narrowed his gaze. "As well as yours. How about you tell us where you really were between six and nine?"

54

Alex

MY HEART RACES JUST WATCHING Marquetta hold the envelope in her hands. Her fingers are trembling. I've never seen her like this before, but I get it. She's waited like her whole, entire life to find out what happened to her dad.

She sits down in one of the chairs and pulls the other one close. I sit next to her. She opens the envelope and we read the letter from Captain Jack together.

March 11, 2014

My dearest Marquetta,

You know me as a man of few words. However, as I approach my final hours, there are so many things I must tell you. I, however, could not bear the thought of you hating me in these last few days, so I have burdened Joe Gray with the delivery of this letter. I trust he will dispatch his duties when, and if, he considers you ready to hear what it contains.

Thirteen years ago, I watched you on the docks when your father set out to sea on his final voyage. It broke my heart to see this precious little girl standing in the wind and rain alone waving goodbye to her daddy. I've shed few tears in my life. I shed many that day.

It was never my intention to lie, but the burden weighed heavily on my soul. My only light was the love I received from you. The thought of jeopardizing our relationship was more than I could bear, so I held my secret in. By the time you were twelve, my load was so great I could do no more than leave the truth buried in the past.

On the morning your father set sail, I was there on the docks. I don't know if you ever saw me, but your father and I argued over him leaving in such foul weather. It wasn't until years later that I learned you believed he valued a treasure hunt more than you. Nothing could be further from the truth. You were precious to him, and he left because of his dedication to you and your mother. Your mother knows their financial condition at the time. I will only say it was dire.

This is the second letter I've written today. The first was to your mother. I owed her an explanation, too. If I had been stronger, I would have done more to assuage your pain. Instead, I chose the same path I have always taken. It's the one that has led me to hurt those I cared most about.

Please accept my deepest apologies for the hurt I caused you, Captain Jack

Marquetta folds the letter and puts it back in the envelope. Her chin is quivering and her eyes are red. "He didn't say," she croaks.

We both look at the letter addressed to Marquetta's mom, then I look at her. "Maybe it's in the other one."

She nods. Picks up the second envelope. Holds it to her heart.

"Your mom would want you to know, right?"

"I've never opened mail addressed to someone else. You see what a bad influence you are on me?" Marquetta smiles.

I lean against her. She kisses the top of my head. She's gonna be my mom. We can be like this forever and ever. A tear dribbles down my nose and drips on Marquetta's arm.

She kisses me again and wipes my cheek with her fingers. "It's okay, Sweetie." She takes a deep breath and opens the second envelope.

March 11, 2014

Dear Madeline,

I have just been told by the doctor that I have only a few days left. Why I'm writing this letter, I do not know. I also do not know if you will ever read these words. I've made so many mistakes in my life. I've driven away those I loved, chased those I could not have, and never been a man prone to second-guessing myself or apologizing. The reality of death, however, has revealed to me the pain I have caused others. In most cases, even that of my own family, I must face another reality—my nearly perpetual absence was driven less by my love of the sea than by my fear of baring my soul to those I loved.

You and Neal, however, were my second chance. You both took me into your lives willingly and wholeheartedly. And Marquetta, dear Marquetta. She treated me as though I were her own grandfather. Neal once told me that he was smitten from the first moment he saw her face. I understood that feeling the first time she sat on my knee at the B&B.

Many times after his death you asked me why Neal chose to sail in such foul weather. Never once was I able to tell you the truth. The responsibility, I fear, was solely mine. I was the one who gave him the coordinates for the treasure he chased. I was the one who told him about another expedition that was due to arrive the following week.

    On the day of the sailing, I went to the docks and halfheartedly begged him to delay his departure. But you and I both know Neal was a man determined to protect his family at all costs—and we both know the financial conditions that drove him to desperation. So when he refused, I wished him godspeed. The truth is we both believed he could succeed where others had failed. I now see how foolish—no, selfish—I was. My weakness cost you your husband, and Marquetta her father.

    Over the years I tried in small ways to compensate for tearing your lives apart, but fear I only hurt you both more. If the B&B were in better financial condition, I would gladly give Marquetta ownership. But I must at last face a second truth—I failed in business, too. You know my folly, and the financial burden I have created for my successor. Your family has borne enough pain. For this reason, I have decided the best way for me to help you and Marquetta is to stop interfering in your lives. How ironic that this epiphany comes only days before my passing.

    If you never read this letter, I have again succumbed to my weaknesses, and for that I will be eternally sorry.

    Jack

When we're done reading, Marquetta holds the letter in one hand and wraps her other arm around me. We sit, holding onto each other, just staring at the empty chair where Captain Jack probably wrote the letters.

55

Rick

RICK AND ADAM SAT AT the kitchen counter going back over the photos Adam had gotten from Christopher Jenks. In Rick's opinion, there were several that stuck out and raised questions. The way Heather Sanna and Gavin Mancini looked in one particular photo gave the impression they were more than coworkers. Was that true? The photo of Will Shelley leaning over the GPS looked incriminating, but was it? And then there was the one of Matthew Redmond at the lighthouse. It put Jenks and Redmond at the lighthouse during the murder window—it also blew apart the alibis of most of the treasure hunters.

Adam pointed at the image. "The timestamp places Jenks at the lighthouse when he was supposed to be preparing for his conference call with England. So England lied about his alibi."

"That also means the alibis for Silverstein and Longstreet are out the window. They were supposed to be with Redmond. We basically have a whole bunch of people who lied to cover themselves and all they did was make things worse."

"I think Mr. Jenks's photos are the key," Adam said. "They're not going to lie."

"Agreed. Do you mind giving me a copy of those photos, Adam? I'd like to put them on my laptop so I can look for more details."

"No problem at all. I need to do the same thing when I get back to my office."

"I'll go grab it. Be right back." Rick hurried out of the kitchen and made his way to the front stairs. He climbed to the second floor, did an instinctive check of the coffee station, determined that it was fully stocked, and continued on to his office.

When Rick opened the door and stepped inside, his breath caught. His legs felt as though they'd been cemented in place. Marquetta and Alex were both sitting at his desk. They both looked like they'd been crying, and there were papers and a picture frame laid out before them. Across the room, the wall where the Seaside Cove map had been was empty.

Marquetta started gathering up the papers. She shook her head. "I'm sorry, Rick. I'm sorry. I didn't mean to come in here without asking."

"No," Rick blurted. He rushed across the room. "I'm the one who's sorry. I don't want to interrupt. I just needed to get my laptop." He forced a polite smile and did his best to not sound hurt. "If you two want to do this without me, that's fine…I mean…it's okay with me."

"I didn't know if I was strong enough to actually have you here," Marquetta said.

Alex stood and squared her shoulders. "It's my fault, Daddy. I talked her into breaking in."

"You did not," Marquetta countered. "I won't let you take the blame for my decisions, young lady."

"Wait." Rick held up both hands. "Nobody's in trouble. Honestly, I don't mind you coming in here. I told you before, anytime you wanted to see those letters, you should feel free. My only regret is barging in on you. That's all." He quickly added, "And if you don't want to talk to me about what's in them, I'll understand."

Marquetta reached up and stroked his chin. She stood on her tiptoes to kiss him. "You should know everything. These letters were written by your grandfather. Captain Jack was a hard man, but I realize now that all that gruffness was really a cover for his insecurities. Do you have time to read them?"

Suddenly, Rick remembered why he'd come upstairs. He groaned. "I wish I did, but I'm supposed to be getting my laptop so Adam can transfer photos to me. No, wait. You two are my first priority—I'll text Adam to let him know I'll be a few minutes."

Alex took a step forward and looked up at Rick. "I can tell him."

Rick decided to let Alex keep Adam occupied while he and Marquetta talked. He sat in the chair Alex had been using. Marquetta showed him her letter first, then the one to her mother. When he handed the second letter back to her, he let out a long, slow breath.

"Wow. I never suspected he was so tormented. I don't think anybody did."

"Except Joe Gray…or maybe my dad."

Rick was afraid to ask his next question, but knew he had to. "Where do we go from here?"

Marquetta didn't answer, but was watching him, her brows knitted, her eyes intense. "What do you mean?"

"Do you still want to marry me? Based on what's in these

letters, if it wasn't for my grandfather, your dad might still be alive."

Butterflies fluttered in Rick's stomach as he waited for her answer. It almost felt as though time had stopped. Finally, Marquetta shook her head and the corners of her mouth turned up slightly.

"All Captain Jack did was give my dad information. I suspect he also was giving my parents money to help us live. My father chose to be a treasure hunter. He chose to go out that day. Not for the reasons I've always thought, but because he knew he'd run out of time. If he didn't find that treasure, he was going to lose everything. At least he died proud and doing what he loved. And for once in my life, I think I'm going to be able to accept that."

"So you're okay with this?"

"Very. I've finally found the answers I always wanted."

"Then you haven't changed your mind?"

Marquetta's mouth dropped open and she shook her head. She put her hand at the back of Rick's neck and pulled him closer. When she kissed him, it felt as though time had restarted and all was suddenly right with the universe. Captain Jack wasn't a problem. The mystery surrounding Neal Weiss's final voyage was solved.

"No. I haven't changed my mind," Marquetta said. "Now, you have the Chief of Police waiting for you in our kitchen."

"Wait—you said 'our kitchen.' I like the sound of that."

"You're right. I guess I did. Now, go, already."

"We're supposed to be trying to find Will Shelley, then we also need to talk to the two crew members."

Marquetta kissed him again and whispered, "Then what are you waiting for? You have a job to do, boss."

"I'm waiting for this to stop." Rick smiled and kissed her

again.

There was a gentle knock on the door. Adam peeked into Rick's office, then stepped inside when Rick motioned for him to enter. Alex followed him.

"Hey, you two. I hate to interrupt what looks like a nice moment, but I really need to find Mr. Shelley." Adam peered at Rick. "Should I leave you two alone? We can catch up later/"

"That won't be necessary." Marquetta pulled away from Rick, then stood and put each letter into its respective envelope. She clutched the letters to her chest. "I'd like to take the afternoon off. I need to go to San Ladron to see my mom."

"Of course," Rick said.

"I'd like to take Alex with me. It's about time they met."

"I'm gonna meet Grandma Madeline?" A large smile spread across Alex's face. "That's awesome!"

"If your dad says it's okay, Sweetie."

Rick didn't hesitate to make his decision. If Alex stayed here, she'd be alone. She'd probably do more investigating. If she went with Marquetta, she'd be too busy to get into trouble. And in San Ladron, which was a good hour away, she'd be perfectly safe. The choice was clear.

"I think that would be wonderful," Rick said. "I'd like to meet her, too, at some point."

"We'll bring her back," Marquetta said.

Rick felt himself trying to stutter out a reply, but the only thing that came out was, "What? Here?" Oh, God, he sounded like a complete idiot.

"That's a great idea, Daddy! She can stay in the Jib Room. Mrs. King is gone and we don't have anyone coming in."

Marquetta smiled. "What do you think, Rick? I was planning on having her stay with me, but if she stays here at the B&B, it will give you and Alex time to get to know her. And while she's here, you can also ask her for the ring."

"The ring?" he croaked. Oh, God, he'd definitely gone brain dead.

56

Alex

Hey Journal,

Me and Marquetta are on our way to meet Grandma Madeline. This is so awesome. I can barely sit still 'cause I'm so happy. This is the first time I'll get to meet one of my grandparents. My dad's parents died before I was born and my mom's never wanted to travel to see us. So this is like a really big deal.

Marquetta's driving right now while I write. It's kinda hard 'cause the road over the mountains is super bumpy in spots, but none of that matters. Just wanted to let you know things are awesome, Journal. Totally awesome!

Alex

"It was nice of your dad and Adam to help us get packed up," Marquetta says.

I put down my pen and tuck the journal in my backpack. I can't believe I've used up over half the pages in it already.

"Daddy and Chief Cunningham sure do get along good. I guess with Deputy Baker leaving, they'll be doing that more."

"Let's hope that's not necessary. We don't need more murders in Seaside Cove. By the way, you should be watching the scenery. This is such a pretty drive."

"I remember it from when Daddy drove us to Seaside Cove. That was the only time I was ever in San Ladron."

"Maybe you'll get to see it more often now. I can bring you over when I come to see my mom. Would you like that?"

"For sure," I say absently. I wonder if Marquetta wrote in her journals as much as I do. "Marquetta, how many journals did you have when you were my age?"

She laughs and taps the brakes for the turn. "A lot," she says. "After my dad died, I poured my heart out to my journal. It felt like the only place I could be myself. That's why I thought it was so important for you to have one."

"I totally feel the same. Did anyone ever read yours?"

Marquetta shakes her head. "I never wanted to share those thoughts." She bites her lip and frowns as she looks at me. The car veers toward the side of the road and Marquetta pulls the wheel back. She's got her eyes on the road when she asks, "Has someone tried to force you to let them read yours?"

"No."

"Good. Those are your private thoughts, Sweetie. Don't you ever let anyone pressure you into letting them read it."

"Did someone do that to you?"

"There was one person who tried." Marquetta sucks in a breath and blinks a few times. "We're on the other side of the mountain. We only have about thirty minutes to San Ladron."

I can't think of one person in Seaside Cove who would read her journal without permission. Marquetta gets along with everybody…well, almost everybody. I suck in a breath. I know who the person was.

She looks at me a couple times like she's super distracted. "What's up, Sweetie?"

"It was Deputy Baker, wasn't it?"

There's another long pause and after a couple of turns, Marquetta says, "She wasn't Deputy Baker then. She was Pamela. My best friend. And she stole my journal to get back at me."

Marquetta's eyes are all watery. Her breath is ragged. "She threatened to tell everyone what was in it if I didn't do what she wanted."

Deputy Baker blackmailed Marquetta?

We come around the turn. Flashing red and yellow lights block the road.

Marquetta slams on the brakes. The car skids. It goes sideways.

I scream, but we don't stop.

We're sliding towards the cliff.

57

Rick

"I'M SORRY FOR THE DELAY." Rick regarded Adam from the passenger's seat of the police cruiser. "You didn't have to help us get Marquetta and Alex ready. They could've handled it."

Adam flicked on his signal light, checked his mirror, then pulled the police 4x4 out onto Front Street. His right cheek inched up in a lopsided grimace. "What? And have you worried they wouldn't get out before dark while we're pussyfooting around with Will Shelley? No way."

"I just hope I can stay focused. That can be a nasty drive to San Ladron."

"Marquetta's a good driver. She'll be fine. If I were you, I'd be more worried about how you're going to handle tomorrow morning's breakfast rush all on your own."

Rick slumped back in his seat. It wouldn't be the first time he'd had to handle the rush without Marquetta, but her presence made it so much more enjoyable. "The same way I've done it before when she's been gone. I'll put in an order at Crusty Buns, buy fruit at the market, and put out the waffle maker."

"Glad to hear you've got a plan. This talk with Shelley shouldn't take too long—unless he tries to lie his way out." Adam paused, then added, "If he does, I'll throw him in the cooler overnight so you can get on with your shopping duties."

"Pussyfooting? Cooler? You really are turning into a seasoned cop."

Adam chuckled. "And don't you forget it."

They turned up Main Street and drove the few blocks to Crusty Buns. As Adam parked, he asked, "What do these guys do, spend their entire day eating donuts?"

"Don't let Angus or Mary hear you call their baking mere donuts. You might be banned for life."

Adam winced and turned off the ignition. "You're right. That is not a fate I want to suffer. I love their cinnamon rolls too much." He patted his stomach. "Way too much."

They entered Crusty Buns and Rick scanned the tables. He spotted Shelley at a two-top near the rear of the store, leaning back in his chair, a scowl on his face. If Rick didn't know better, he'd say the man had been expecting them.

When they were a few steps away from the table, Shelley stood. "I was just leaving. Table's all yours."

Adam held up his hand, then motioned for the man to sit. "We're here to ask you a few questions. It shouldn't take long."

"I really need to be going."

Shelley tried to sidestep them, but Rick and Adam blocked the two exit paths.

"I'd like to do this quietly, Mr. Shelley," Adam said.

Shelley's craggy face contorted into something of a cynical smile. "Have a seat, then. By all means."

Rick pulled a chair from a nearby unoccupied table. He and Adam sat, then Adam deliberately pulled his notepad from his pocket, flipped through it, and jotted a quick note. "Don't want to forget anything. Mr. Shelley, why did you book yourself on this cruise?"

"Are you kidding me?" Shelley laughed. "How many times are you people going to ask that? For a chance to make millions from the *San Manuel*, of course."

"So you're tired of being a line cook?" Rick asked.

"I've been trying to work my way up, but there's a lot of competition. I thought if I could get enough money out of this venture, I could start my own restaurant. Or just retire."

Having been in Seaside Cove for a year and seen how cutthroat and difficult treasure hunting was, Rick found Shelley's logic overly optimistic at best. "Have you ever done any treasure hunting before?"

"Done some dives," Shelley said casually. "Mostly offshore stuff. I've explored a few wrecks."

"How did you hear about this one?"

"It was on one of those treasure hunting message boards. There was a lot of skepticism in the comments, but enough people said it could be a huge score."

"How many people is 'enough people'?" Rick asked.

"Maybe…a half dozen. A couple of them are on this trip. That's Ed and Isaac. After we set sail we all started comparing notes. You know, kind of like one of those how-did-you-get-here moments."

Adam looked up from his notepad, scrutinized Shelley, then made another note.

"Did you feel this cruise lived up to your expectations?" Rick asked.

"Not even close. Captain Carroll had us all sold on how he knew the location."

"Is that why you hacked the GPS on the boat? To find the location of the *San Manuel*?" Rick asked.

Shelley's face fell. "The GPS? I wouldn't have any idea how to do this hacking thing."

Adam pulled out his phone and held the screen so Shelley could see it. "Looks kind of like you knew what you were doing to me. Are you sure about that?"

"I…um…okay, fine. I tried. Christopher must've been prowling around taking photos. Should've known." Shelley sighed. "The reason I tried is I thought I might get lucky. The night before, Ed was talking about how these GPS things keep track of all your previous locations. The more I thought about it, the more I got curious. So the next day I waited until Gavin wasn't on the bridge. I snuck up there expecting it to be easy, but I couldn't figure out where anything was. All I got for my trouble was a bad case of nerves."

Shelley looked to be so sincere. Was he telling the truth now? Or weaving a story? And what about Ed Silverstein? His name had surfaced again. Rick suspected he and Adam would be talking to Silverstein soon. "Did anyone else besides Mr. Jenks know what you tried to do?"

"I doubt it. The last thing I wanted to do was let it get back to Ed that I'd had a shot and blown it. He would have made my life miserable."

"Were you aware that Mr. Jenks probably shared this photo with Mr. Silverstein?" Adam asked.

Shelley groaned and buried his face in his hands. "No, I wasn't. But it explains why Ed was acting all high-and-mighty."

"It sounds like nobody on the boat really believed Captain Carroll knew the location of the *San Manuel*."

Shelley let out a heavy sigh. "He said he'd gotten it from a reliable source."

Adam looked up quickly, his interest obvious. "Did he tell you who this source was?"

"No. One thing about Carroll, he never gave specifics. He said it was a security measure. All he told us was that he had a source in Seaside Cove."

"Here?" Rick exclaimed.

"Are you deliberately trying to obstruct justice, Mr. Shelley?" Adam asked flatly.

The look of annoyance Shelley had been wearing turned to worry. "Okay. Fine. I heard it was an archaeologist who wanted to make some money on the side."

The hairs on the back of Rick's neck rose. He and Adam made eye contact. They both frowned. There was only one archaeologist Rick knew of who might have that kind of information. And she claimed she didn't.

"Captain Carroll told you he got the information from an archaeologist? When?" Rick demanded.

Shelley cleared his throat. "Well." He crossed his arms. "He didn't exactly say it to me directly."

Adam inched closer to Shelley. The move was subtle, but seemed to have a profound effect on the man's confidence. Beads of sweat formed on Shelley's forehead; he looked back and forth between his questioners nervously.

"Then how did you hear about this mysterious source?" Adam asked.

"Ed was talking about it. I don't know where he got the information. Really. I don't." Shelley looked at Adam. "Can I... can I go now?"

"Not quite yet," Adam said. "Previously, you told us you'd gone to see your niece in San Ladron the night Captain Carroll was killed. Is that right?"

"Yes," Shelley said cautiously.

"Do you regret your choice of alibis, Mr. Shelley?" Adam asked.

"What? Why would I regret telling you the truth?"

"Because your alibi can't be verified. Whereas those of…say, Mr. Silverstein, Longstreet, and Redmond, all conveniently match up."

Shelley dabbed at his forehead with a napkin. "What are you implying, Chief?"

"I might be wondering about those alibis. It's always possible they compared notes…or that you weren't where you said you were. For instance, I've spoken to the only rental car agency with an office here and they tell me you didn't rent a car that day. How exactly did you drive to San Ladron without a car?"

"I…um…didn't. I was supposed to, but the rental car office was closed when I got there."

"You told me you rented that car in the afternoon," Rick said.

"Which means you lied about your alibi." Adam looked down at his notepad. He spoke as he wrote. "Obstruction… perjury…"

Shelley's eyes widened. He shook his head quickly and stammered, "Carroll…suckered us, man. He took my life savings. That was money I was gonna use to open a restaurant. That's all true. The alibi was stupid. And those other guys? I don't know if they were together or not. My guess is they weren't because they were all comparing stories. That's the truth."

"Then where were you between six and nine?" Adam asked.

"I was on the navigation deck trying to hack the GPS again until about seven-thirty." Shelley sighed. "I couldn't figure it out, so I went to my cabin and felt sorry for myself for the rest of the night."

While Adam made a note, Rick asked, "Did anyone see you?"

"No. I saw Isaac at one point, but I ducked down and I doubt if he saw me. He was wandering around on the main deck."

Rick pulled out his phone and brought up the photos from Christopher Jenks. He turned his phone around and showed Shelley the shot of Silverstein, Longstreet, and Redmond huddling on the tail end of *The Treasure King*. According to the timestamp on the photo, it had been taken after the announcement of Captain Carroll's death. In the background, Heather Sanna was busy polishing the metal railing.

"Is that what this is all about?"

"Yeah. We'd just heard the captain was dead. Ed called the meeting with those two and said they needed an alibi. They all agreed to say they were together."

"But you're not in this photo, Mr. Shelley," Rick said. "How do you know about it?"

Shelley pointed at the photo. "Because Matthew told me the whole story. You can ask Heather, too. She probably overheard them talking."

58

Rick

IT WAS AFTER FOUR BY the time Rick made it to the market. He'd already placed his order at Crusty Buns so all he had to do was grab the fresh fruit and a few staples. He didn't feel much like cooking for one, but had to eat. To make things easy, tonight's menu would be grilled salmon paired with a veggie he could also grill. Simple. Easy cleanup. And boring—mostly because he already missed Alex and Marquetta despite a house filled with guests who were counting on him.

He was checking out the asparagus when he spotted Heather Sanna approaching. Her basket contained only two items—a carton of milk and a half dozen eggs. He watched as she picked up a couple of apples, weighed them, and grimaced when she looked at the price. She consulted her list, then put the apples in her cart. She looked up at the aisle signs hanging from the ceiling. Rick approached, gave her a friendly smile and a wave.

"Looking for something in particular?" He made a show of looking up at the aisle markers as he waited for her to answer.

"Cookies." She threw up her hands. "I'm having sugar

withdrawal."

"Two aisles over. There's also Crusty Buns. They can satisfy any sweet tooth."

"I need cheap. I can't afford to be spending money at bakeries and restaurants."

"I get it—living on a budget. I wish my daughter understood a budget. She doesn't yet understand how hard it is to make money." Rick watched as Heather fidgeted.

"I should get the rest of this done," she said.

"Sure. But before you go, I have a question. If you don't mind?"

"What's the question?"

"Chief Cunningham and I were wondering if you overheard a conversation between Ed Silverstein, Isaac Longstreet, and Matthew Redmond that took place on the tail end of *The Treasure King*."

She sighed and looked away. While waiting for her to process whatever was going on in her mind, Rick noticed her gripping the handrail of her shopping cart.

"I don't know what those three were thinking. Actually, I know what Isaac and Matthew were thinking—don't mess with Ed. None of them, with the possible exception of Christopher, want to cross him."

"Why's that?"

"Ed can be very…forceful. He's a strong personality."

"Did he challenge Captain Carroll?"

"Ed seemed to enjoy seeing how far he could push Morris."

"Meaning?" Rick insisted.

"Morris was tired of Ed. I don't think he would have tolerated him much more."

"What would Captain Carroll have done? The man was a

paying passenger."

"Morris had his ways. There's no telling how he'd have handled it, but he could be very vindictive."

Rick raised his eyebrows—wasn't that exactly what they'd seen during the confrontation at the Crooked Mast? "Were there conflicts between Ed and the captain?"

"Always under the surface. It was never overt, but it was there." Heather shrugged. "I suppose you're wondering if Ed would have killed Morris. I really don't know."

"Actually, that wasn't my next question. What I'd really like to know is why Ed and the others felt they needed to coordinate their alibis."

"I don't know. Ed likes to cover his bases."

"Personality clashes don't require an alibi. And, it's a long leap from two guys not getting along to murder. What would have been his motive?"

"I wouldn't know." She looked at Rick and smiled. "Isn't that what you're supposed to be finding out?"

"It is." Rick stared back at her. "And that's why we have so many questions. We're looking for holes in stories. Like the one about Will Shelley hacking the boat's GPS."

Heather's smile fell. She cleared her throat, turned away, and said, "I really must be going. Gavin and I are eating light until we can somehow get cash. The store won't give us credit because Morris never bothered to set anything up. If you'll excuse me. I need to find those cookies."

She pushed her cart forward, and Rick watched her leave. There were still so many questions unanswered. As far as Rick was concerned, Ed Silverstein's name had come up a little too often. Standing between the Gala apples and the Fujis, Rick dialed Adam's cell.

When Adam answered, Rick said, "I'm at the market and I just ran into Heather Sanna. I was asking her a few questions. She confirmed that Silverstein, Longstreet, and Redmond coordinated their alibis. According to her, Silverstein was the mastermind, the other two just went along so they wouldn't cross him. Which has me wanting to take a closer look at Silverstein. The other thing is when I mentioned Will Shelley and how he tried to hack the GPS, she bolted. From the look on her face, I hit a chord."

"You want to talk to her again? Officially? We'd better do it quick. By tomorrow morning, I'm probably going to have to let them leave. After that happens…"

"I know. But there's something we're missing. These people are either protecting the killer or covering up something about *The Treasure King*—something big. We need access to that boat."

"I could haul them all in for questioning and we can play hardball," Adam said.

"The way these clowns have been lying, I don't know how much good that would do."

"Well, to get access we need something concrete for the DA. Why don't you come over and join Traci and me for dinner? We can kick around some ideas. Maybe we'll come up with something brilliant."

Rick picked up one of the Gala apples. He weighed it in his hand. It felt solid, unlike anything they had on Carroll's killer. "Tell you what. Why don't you both come to the B&B? I was just going to grill some salmon. I could throw a couple more filets on and we can set up the telescope."

Adam paused. Grunted. "Are you crazy? It's way too overcast for stargazing."

"I wasn't planning on pointing it at the sky. From our back patio, you can see *The Treasure King*. We could keep watch. Because their alibis are breaking down, I'm betting something's going to happen soon."

"Traci might not want to be sitting out there freezing while we take turns on your telescope."

"I've got that covered. I'll set up the portable heater on the patio. It will be toasty out there, and she can even take a turn spying if she wants to."

They agreed that dinner would be at six. Rick bought more asparagus and grabbed a half dozen small red potatoes. The B&B was quiet when he arrived. The Carstons sat in the living room talking with Mr. West and Mrs. King. Rick waved as he passed, but Stephen Carston motioned for Rick to join them. Each couple sat on one of the couches, and the older pair were holding hands. Rick felt a small flush of satisfaction that the B&B had helped them find each other. He'd have to tell Alex and Marquetta about this when they returned.

"It looks like you all are getting along quite nicely," Rick said.

"We're having a lovely time." Mrs. King snuck a quick peek at Mr. West.

"We've decided to double date for dinner," Stephen said. "We've been to the Crooked Mast every night and were thinking of trying your other restaurant, the Rusty Nail. Any thoughts on that one?"

"It's a good place," Rick said. "Did you see our attractions display? They've got a coupon for free appetizers with the purchase of an entree."

Winnie held up one of the coupons. She flashed him a smile. "Already got one. That's what gave us the idea. It's pricier than the Crooked Mast, but their menu looks very nice."

"It's excellent," Rick said as he hoisted his bag of groceries. "Now, if you'll excuse me, I have work to do in the kitchen. I've invited some friends over."

Adam and Traci arrived at exactly six. Rick put the potatoes on the grill. He'd blanched and seasoned the asparagus and had it on a foil tray with some lemon juice and butter. After opening a bottle of wine, he started the potatoes. Half an hour later, he put on the salmon. Four minutes after starting the salmon, he flipped the filets and put the asparagus over the third burner. While he kept watch on the grill, Adam and Traci took turns peering at *The Treasure King* through the telescope.

"So what exactly are we looking for?" Traci asked.

Adam stood behind her, massaging her shoulders with both hands. "Something suspicious."

"Well, Mr. Smarty Pants, does it seem odd to you that they would be taking out the trash in the dark?"

Rick looked up from the grill, but Adam already had his eye glued to the telescope. "Rick? You know that break we were needing? We might have just found it."

59

Alex

DADDY'S EXPRESSION WHEN HE SEES me and Marquetta step out onto the back patio almost makes me laugh. He looks super confused.

"What are you doing here?" All of a sudden, he rushes forward and picks me up. He gives me a big hug, then looks at Marquetta. "What happened?"

Marquetta looks at the table. "Rick, could you pour me some wine?"

"Already done," Traci says as she hands Marquetta a glass.

"The road was closed." Marquetta shudders, then says thanks and takes a sip.

"What are you not telling us?" Daddy asks.

"We almost drove off the road, but Marquetta saved us."

Marquetta takes another sip from her glass. "I wasn't paying close enough attention to my driving."

I totally don't want Marquetta to take the blame for what happened. It was my fault 'cause I was distracting her, but we already agreed not to give anyone the details. "It was a sharp turn, Daddy."

"Anyway, when I saw the roadblock, I panicked and we spun out."

"Roadblock?" Chief Cunningham asks. "They don't close that road unless…were they doing rescue operations?"

"Yes. They were trying to get to a car that had driven off the road ahead of us. Frightening. We could have joined them. Can we talk about something else? I'm still shaking. I don't want to think about it."

"Sure. Have a seat here by the heater." My dad pulls a chair into the space where it's nice and cozy.

"What's going on out here?" Marquetta asks.

"I ran into Heather Sanna at the market. The conversation raised more questions, so I decided to set up a surveillance of *The Treasure King*. I figured I could have Adam and Traci over for dinner and we could kick around a few ideas." Daddy looks at me. "Don't get your hopes up, kiddo. We haven't come up with anything other than the trash being taken out."

"Oh my God," Marquetta says. "With everything that's happened this afternoon, I forgot to tell you about our trip to Crusty Buns."

"Okay," my dad says. "You got a snack."

"No, Daddy, we overheard the treasure hunters talking and they lied about their alibis."

"To be more specific," Marquetta says, "Ed Silverstein got very upset with Matthew Redmond because he's having second thoughts about what they told you."

"I definitely want to bring Redmond in for a little chat," Chief Cunningham says.

I step closer to the telescope. "Can I see?"

"Sure," my dad says.

It's a long ways to *The Treasure King* from here, but the telescope makes it easy to see what's happening. I adjust the eyepiece to fix the focus. That makes everything super sharp. I can see everything on the boat like I'm right there. I check out the whole thing. All I see is the lady crew member on deck. There's nobody else around.

There are footsteps behind me. It's my dad, and he's standing there looking over my shoulder. "Did you get it focused?"

"Uh huh." I swivel the telescope so I can see the big trash bins. Seaside Cove only has one trash pickup each week, and that's tomorrow. Anything that's in the trash tonight will be picked up in the morning and will be gone forever. "Who took the trash out? Was it the lady crew member?"

"I don't know," Daddy says. "Traci, who took out the trash?"

Traci gets up and comes to where we're standing. "It was Heather. Why?"

I aim the telescope at the boat again. There she is. She's tying down the cover on the lifeboat. "Because when we were watching the boat, we saw her put three plastic bags in the lifeboat. And now she's doing something in that same spot."

"But she only took out one bag," Traci says.

"What color was it?" I ask.

"Black."

"Let me see." Daddy leans down and adjusts the eyepiece. "Alex, how big were these bags?"

"They're like the kind we use for the kitchen."

"Were they white?"

"For sure. And small."

My dad looks at Chief Cunningham and rubs the back of his neck. "Maybe she combined her bags from the rest of the boat with whatever was in that lifeboat?"

I can feel my eyes getting real big. "That's it! That's how she got rid of what she was hiding!"

My dad looks at Chief Cunningham. He comes to join us and takes a turn looking through the telescope. It looks like he's going back and forth between the boat and the trash bins.

He stands up and huffs as he looks at me. "Huh, nice work, munchkin." Next, he looks at my dad. "Rick, I don't know about you, but I have a sudden itch to do a little dumpster diving."

"Yeah," my dad says. "Me, too."

60

Rick

RICK HELD THE ELECTRIC LANTERN high while Adam lined up plastic bags in front of the dumpster. They were standing at the end of the marina parking lot furthest from the B&B. In truth, the lot was barely big enough to have what could be considered a far end, and the dumpsters were seldom full by trash day.

A gust of wind coming off the cove sent chills through Rick's spine. "This is pretty cold work, Mr. Police Chief. And this lantern's getting heavy."

Adam chuckled as he lined up another bag. "Well, Assistant, that's why you're holding the light and I'm the one down here."

They'd both changed into old clothes, donned heavier jackets, and nitrile gloves. Rick had mentally prepared himself for the stench of garbage, but there were enough gusts coming off the bay to prevent any foul odors from lingering. He shifted his grip on the lantern.

"Hey, Assistant, keep the beam down here. Not on the sky."

"Adam, you don't pay me enough to take this kind of abuse."

"I don't pay you at all." Adam snickered. "But you get a

fancy title."

Rick rolled his eyes, but aimed his lantern at the lineup of plastic garbage bags Adam had organized on the asphalt. There were now twelve bags ranging in size from small ones like those used in a kitchen to some large enough to accommodate yard waste. He gestured at the three largest. They looked the same as the ones the B&B used for yard cleanup. "You could fit a body in one of those."

"Now you're sounding like Nancy Drew. I'm pretty sure those are from the Ugly Worm. Jennifer's been throwing away a lot of stuff because of her remodel."

Rick wrinkled his nose. "I wish you'd stop that."

"Stop what?"

"Calling my daughter Nancy Drew. The last thing she needs is encouragement."

"Gotcha." Adam kneeled next to the first bag. It was large and black with sides that bulged from an object with sharp edges. "Okay. Let's see what we've got here."

"I hope those Ugly Worm bags aren't filled with something that's been decomposing for a few days."

"Me too, buddy."

Adam opened the bag, and Rick took a photo of the contents.

"Just packing material," Adam said as he reached inside. "And this." He pulled out a small section of drywall. "That explains the sharp edges. And here's a label addressed to Jennifer Martin. This is definitely from the Ugly Worm. I'll tie it up and put it back in the dumpster."

The next bag was also from the bait shop. With the exception of the one piece of drywall, they both had similar contents. With those out of the way, Adam turned his attention to the third large bag.

"I don't think my predecessor ever went dumpster diving. I should've made Baker do this," Adam said.

"Now, now. She's leaving." Rick paused, then added, "She is still leaving, right?"

"Haven't heard anything different." Adam stretched, then reached down to undo the tie at the top. Here we go."

"Wait. Do you want to video this? I have a feeling this is what we're looking for."

"You're right," Adam said. "Can you juggle your phone and the lantern?"

"I think so." Rick stuffed the light under his arm and then started recording video. "Go."

"My name is Chief Adam Cunningham of the Seaside Cove Police Department. Richard Atwood, my consultant, and I have been going through a public trash receptacle at the Seaside Cove Marina. I believe the black plastic bag before me contains evidence collected pertinent to the murder investigation I'm conducting."

Adam bent down, removed the twist tie, and scrutinized the contents of the large bag. "There are a number of smaller white plastic bags inside. I'm going to remove the smaller ones and inventory them."

He lined up six bags. They looked like little sentries, standing there with the wind fluttering their plastic coverings. Rick's blood pounded in his temples as he watched Adam work.

In addition to the miscellaneous trash contained in the first three bags, there were a couple of scratch pad notes written on *The Treasure King* stationery. When Adam opened the fourth bag, he froze, then looked at Rick. His voice was somber as he spoke.

"This contains what looks like a bloody tee shirt. It's a men's size medium. It also contains a pair of men's shorts. There are no obvious signs of blood on the shorts, but I'm closing the bag and will do a closer inspection back at the police station under better lighting."

Adam sealed the bag with the twist tie, then motioned for Rick to stop the video recording. A gust off the bay sent up a chorus of rustling plastic.

"I need to go through and catalog everything," Adam said. "We should do it at the station. I'll lock this one in the back of the cruiser."

"Wait, Adam. We're standing a hundred feet or so from *The Treasure King*. If Heather put this in the trash, she must be covering for Gavin. They probably thought it would be gone in the morning. But if they see us and think we're onto them, maybe we can force their hand. And, if you still want to get all of them together so we can break down some alibis, we need a spectacle."

Adam's cheek quirked up. He rubbed the back of his neck and looked in the direction of the boat. "We're going to need a few things to avoid contaminating any evidence. I'm calling in Baker."

While they waited for the deputy to arrive, Rick and Adam went through the remaining bags from the dumpster. All they found were the usual types of household refuse—food scraps, plastic wrap, used tissues and paper towels—making the question of which boat the bags had come from irrelevant. They'd finished the last bag when Deputy Baker arrived with a tarp, crime scene tape, more lanterns, and index cards to number the items.

They laid the tarp over the wooden planks of the dock, secured the corners, then began inventorying the contents of the bags. Deputy Baker pulled out the first item, the tee shirt with blood spatter on the front. Rick took pictures to document the process while Adam logged the tee as Exhibit 1. By the time they were done, a small crowd had gathered around them. Most of the passengers from *The Treasure King* were there.

While Adam and Deputy Baker packaged up the evidence and their equipment, Rick drifted over to the small crowd. Heather Sanna watched from near the rear, but her fellow crew member, Gavin Mancini, was missing. Also on the missing list was Matthew Redmond. Rick approached the group from *The Treasure King*. The passengers were talking among themselves.

"Gentlemen," Rick said. "We found a bloody T-shirt that had been discarded from the boat. Any of you have an idea who it might belong to?"

Ed Silverstein took a step forward. In the marina lighting, his skin looked almost pasty white. "We were just discussing that." He looked over his shoulder at the other men. One by one, they each murmured their agreement. Silverstein spoke in a voice loud enough for everyone nearby to hear. "Mancini's run off. We all agreed he has to be the one who killed Carroll."

Rick eyed the men as a group, then narrowed his focus to Isaac Longstreet, who was fidgeting with his left ear. "You all agreed? As in, you held a trial and found him guilty?"

Longstreet gave his ear a final tug, then regarded the others. "Kind of."

Silverstein shifted from one foot to the other, looking irritated that anyone had questioned his conclusions. His tone made it obvious he felt he needed to reassert himself. "He was in competition with Carroll for her attention." He cocked his head in Heather's direction.

Heather crossed her arms over her chest, then turned on her

heel and began a purposeful walk back to *The Treasure King.* Rick sighed. Grimaced. What was that all about?

"Wait here. The chief has questions for all of you," Rick snapped. "And where's Redmond? Why isn't he here?"

"Haven't seen him," Silverstein grumbled.

Rick pushed by the men and hurried after Heather. When they were about halfway back to the boat, he called out. "Ms. Sanna? Would you hold up for a minute?"

She stopped, turned to face him, and rolled her eyes. "What now?"

"Where's your coworker?"

"How should I know?" She raised her hands in the air, palms up. "If you want, search the boat. Be sure to check his bunk. Maybe he crashed early."

"In the market you led me to believe you were having dinner with him. Was that not the case?"

"As far as I'm concerned, I have no reason to share a meal with any of them. They're all a bunch of misfits."

She glared in the direction of the onlookers, but Rick suspected she was really looking at one man in particular—Ed Silverstein.

"Were you offended by what Mr. Silverstein said?"

"Ed is a loudmouthed jerk. Have you checked him out as a suspect?"

Rick ignored the question. "You haven't answered me."

"No. I wasn't offended." She turned away as though she might storm off. Instead, she bit her lip and gazed north. "Just because Gavin is missing doesn't mean he killed Morris."

"Ms. Sanna? Please. Answer my question. When's the last time you saw Mr. Mancini?"

"This afternoon."

"She's lying," Christopher Jenks said as he approached. "Here, look at this. It was taken about an hour ago."

He held out his phone. On the screen was an image of Heather and Gavin. They were sitting together in the chairs up on the bridge. In the middle of the image was a large triangular play button. Jenks tapped the button and the video picked up with Gavin speaking.

"He's gone. There's no need to hide anymore."

"Gavin, I've told you. This is not the right time."

"But I love you, Heather. I want to be with you."

"Shut up, Gavin. I don't know what you're talking about. Whatever you think we had…" She gestured back-and-forth between them with her fingers. "You were wrong."

"But you said…"

"Stop acting like a lovesick puppy and grow up. If you've got fantasies playing in your head, those are your problem, not mine. I'm tired of you and your insecurities." Heather stood and the video ended.

Jenks looked expectantly at Rick. What did he think he was going to get? A medal?

"Thank you, Christopher. I'll take it from here. Would you go back with the others and wait for me?"

The expression on the other man's face fell, and he seemed resigned as he slowly retraced his path to the group. Rick turned his attention to Heather. "Well, Ms. Sanna? It appears you lied to me."

She stood with her weight on one leg, the other stretched out, and her arms crossed. "Fine, I had dinner with him. And yes, I slept with the guy a couple of times. Now he thinks we're a thing and wants to get married."

"So where is he?" Rick waited until she turned away and

again looked to the north.

"I told you. I don't know. As you can see, I blew him off. I can't help it that he thought we were in some big love affair. Can I go now? I'm freezing my butt off."

"You can return to *The Treasure King*, but Chief Cunningham and I may have more questions for you later." Rick watched her walk away, then let his gaze follow the shoreline north of the marina. "Of course," he muttered.

On his way back to share his suspicions with Adam and Deputy Baker, Rick pulled Jenks aside. "When you were at the lighthouse taking photos the night of the murder, did you see Gavin Mancini?"

Christopher shook his head and peered at Rick. "No. Why?"

"You're sure?"

"Positive. Why? Did he say he was there?"

Rick looked over at Adam and Deputy Baker, who were in the process of moving the remaining bags into the back of Baker's cruiser.. He nodded absently, and said, "Thanks, Christopher." He hurried over and caught Adam just as they were closing up the rear hatch.

"We still don't have a murder weapon," Adam said. "Tell me you got something and that this little dog-and-pony show was worthwhile."

"Mancini's disappeared. I think he's gone to the lighthouse."

"You've got to be kidding me," Deputy Baker grumbled.

"Are you sure?" Adam asked. "That's a fair walk from here."

"Alex and I were standing in line behind him at the market. He told me he was going there for a picnic and I gave him directions. Just now, Heather kept looking in that direction. If he's got the speargun with him, he could toss it and we'd never find it."

Adam and Deputy Baker exchanged a glance, then looked to the north. The old lighthouse stood atop a jagged cliff, it's black silhouette in sharp contrast to the reds, pinks, and grays of the sunset.

"Baker," Adam said. "Corral this band of misfits and put them on the boat. Then take the evidence back to the station. Lock it in the evidence room. When you're done, come out to the lighthouse unless you hear from me. If Rick's right, we might have to set up a search party."

"Got it, Chief." Baker marched off toward the group, who were still huddling on the dock.

Adam shrugged down into his jacket. "Let's see if we can find this guy before he tosses our murder weapon."

61

Rick

THE DRIVE TOOK ONLY FIVE minutes. Adam parked the cruiser in the empty lot, but left the lights on. As they got out of the vehicle, Rick said, "Alex said they call this place Lover's Leap."

"Kids." Adam laughed. "I'll say one thing, that munchkin sure knows how to dramatize things. Nobody actually ever jumped out here. The incident she's referring to was an accident." Adam opened the rear hatch and pulled out two lanterns. "Take one of these. Let's go."

Rick fell into step astride Adam. As they walked, they swept the surrounding area with the beams of their lanterns. When they passed the trail marker a short distance beyond the parking lot, Rick spoke in hushed tones. "You mean there were no spurned lovers?"

Adam stopped, aimed his beam directly ahead, then said, "I fibbed when we were here talking to Christopher Jenks. The fence was actually put in after just one incident. Two kids got too close to the cliff. Back in those days you could go right to the edge and look out. The story goes that a local boy brought his girlfriend out here to propose. He took her to the edge, got down on one knee, and told her he wanted to marry her. She accepted, but when they kissed, the outcropping gave way."

An involuntary shiver coursed down Rick' spine. "Yikes. Let's go find Mancini."

They continued on to where the trail bent to the left and turned back into a stand of trees. Adam aimed his light to the right and lit up a sign not more than ten feet away. It read, *Unstable ground. Stay back.*

Adam's beam swept the area in a wide arc. "Mancini might have chosen the spot over by the lighthouse. The trail is even closer to the cliff."

"Let's go check," Rick said.

Their footsteps crunched on the decomposed granite as they followed the trail into the trees. Overhead, silvery clouds glimmered in the sky behind a spiderweb silhouette formed by the branches of alders, cottonwoods, and firs. It was a beautiful sight, yet a lonely one, thought Rick.

"Did they ever find the bodies?" Rick asked.

"No."

"So this could be another one of those Seaside Cove legends nobody can prove."

"You mean like Juan Murrieta's treasure and the *San Manuel?*"

"Exactly. Nobody's found either of those. Right?"

Adam stopped, flicked his beam in a wide circle, and frowned. "Thought I heard something. These woods always give me the creeps." He continued on, speaking as he walked. "The details were reported by a couple of high-school kids. They weren't supposed to be out here. Nobody knows for sure whether they were telling the truth, but a boy and a girl did disappear."

A black spire came into view as they broke into a clearing. Rick flicked his beam toward the top as they approached. "Looks a lot more imposing in the dark."

"Yeah," Adam muttered as he swept the area with his light. The beam caught the figure of a man dressed in jeans and a light windbreaker standing on the trail. "There he is."

"I'll go talk to him while you call Baker for backup." Rick stepped toward the figure. "Gavin! Stay where you are. I just want to talk. That's all."

"Don't come any closer!"

Rick stopped, momentarily stunned. This wasn't Gavin Mancini. The man was shorter, thinner, and the tips of his hair were blond. It was Matthew Redmond. Rick took a cautious step forward and spoke loud enough to be heard over the sound of crashing surf fifty feet below.

"Mr. Redmond. Why are you out here?"

"I've got nothing left. That slime Carroll took me for everything I had. He totally deserved what he got."

Rick walked slowly toward the fence, still calling out over the sounds of the surf. "Tell me about what he did. It sometimes helps to get these things out."

Redmond faced Rick, holding up his hand to shield his eyes from the intense light. "I know what you're trying to do. It won't work. I quit my job; my wife divorced me; and Carroll took the last of my savings. He duped me into thinking I could make a killing. I wanted to get rid of him so bad."

Rick's heart thudded in his chest. "Are you saying you're the one who shot Captain Carroll with the speargun, Mr. Redmond?"

"What? No. I could never kill someone."

"Then what are you doing out here?" Rick asked.

Redmond pointed to his right. "She told me to bring that here and wait for her. She said she'd get me my money back."

Rick aimed his beam to the spot where Redmond pointed. His breath caught. A long, skinny cardboard box had been placed next to the fence. "What's in the box?" Rick asked suspiciously.

"I have no idea. She told me not to open it."

"Adam!" Rick called over his shoulder. "I think you should see this."

A second beam of light joined Rick's. "What've you got?" Adam asked as he approached. "Is that our missing speargun?"

"Speargun? What?" Redmond stammered.

"I thought you should open it," Rick said.

"Get your video camera going." Adam did another video introduction, then slit open the top, which had been taped together. When he opened the box, his jaw dropped. "What the heck?"

"Is it the speargun?" Rick asked.

"Not exactly," Adam said. He reached into the box and pulled out a roll of toilet paper. "What kind of game are you playing, Mr. Redmond? You pack this with toilet paper and then you carry it out here? You're looking an awful lot like an accomplice to murder."

"No! It was all Heather."

"I need details or I'm taking you in right now."

"The night we docked in Seaside Cove she came to me and asked if I could get everyone to the Crooked Mast." Redmond's breathing quickened and he squinted at Rick against the light. "Honest. I didn't know what she intended to do. You're not going to charge me, are you? I'll tell you everything I know."

"You'd better," grumbled Adam.

Rick took a more consoling tone. "I'm sure that if we all work together we can set this right."

"You think so?" Redmond asked, hope evident in his tone.

"I'm sure of it." Rick tried to sound positive despite the knowledge that Redmond's fate was still very much up in the air. "Let's go." Rick extended his hand. Stepped forward. When Redmond held out his, Rick took it.

Adam immediately grabbed Redmond's other arm, then secured his hands behind his back. "Matthew Redmond, I'm taking you in as a material witness in the death of Captain Morris Carroll."

"You're arresting me?" Redmond wailed. "After I promised to cooperate?"

"I'm detaining you."

Redmond's shoulders shook and he choked back a sob. Rick started to console him, but stopped when his phone rang. He checked the display before he answered. "What's up, Marquetta?"

"Have you seen what's happening at *The Treasure King*?"

"No. What?"

"Gavin Mancini just forced all the passengers off the boat at gunpoint. Alex saw the whole thing."

Rick looked toward the marina. *The Treasure King* had moved away from the docks. Water churned behind the boat and the sound of the engines mixed with the crashing surf from the base of the cliff. Even at this distance, he could see a group of people standing on the docks nearby.

"Adam, *The Treasure King* is leaving," Rick said.

Redmond straightened up and peered into the distance. "Are you kidding me? They're getting away?"

"Not on my watch," Adam said. "Keep this one under control."

"Thanks, Marquetta," Rick said. "Adam needs a hand. I'll

call you back."

Adam handed Redmond over to Rick, pulled his phone, and stepped away. When they were alone, Redmond's tone turned bitter, "I don't believe this. She lied to me and now she's trying to stick me with the murder. The whole thing. My life's already ruined, but I'm not taking the fall for her."

"For Captain Carroll's murder?"

"That's right."

"Who's piloting the boat?" Rick asked.

"It's probably Gavin. Heather doesn't have the skills. I'm not going to be the patsy on this thing. I want to make a statement."

"That's good," Adam said as he returned. "Because I've alerted the Coast Guard. Once they board, it's game over."

62

Alex

Hey Journal,

It's been kinda quiet around here since the Coast Guard brought back The Treasure King. Chief Cunningham and my dad talked to both of the crew members. They confessed, but tried to blame the other one. Chief Cunningham says they have enough to put them both on trial. It sounds like Miss Sanna tricked Mr. Mancini into thinking she was in love with him. That's like a major bummer 'cause I kinda liked her.

Chief Cunningham says it will take a long time, but eventually they'll both 'go away for life.' He said that in a deep voice like he was on a movie or something. It was super funny 'cause he hooked his thumbs in his belt, too.

Writing about The Treasure King now is kind of a let down. I mean, everybody already knows the Coast Guard boarded the boat and searched it. They even found a speargun in the freezer, so it looks like the cops have everything they're gonna need for their case.

Now the investigation is out of the way, I can start looking forward to Grandma Madeline's visit. She wants to meet me and Daddy. Isn't that awesome, Journal? My Grandma Madeline wants to meet me! I'll have my very own grandma. At least until I get a baby brother or sister. I know, I know, Daddy and Marquetta have to get married first, but I think they're gonna need all the help they can get.

Uh oh, my dad just knocked.

Gotta go!

Alex

"Come in!"

Daddy opens my door and wiggles his fingers. "Come with me. Flynn O'Connor is with Marquetta in the kitchen. She has something to tell you."

"Really? Flynn is here? Awesome!" I rush out the door and down the stairs. When I get to the bottom, I go through the living room and dining room and into the kitchen.

"Flynn!"

She's wearing a camp shirt and khaki shorts, but this time the shirt's a pretty gray. Her face lights up when she sees me and she gets off her stool. She gives me a big hug. When she pulls away, she says, "Congratulations to the girl who broke things open."

I look at her, and she's like, serious. "What did I break?"

"So you haven't heard? The coordinates for the location of the *San Manuel* were written on the back of that cheap treasure map you discovered in Captain Carroll's cabin."

"Who would do a thing like that?" Daddy laughs and rolls his eyes.

Flynn looks at my dad and raises her eyebrows. "I don't understand."

I look at Daddy, then Marquetta. "Can I tell her?"

They look at each other, then Daddy says, "Go for it, kiddo."

"Captain Jack did almost the same exact thing. He had letters he kept behind a map of Seaside Cove up in his office. Daddy looked at the map for more than a year and never knew what was there."

"Really?" Flynn says. "Doesn't seem terribly creative."

"I don't know, Flynn," Marquetta says. "I've dusted that map for years and never suspected a thing. It was a very effective hiding place."

"Hiding in plain sight." Flynn nods. "I guess it is effective. In fact, that's almost exactly what happened with the *San Manuel*. I did a preliminary dive the day I got the coordinates and confirmed we have a wreck of what appears to be an old Spanish galleon. The artifacts are scattered, but we deal with those conditions all the time."

"How'd he find it?" Marquetta asks, then she stands and looks at Flynn. "My manners. Would you like a cup of coffee?"

"I'd love one, thanks. It happened after a storm forced *The Treasure King* to seek shelter down the coast on a previous trip. I guess you'd call it beginner's luck."

I climb up on my stool and think about what Flynn said. "I thought Captain Carroll was some big treasure hunter. He wasn't?"

"Chief Cunningham told me when they checked the captain's prints in the autopsy, they discovered his real name was Morris Carleton. The name sounded familiar, so I did some research. He was a smuggler. His only relation to treasure was taking pirates out to a site, then returning them and their booty to a port where they could fence it. I guess he decided it was high time he got some of the big money. He was in hock up to his eyeballs because he wangled a loan from a former employer for *The Treasure King.*"

Marquetta pours Flynn's cup and hands it to her. "So it was just pure luck that he found the *San Manuel*? Amazing."

"Especially because it's outside the search zone. It's nowhere near where we thought it was. Now that we know the location, the trick is going to be keeping the treasure pirates from looting the site. And we might not have found it without your help." Flynn looks at me. "Good job."

My dad watches Flynn as he leans forward with his hands on the countertop. "When Silverstein told us that Captain Carroll got the coordinates for the *San Manuel* from an archaeologist working here in Seaside Cove, I was getting worried. I thought maybe you'd gone to the dark side."

Flynn shakes her head. "Never. I would never sell my soul like that."

"It was just a rumor Heather started," Rick said. "When Adam interrogated her, she told him she planted it with Ed because she knew he'd go for it. He was duped just like all the others."

I feel kinda warm and happy inside. I guess getting in trouble was worth it 'cause now Flynn's gonna be able to start bringing up the treasures of the *San Manuel*. And now I totally have a story I can write for the Cove Talkers.

"I see that smug look on your face, young lady," Daddy says. "Don't think you can get away with disregarding the rules. You got lucky this time because it worked for the greater good and Chief Cunningham wanted me to go easy on you. You also got lucky because Deputy Baker responded to your call for help so quickly when you were in trouble."

"What happened to her, Daddy? Did she quit?"

"See what I have to deal with?" Daddy looks at Flynn and throws up his hands. "She's a professional at changing the narrative to suit her needs."

Flynn laughs as she watches me over the rim of her mug. "You do have a challenge on your hands."

"Why, Mr. Atwood," Marquetta says as she steps closer to Daddy. "I do believe that's a gray hair I see."

Daddy closes his eyes and shakes his head. When he opens them, me and Marquetta and Flynn are all grinning at him. He's so in over his head.

63

Alex

APRIL *14*

Hey Journal,

Daddy read my story for the Cove Talkers newsletter and said it was good. He marked it up with a red pen—he says that's what his editor always did to him—then gave it back to me and said to bring him the next version. Whew! This writing for the press stuff is a lot of work!

We got a postcard today from Mr. West and Mrs. King. They've finished their cruise and have decided they're gonna travel together some more. They might even get married! Can you believe it? That makes me super happy 'cause me and Marquetta helped bring them together.

I'm totally stoked because it's Friday night and Grandma Madeline is coming to visit tomorrow. We had to wait a couple weeks 'cause things got crazy after the Coast Guard brought back The Treasure King, but we had a last-minute cancellation yesterday, so Daddy asked Marquetta to see if her mom could come. I'm all nervous 'cause I've never had like a real grandma before. If Grandma Madeline is anything like Marquetta, we're totally gonna get along. This is gonna be super awesome!

Xoxo

Alex

PS I caught Daddy and Marquetta kissing in the laundry room again. They got all embarrassed, but I think it's super cool. Project Baby Sister is off to an awesome start!

AUTHOR'S NOTES

While *Secrets of the Treasure King* is a work of fiction, I have also woven in historical fact. The *San Manuel*, the Spanish galleon described in this book, never existed, but it easily could have. The Spanish empire sailed these galleons until 1815, when a four-year voyage by the *Magallanes* concluded in Manila. For 250 years, these ships were used to bring New World gold and silver from the Americas and exotic goods such as silk, china, ivory, and spices from the Far East.

Manila galleons such as the *San Manuel* traversed a course from Japan to California, then down the coast to Acapulco. Despite the dangers, the Spanish galleons sailed this eastern course regularly by the 1560s. The journey, which could take eight months, was one of the most dangerous in the world. The waters were unpredictable, the conditions onboard deplorable, and the potential for raids by privateers high.

One of the earliest known shipwrecks off the California Coast is the *Santa Domingo*. This galleon sank in 1540 near the South Channel Islands according to the California Lands Commission. Another galleon lost along the California coast is the *San Augustin*, which sank in Drake's Bay north of San Francisco. Altogether, there are more than 1400 other wrecks lying on the bottom of the sea, most from the last 150 years.

The value of a Spanish galleon's cargo would depend on many factors. However, it's not unreasonable for that value to be millions of dollars. The ship mentioned by Alex in her conversation with her friends Sasha and Robbie is real. The *San Jose* lies on the sea floor and is anticipated to have a value of $17 billion. She is the subject of a custody battle between multiple countries and private companies, all of whom claim an interest in the salvage rights. The *San Jose* typifies the battle between those interested in preserving history and those interested in private gain.